enjoy!

Nita Joy Haddad

GHOST RANCH

By

Carole T. Beers

Carole T. Beers

W & B Publishers
USA

Other books by this author—

Over the Edge

Saddle Tramps

*****

Ghost Ranch © 2018. All rights reserved by Carole T. Beers

No part of this book may be reproduced or transmitted in any form or by any means, graphic, electronic, or mechanical, including photocopying, recording, taping, or by any informational storage retrieval system without prior permission in writing from the publisher.

W & B Publishers

For information:
W & B Publishers
9001 Ridge Hill Street
Kernersville, NC 27284

www.a-argusbooks.com

ISBN: 9781635541113

This is a work of *fiction.* All of the characters, organizations and events portrayed in this novel are either products of the author's imagination or used fictitiously.

Book Cover by Cheryl F. Taylor from a photo by Jenny J Jaks Grimm

Printed in the United States of America

DEDICATION

Never lose faith in dreams born of love and hope

ACKNOWLEDGEMENTS:

I am indebted to all you people, critters and spirits who shared your lives and thoughts with me, and gently or aggressively prodded me forward. Sometimes from a distance of many years and miles. Other times teaching in a *heyoka* way—the Lakota "clown" way of instructing by doing the opposite of the desired action. Once you even spoke to me through a dream.

To the early readers whom I confused with out-of-order scenes and indecipherable sentences—as per your suggestions, I tried to "make better." Later readers, thank you for the time and interest you've given this story. I hope it brightens your life in some small way.

Hugs to publisher William J. Connor, and writing colleagues Jenn Ashton, Melinda Bargreen, Susan Clayton-Goldner, Sharon Dean, Michael Niemann, Clive Rosengren and Tim Wohlforth. I also thank bestselling authors Stella Cameron and J.A. Jance for cheering me on.

Authors Innovative Marketing and Joy Luck Book Club offer valuable support, as do my faithful Facebook friends: Patty Baker, Jan Crossen, Barbara Boronda, Kari Lynn Dell, Laura Drake, Jo-Ann Mapson, Staci Nauert and Ken Shoemaker. Can't forget friends at Bethany Presbyterian Church and Oregon Paint Horse Club. Plus you buttercups I have no room to mention. Your honest reviews on Amazon and Goodreads are appreciated!

Writing this book I broke a few rules and invented my own. Or went rogue and rule-less. All in the service of my mysterious Muse—a Muse with a message and a great sense of humor. Thank you, Lord.

PROLOGUE

September 26, 1953

The man standing in the great room of the log house in the wood noticed the world had turned very still. It was as if birds in the meadow, the breeze, the leaves—even the river gliding beyond the window—waited to see what he would do.

Spying his ghostlike reflection in the glass, he saw a stranger. This was a tall stranger, six feet or more, and gaunt. Like a hunting hound who himself is hunted. A hound who once freely roamed the Oregon hills, waters and deserts. One who never failed to turn up treasure, whether tales beloved by many or riches known only to his own heart. But who now, exhausted and starved, stood immobilized by the jaws of a virtual bear trap. Cut off. Alone. Not even hope was an ally.

He'd done all he could. The National Lawyers Guild had done all they could, given the times. Given the fear, the bloodlust hatred of anything the least tinged with unfashionable ideals or morals. But it was not enough. The jealous, the paranoid, the witch-hunters had taken everything.

His gaze drifted to the redwood mantel of the river-rock fireplace. The fireplace he had built himself, choosing only the most beautiful red and blue-green stones interspersed with dark, violently pocked lava rocks. On that mantel stood the two Oscars, bookending his masterpieces bound in leather with gold lettering. Then he took in the portraits and movie posters on the walls, the cowhide-covered couch and chairs, the pine table adjoining the kitchen along the wall opposite the window. Where she had created her own masterpieces using roots, greens, wild fruits and game before their baby passed to the Spirit World, taking her along shortly after.

He dragged his thoughts back to happier times. To when Preston O'Hara was the golden boy of adventuring American literature. Critics called him a successor to Zane Grey, the new Jack London, a rival of Hemingway. His books shot to the top of best-seller lists and were made into award-winning films starring Hollywood royalty.

What was this to him now? His fame had turned to infamy, the endless gold to brass. He was bankrupt. Robbed of love, health, livelihood. No family, no future.

His insides felt leaden. The feeling was not new. It had gone on for some time now. Two years? No, three. He'd known it was a losing battle. Yet still he had fought. Gone to the hearings. Recited his love for America. Argued that his writing proved it, honoring both frontier and Indian ways. Showing how each culture thrived by taking care of its own.

That's why he'd mailed the letter to Marguerite on the reservation. He had made his late-wife's sister pregnant that summer when all looked darkest. He had now offered her atonement, a small gesture that might bring a measure of comfort. His seed would know its legacy, however compromised. A baby faced difficulties enough, healthwise, workwise, growing up on the reservation in the 1950s. Even if what lay beneath were snatched away, the child would at least know who it was.

An owl hooted. The Indian's bird of death. He'd always considered owls a sign of life. Beings that saw in the dark, rose up on silent wings and dove swiftly to claim sustenance. He remembered how his baby boy had laughed, hearing the owl call. At that infant's gurgle, the man had hooted and flapped his arms, causing more laughter that devolved into hiccups.

Looking now at the overhead beam, he ran the sisal rope through fisted hands. It prickled his skin. At least he could feel that. He pulled a two-foot section taut, yanking it harshly to test its give. There was none. But he already knew this. How often had he hung an elk or a deer from that same rope pulled over the pole-barn beam to bleed the carcass and age its meat during cool November days?

The simple note he had written to those who would find him was folded in his pocket. It kept company there with the truck keys and the first small gold nugget he'd panned from the river. What, twenty years ago? Just as the Great Depression was gathering steam before the war, with him kept home by the polio-crippled leg.

He cracked a weak grin thinking of the note, the keys, the nugget. The truck didn't run. The nugget was barely worth the trouble to assay it. And the note should make the cabin a pariah to a future owner. It would serve the greedy bastards right.

Even if such things did have value, he'd need none where he was going.

1

May 26, 2017

On this steamy twilight in May, I slipped off my Mom's old barrel-racing horse and stood with her and Dad's dog at their back fence. I gazed across twenty-five overgrown acres ending in a rise of oak, cottonwood and pine. The Applegate River whispered beyond the trees. An ancient log cabin hunkered there in purple shadows.

I could just see this gem all gussied up, annexed to my folks' forty acres outside Grants Pass and thriving as a guest ranch. I'd often dreamed of that in the five years I'd been back in Oregon's Rogue Valley after twenty-five years as a reporter for a Seattle newspaper. My friend Tulip Clemmons and I struggled to support our horse-showing habit. We also busted our hump to keep our tack shop, The Best Little Horsehouse in Oregon, in the black. We might do better selling our houses, tapping our 401Ks and bringing our horses home from the trainers. Then incorporating the store into a proposed B, B & B—a western-theme bed, barn and breakfast.

Now Tulip and yours truly, ex-reporter Pepper Kane, had a chance to make our dream come true.

Over dinner that night my father had spilled the news: The old place might be going on the market. Because it was not listed, we might cobble together a by-owner sale, saving us thousands in real-estate fees. At once I decided to hop on Mom's old sorrel. He needed exercise and I needed to go to see if the place was as desirable as I recalled. If so, I would contact the owners, recently moved to a senior residence.

Now I saw that repairs to the barbed-wire fence dividing the properties blocked my way. I'd have to go on foot. Untacking the horse, I set down the saddle to tote back later, and shooed the sway-backed animal back the way we'd come.

While the yellow Lab-heeler dog sniffed the air, my mind dredged up childhood memories. Tulip and I riding through fields and forest owned by a succession of slightly odd neighbors. Fishing or tubing the river that joined the Rogue farther down. Picking blackberries that bled purple on our thorn-torn fingers. Sneaking into that cabin, rumored to be haunted.

A mosquito pricked my arm. I slapped it dead. I'd soon take a pinch of dirt, spit in it and rub the slurry on the bite to calm the itch, an old Lakota trick my elusive lover, Sonny Chief, showed me in November on his last visit. Right before my Brassbottom Barn buddies and I traveled to compete in the World horse-show in Texas.

Now, under a darkening sky, this peaceful country scene was much as I remembered. It was sure to please the scores of guests that Tulip and I, aided by family and friends, would entertain when we opened the Western mini-resort of our dreams.

Yes, the fields and trees were heart-fillingly beautiful. But it was the rustic cabin that drew my eye. Did it still carry the curse imposed by the famous writer, its first occupant, as neighbors claimed? As its current owners and prospective realtors would be loath to disclose?

Pulling strands of rusty barbed-wire apart to spare myself pain or disfigurement, I bent over and eased through. Heller paced back and forth, ignoring my commands to come. Farther down that darned dog found an entry more to his liking and crawled under the wire, getting a free backscratch in the process.

I had to grin. He was yellow-Lab sweet, cow-dog clever and bulldog stubborn.

Keeping the cabin in sight, aware of jays and doves calling in the trees, I made my way through thick weeds and past oak, pine and madrone seedlings. I followed an old truck track toward the cabin. Old Heller bounded ahead, drawn by some enticing scent or other.

"Heller," I said. "Stay close." I didn't want him crashing through poison oak and then making me itch when I petted him. Nor did I want him startling some rattlesnake curled behind a bush or boulder. True to form, he semi-obeyed.

As I brushed past low grass, seeds leaped onto my jeans. Spicy herbal scents filled my nose. A gamey whiff wafted past, then as quickly wafted away.

I continued walking toward the cabin in the trees. I was sad to see how the once-sturdy four-room abode had deteriorated in the forty or so years since I'd last seen it. Its river-rock chimney leaned precariously and its cedar-shake roof sagged under moss and leaves. Its windows were cracked and fogged. You once could spy the river from the great-room window on the left. I doubted you could see it now for the trees.

A support pillar of the front porch, if you could call it that, was kicked askew. The cabin's lopsided back section with the bath and two bedrooms listed perilously.

What a handsome little place it must have been when Preston O'Hara had lived there, when his pioneer sagas and shoot-'em-up Westerns were all the rage in the 1930s and 1940s, and made into movies. In the time he hunted deer and elk from horseback, fished the river and panned it for gold. We used to watch his movies at the theater downtown on Saturday afternoons. By then he'd been gone twenty years.

This offshoot of the semi-rural community called Jerome Prairie was considered the wilds back in the day.

In the mid-1950s people thought my parents nuts for buying out so far—nearly eight miles from Grants Pass—a thriving timber town with a river and railroad tracks running through it. And buying so near a property with a troubled past, despite that a newer cottage was built out by the road, allowing the cabin to continue its return to earth.

When I drew within a hundred feet I glimpsed the collapsed pole-barn behind and to one side of the cabin. The old corrals where Tulip and I stashed our horses while we explored the property years ago were invisible, likely pulled down by towers of long grass and wild-pea vines.

Rumor had it that O'Hara in his heyday had entertained celebrities such as Clark Gable and John Wayne at this rustic retreat before a lawsuit accusing him of plagiarism, and then Communism, drove him to hang himself from the cabin's main beam. He'd left a note saying he'd put a curse on the cabin, saying "they" had cost him his home and his life. Threatening that whoever else tried to make this their home, would lose their life, as well.

It was the stuff of legend. And of his blockbuster books and movies.

However, all that had taken place so long ago, when Tulip and I were young in the late 1960s and early 1970s, that we could barely fathom it. We just thought it an apocryphal tale from an era we'd only read about, and embroidered over the years. Events worthy of a horror film couldn't have happened so close to our homes where everything was boringly normal.

We whispered about it anyway through long summers of roaming fields, forests and rivers that included this end of the neighbors' dogleg-shaped farm. The cabin had lain undisturbed as owners in the newer house refused to have anything to do with it.

Tulip and I, along with a few other friends when a wild hair got up our shorts, sometimes peeked in the windows, tiptoed through the rooms and dared each other to spend a night inside—though we never did. Now, ironic as it seemed, we might get a chance to, if the property became ours. We'd even talked of restoring the cabin as an attraction of our guest ranch, tricked out with O'Hara's books, movie posters and era furnishings.

I stopped some fifty feet from the cabin. Heller stopped, too, lowered his head and growled. There was that odd smell again. Cloyingly sweet and rancid at the same time. Something dead. As if predatory animals had brought kill to the cabin, or to the ramble of blackberries creeping over its mortared-stone foundation.

A breeze came up, momentarily dispatching the scent and blowing a hank of red hair over my eyes. I pushed back the locks and took a few more steps forward, kicking aside honeysuckle vines snaked around my ankles.

Heller raised his head. His tail stood stiffly at attention. A questioning whine.

The scent returned, even stronger. Standing fifteen feet from the porch, I almost gagged. The meal my mom had lovingly prepared was at risk of being lost. While the stench filled my nose and mouth, foreboding filled my heart. I knew the odor emanating from the cabin was more than that of some small unfortunate animal.

As a reporter I'd been to crime scenes, sometimes with first responders. I knew this was no coyote—or cougar—kill, although I'd come across those, too, since I'd been back in the Valley. I pulled my cell phone from my pocket, saw the Reba McEntire lookalike on a chestnut horse staring back, and noticed I had "no service."

The dog whined and started toward the steps. I grabbed his collar.

"Heller, sit," I commanded. The dog squatted, body rigid but trembling, eyes fixed on the cabin door. He lifted his snout, nostrils fluttering to absorb every nuance.

I ducked under the drooping porch roof, breathed through my mouth and took one creaking step up. Then another. I felt inexplicably chilled. In the trees an owl called. The mournful staccato hoots sounded like a warning.

It was darker on the porch. A cobweb plastered itself to my face. I pulled it off and wiped my fingers on my jeans. I flinched when a rat skittered from a stack of kindling to the left of the door.

I paused to calm myself. But my blood pressure had already shot up. My ears rang as if I'd been to a rock concert.

What in hell am I doing? Out here alone, with no weapon, no phone service, in a place where death is no stranger?

The door was open a crack, askew on loose hinges. When I kicked it open, it gave an ominous screech. The dirty windows let in little of the day's remaining light, but let in enough. A woman's body lay face down, head turned to reveal a pale, prominent left cheek. She was short and obese, wearing a white peasant-blouse bearing an enormous, black vase-print over a full skirt. The skirt fanned out from her cowboy-booted legs the way her dark hair spread out from her face on the wide-plank floor.

"Hello?" I said, voice cracking.

Nothing.

I hadn't really expected an answer. She was too still. Plus there was the stench. Bile pushed into my throat. Heller lunged forward to sniff at her furiously.

"Heller, no!" I shouted. The dog slunk back to my side. "Sit." For once, he did.

Cell phone still in hand to call 911 when I got out of the cabin and had service, I swept my gaze around the dim room with its cathedral ceiling and rough-hewn overhead beam. A chunky armchair with spots of exposed stuffing stood in a corner by the main window. Books and papers littered a small table next to it. A medium-sized mug lay near the woman's left hand—as if she'd been toting coffee from the wall-kitchen to my right.

Operating on reporter instinct before getting the hell out and calling 911, I shot a half-a-dozen cell-phone flash photos. You never knew when your images of a scene might come in handy. They had helped beef up stories several times in my career.

It struck me this woman might have been homeless and squatting in a vacant shelter as did many displaced souls in the Rogue Valley. Had she suffered a medical event? Tripped and hit her head?

My eyes darted back to her body. I stared a minute longer, breathing through my mouth. Then I felt punched in the chest. Some kind of short stick protruded from her upper back. I leaned closer. Shock rolled through me. The stick was a hatchet handle, the blade's butt visible but its cutting edge buried between her shoulder blades.

That dark vase-shape I had considered a printed pattern on the woman's blouse? That was no fashion image. It was blood. I held my phone flashlight to it and saw it had pooled and coagulated beneath her. And there was a lot of it.

A scream froze in my throat. I glanced around, goosebumps needling my skin. The woman must have died a few days earlier and begun to decompose rapidly as the afternoons heated to the unseasonable nineties. Hopefully whoever had killed her was long gone, and had not seen me enter the cabins. But if he or she were still in the area, I didn't need to announce my presence with a scream.

Heller at my heels, I turned and bolted out the door and into the twilit field where a full moon was rising in the south. I speed-walked back toward my parents' fence. I looked around as if I were being watched. My foot hit a stone, pitching me forward. Recovering, I touched my phone home button, saw one bar of service and punched the emergency icon.

"911, what is your emergency?" said a clipped female voice.

"I just found a deceased woman in a cabin next to my parents' farm in the Jerome Prairie neighborhood."

"Are you in any danger?"

"Maybe. Just hurry." My voice wavered.

I quickly gave the dispatcher further details. Then I tapped my parents' number while crickets tuned up for their nighttime serenade.

Mom's melodious voice came through the phone's speaker.

"Pepper, honey, where the hell are you? You said you'd only be gone ten minutes. Just took the apricot pie out of the oven."

"Mom. Listen. I found a woman's body in the cabin on the farm behind yours."

"What? You found a body?" Her voice became muffled. "Gus! She found a body." Then louder as she came back on. "Where are you now? Are you OK?"

"I called 911. They'll be coming up your drive-way. I'm OK and on my way." I pulled apart the fence wires and wriggled through, taking a blood-drawing tear on the forearm as I passed. Heller could find his own way through.

"Sure there's nobody on your tail?"

"Mom," I said, retrieving her lightweight saddle and balancing it on one hip as I started across the hayfield. "Turn on all the lights. Have Dad come out with a shotgun. Woman's been dead awhile, but her killer might still be around."

2

Despite the saddle, I made like a scalded coyote toward my folks' outbuildings and their lit-up house beyond. Halfway there I met my short, wiry father toting a flashlight and a shotgun. He aimed the light beam at me. I raised an arm to shield my eyes.

"That you, Pepper?" Dad said, though he could see perfectly well. "You OK?" He waved the beam around the hayfield and back toward the fence. His usually bent form looked straighter tonight, his step surer. He had come to the aid of his fifty-five-year-old baby girl. Ready to take on the world, if needed. But first he took the saddle.

"Where's the horse?" He raised the saddle to one shoulder and balanced it there with one hand.

"Sent her back to the barn," I said, giving him a hug. "Someone's patched the old fence, and we couldn't ride through."

"But you're OK."

"I'm OK, If you call my just finding a body OK." I felt his worried eyes on me as we hurried back to the old yellow farmhouse. "I feel a bit sick. But with you here and police coming, I'll be fine."

"That's my girl." He reached out his free hand to touch mine as we walked.

I took his hand and squeezed it, looking at his profile faintly outlined in light from lamps mounted on the barn, garage and workshop.

"I love you, Dad."

Augustus "Gus" Kane, the best accountant the Valley ever saw, and grower of the zingiest hot peppers this side of New Mexico, might not be much help in a real crisis, what with age and dementia nibbling at him. But I was glad he'd come.

"Told you not to go back there," he said, shaking his head as the bright windows of the house beckoned. "Especially not with dark coming on."

"When have I ever listened to you, Dad? And it wasn't dark when I left."

"You could've explored that place in daylight, taken someone with you. I thought Tulip was interested in it, too. Isn't Sonny due for a visit soon?"

"Couldn't wait, Dad. You said the owners might put it on the market next week, and I don't get over from Gold Hill that often. This was an early chance to check it out, make sure it was right for our guest ranch."

"Not right if that curse is still in place, which it sounds like it is."

"Not sure I believe in curses, Dad." But I might now, after tonight.

Heller loped to the house ahead of us. He stopped to look back every so often to make sure we were coming, and then bounded forward again. I wasn't sure how much help that decrepit mutt would be in a crisis, either.

"How'd the woman die? Any idea who she was?"

"Hatchet in the back." I shuddered. "No. Didn't recognize her."

"Was there much blood? How'd she look?" He was panting from walking too fast while carrying a saddle. I slowed for him. I could have taken the saddle but didn't want to dent his pride.

"Yes, Dad," I said. "Some blood. An older lady, short and obese, dressed nice, face down on the great room floor."

He tightened his hand holding mine. My mosquito bite on my arm began to itch. I stooped to take a pinch of soil, spat into it and rubbed it on the bump.

Sonny was right. It stopped the itch. God, I wished he were here. It had been six too-long months. We had not been apart that long ever in our long-distance romance. Four months at most. But I would see him when I traveled to Seattle in less than two weeks to compete in a regional horse-show. It wouldn't be too soon.

"Don't know why you always gotta get yourself in trouble, Pepper," Dad said. "Put yourself in danger. You don't know how your mother and I worry."

"Oh, I think I do, Dad. I have kids, too, remember? Your granddaughter and grandson? Chili and Serrano put me through the ringer when they were young. Even now, at times. In their thirties and still not settled down."

My adult children's father, the first of two controlling husbands I'd caught and released, had been no help. He might even have been part of the problem.

"At least your kids are not always chasing down killers," Dad grumbled.

I had no answer. We were at the back porch. Mom stepped out just as I heard a vehicle roar up the gravel drive out front. Colored lights swept the right side of the house yard. Police radio chat overtook the buzz of the cricket chorus.

Mom propped her bull-pizzle cane on the back-door frame, stepped down and pulled me into a hug before I climbed to the kitchen.

"Thank God you're safe," she said, pressing her bony, sweet-smelling cheek to mine. Hot pie-smells floated past us. White hairs that had escaped her thick topknot tickled my ear.

"Sorry I gave you a scare," I said, patting her erect back. Martha Mosey Kane might be past eighty, but she still had the trim, firm body of a younger cowgirl. And fitted Western shirts, jeans and trophy-buckles to show it all off. Her late older sister Connie, who'd run a dude ranch up in Washington, had been the same. Pistols to the end. Proudly—though distantly—related to Annie Oakley; it figured.

A loud banging on the door and the ringing of the doorbell set Heller to barking and drew us into the house. Dad reached the front door first. He yanked it open to reveal two officers wearing Smokey hats and tan-and-olive sheriff's uniforms. Behind them under the ancient oak stood a black-and white sheriff's unit, its light bar shooting rainbows around the house and yard.

I recognized the taller officer as Josephine County Sheriff Grant Welles from TV coverage of area crimes. Stepping forward, he seemed taller than he appeared on the small screen. His face looked craggy and pale in the porch light's glare.

"Sheriff Grant Welles," he said. He stood with his long legs slightly apart and gave a smart nod of his hat. "Responding to a report of a body?"

I was momentarily stunned at seeing the handsome sheriff in real life. Fit, fine and forty-five, he was all business. Close-cropped hair, serious eyes and mouth. But something about the guy set my socks on fire. I loved Sonny with all my heart. Inexplicably, the rest of my body sometimes had its own ideas. Not that I would consider acting on them.

"Pepper Kane," I said, pulling myself together. "I called it in. I was walking the neighbors' farm I'm interested in buying—behind my folks' farm—and found a deceased woman in the old cabin by the river. Fifteen, twenty minutes ago."

Sheriff Welles stood a few inches shy of Sonny Chief's six-foot-six altitude. But he carried himself with the same manly confidence. Dark hair showed behind large, flat ears and in straight, bushy eyebrows above deep-set eyes. Long laugh lines framed a wide mouth. He reminded me of someone but I couldn't think who. What a pleasant change from the pushy-grizzly sheriff in my home county some miles south.

He listened with professional attentiveness. But he took my measure with deep-brown eyes that didn't miss a trick, and might know the whereabouts of a hidden ace.

I jumped when Dad clapped a hand on my shoulder.

"My daughter was a big time newspaper reporter," he said in a prideful tone. "You've probably heard she's helped you guys solve some crimes around the Valley. Down there in Sam Houston's territory, too. Why in Fort Worth just last fall, Pepper—"

"Oh, Dad." I smiled sheepishly at Sheriff Welles. Behind him a skinny, younger deputy hung back with one hand at his side, the other on his service weapon. "Evening, deputy," I said. "Thought you guys didn't work this late, what with the funding cuts."

"County gave us extra hours because of Boatnik," Welles said.

I nodded, saying nothing. But my eyes must have asked the question I was thinking, because he gave an answer a heartbeat later.

"City police have their hands full downtown on Memorial Day weekend, at Riverside Park and everywhere else. So we keep an eye on the riverbanks and roads outside of town. Drinking, driving and illegal fireworks aren't a good combination."

"I haven't been to the boat races or night carnival in years," I said, thinking how I'd watched the races from the riverfront park when I was a teen. "Got to get back there one day, but watch from a safe distance. Like a deck at Taprock Northwest Grill."

Welles and the deputy nodded as a black-and-yellow Oregon State Police unit roared up the drive. Lights from both vehicles danced across our faces. The OSP unit parked, engine running. The driver's-side door swung open. A female voice, radio static and chatter stuttered through the night air. A sturdy-looking uniformed woman got out. She played her flashlight beam around the yard.

The light picked up the ghostly eyes of Cootie Three, Mom's gelding now safely ensconced in the pasture, and the lights and chrome of a swoopy silver car tooling by on the road–likely a driver curious about the police presence on his quiet country lane.

"Be on your way, dude," I muttered. "Catch it on the news tomorrow."

The OSP officer walked closer. Her name tag read "Broughton." She greeted the sheriff and deputy, and introduced herself to my folks and me, now out on the porch.

"Ma'am," I said.

"Where's the cabin where you found the body?" she asked.

"Back of my parents' house about a quarter mile," I said. "It's on the neighbors' property bordering the river. It's farther, but you can access their house from the road, one driveway down." I pointed ahead and to my right.

She nodded, clicked on her service flashlight and headed across the yard.

"Go ahead," she shouted back to Welles and the deputy. "See you in a minute."

On the porch, we got back to business. I gave Sheriff Welles details of my grisly discovery plus a backstory on the cabin and its owners. Also the address of the main residence on the property, down the road a few hundred feet. He jotted notes while Broughton vanished around the house corner.

Partway through my debriefing Dad went to find a note he'd written with contact info for the Robertsons, the adjoining property owners. No one had really known them. They kept to themselves the two or three years they'd lived there. But Dad had briefly spoken with the oldsters five days ago by their house where their fifty-something son, Cleve, and a teenage boy loaded a pickup and van with furnishings. The Robertsons were moving to a retirement community.

"That's when I heard they were thinking of putting their place on the market," Dad concluded. He held out the note with the Robertson information to Welles. "My daughter and a friend hoped to buy it if it ever came up for sale."

"Can I see that, Dad?" I said. I grabbed my cell phone and copied the info into Contacts. "Thanks."

Broughton approached the porch again as Welles took Dad's note. She told us she'd walk with us to the cabin, do her own recon, call EMTs if necessary. Then she would secure the scene and call the state forensics team. They'd bring their van first thing in the morning.

"An OSP detective will be assigned to the investigation, if one is deemed necessary. We'll be in touch." She returned to her unit and cut the engine.

I turned to Welles.

"Too bad you guys have no funds to hire your own investigators," I said.

Dad wasted no time jumping in to beat one of his favorite drums.

"Rural property owners have the lowest taxes in Oregon," he groused. "Yet they vote down propositions that fund county services like you guys. So we're on our own."

Uh-oh, I thought. Here we go. I touched his arm, but he pulled it away. He was just warming up.

"Thank the tree huggers who killed timber harvests that funded half the county budget before 1992," he said, gathering steam. "Now overgrown forests burn out of control rather than benefitting from smart, income-generating management." His words were ripped from one of his frequent letters-to-the-editor.

Welles listened patiently, but probably thought, 'Tell me about it.' When Dad was done, the sheriff nodded and gave us a courteous smile.

"Thanks for your help, Miz Kane, Mr. and Mrs. Kane." Welles touched his hat brim. Broughton waited in the side yard.

"No problem, Sheriff," I said. "I'll show you the way." I told him how the cabin also could be reached via pastures beyond the newer house on the Robertson farm.

"You've been through enough tonight," he said. "Just get us started. We'll find it. We may have more questions, but don't feel you have to stay. You can give a statement downtown on Monday depending on what we find." He handed me his card.

I took the card and rubbed my bare arms, though the night was still warm.

"Oh, Sheriff?"

He looked back.

"I doubt the cabin has power," I said, "although there used to be lines out there."

"We have lights. We'll take a quick look around tonight. Secure the scene until OSP brings their team tomorrow. If it turns out to be complicated, investigators could be there two or three days."

"It's this way," I said, gesturing toward the side yard. He swept his light beam over the lawn as I skipped down the steps. Passing him, I smelled clean uniform and warm man. Not at all unpleasant.

I jogged toward the house corner with Welles and the deputy bearing gear in my wake. Their flashlights picked out Broughton a few yards ahead. I broke to a walk as I passed the garage, chicken coop and Dad's newly planted chili patch. The horse stalls and covered arena ahead and to our right appeared decent enough by moonlight. But Tulip and I had our work cut out for us, to make them presentable for future ranch guests—if, after tonight, there would be a ranch.

We continued on through the hay field lush with new grass. Crickets sang while Heller bounded ahead, tail wagging. Finally we stood at the barbed-wire fence. Sheriff Welles and the others swung their light beams around the landscape, focusing on the distant trees and the wreck of a cabin faintly visible among them.

"That the place?" Broughton said.

"It is," I said. "Again, far as we know, no one's lived in the cabin for years." I thought of the dead woman and how the mug, papers and chair suggested that she or someone else had made a rude home there. "Be careful, though. Pretty run down."

Welles, his face faintly lit from the flashlights scanning the area, smiled down at me. His eyes lingered on mine. At least that was my read.

"We've probably dealt with worse."

I blushed, hoping he wouldn't notice. *Of course he'd seen worse.*

"Let us know if we can be of any further help."

He watched his deputy and Broughton lift gear over the fence. As if reading my thoughts, he said, "I wouldn't worry too much that a killer is still around. We'll have someone there all night. We've put extra patrols past your parents' house, as well."

"Thanks. I just hope my folks aren't in danger."

"Is the river past those trees?" He nodded in that direction.

"Yes, a hundred feet give or take."

"Did you go there, or know of any activity down there tonight?"

I thought that an odd question.

"No reason to. Why?"

"People have been known to party along this stretch of the Applegate, especially in warm weather. Some cult activity, but it's been awhile. You may've read there was a drowning five, six years ago."

That nudged something in my mind.

"I was working in Seattle then, but I heard about it. Wasn't it a pagan baptism or something like that, gone wrong?"

"That was the theory. Not proven, though. No convictions." He ran his light beam along the fence line.

"The wires are pretty loose where I crawled through." I motioned to my left.

"Thanks. We'll be in touch." He tapped a finger to his hat, bent over and crawled through the fence where the deputy held apart the wires.

3

I watched the three make their way across the long moonlit field. Then I turned and walked to my parents' rear door opening onto their warm, bright kitchen. We sank into ladder-back chairs to rehash the evening. Mom offered coffee, which I took, and offered pie, which I declined.

"I might take pie home for tomorrow, though," I said, not wanting to offend.

She pursed her scarlet lips and ran a hand over her topknot. She pushed in a hairpin that had partially popped out. "Right before eating, dust the pie with parmesan," she advised. "That really kicks up the flavor."

That did it. My appetite for a sweet fix made itself known. It never ceased to amaze me how often I craved something to munch after a crisis. And, as just about everyone knows, I have a weakness for pie. Even after a crisis. Sometimes, *especially* after a crisis.

"Maybe I'll have just a tiny sliver," I said. "For the road."

As we savored warm apricot pie, my folks kept their questions to a minimum. We were bushed. The evening's developments were just too stunning. But Mom and Dad did probe a bit, and who could blame them?

"So, you still interested in buying that place?" Dad said, blotting his mouth.

"I'll have to get back to you on that," I said.

"Did you have any sense of the poor woman's face, who she was?" Mom said.

"Not really," I said. "But she had long, dark hair. And high cheekbones. She was short, overweight, older." While describing her, I recalled something I hadn't thought I'd registered at the time, when I was probably in shock. "She wore cowboy boots. Pointy-toed. Vintage."

Experienced a reporter as I was, as curious as I was, it still surprised me to later recall details I hadn't thought I'd noticed when first seeing a crime or accident scene. I knew that was one reason reporters and detectives asked the same questions over and over of witnesses or suspects. To tease out something they'd buried in their subconscious during a discovery. Or see if their story changed, raising a flag.

I'd taken photos. But I wasn't in the mood to look at them then. I could do that later when I had more of my wits about me. Besides, I didn't want to cause my parents further distress.

"Now that's odd," Dad put in. "Saw a gal like that—flouncy skirt, long dark hair, old-timey boots— over at the Farm Co-op last week. Rammed my cart. Cussed a blue streak. Made me feel like I was the one who should be apologizing."

I pondered that. *What kind of person would do that to an old guy? To anyone?*

"Probably a coincidence," I said. Then another, more worrisome thought arose. "Did Mom take you to the store, Dad? Or are you driving again? After that accident with Lone Ranger last year?" They still hadn't fixed the dent in the F250.

"Like, you need to ask?" muttered Mom. "Never listens to anything we say."

I gave Dad an exaggerated wink.

"Runs in the family," I said.

Dad rolled his eyes and forked another piece of pie into his mouth.

'I wonder how much more time they'll take out there tonight," I said. "Or if they need me for anything more."

"They know where to reach you," Mom said. "It's getting late, it's Friday night, so you'd best hit the road for home. Drunks'll be out before you know it, if not now."

"You're right," I said, rising. "Hey, good pie. Wish I felt like more. So I can take the rest of it home?"

She eyed me and nodded, but refrained from her usual comment about my need to watch my weight. Mom didn't seem to be aware she was a big reason I had put on a few pounds. Bracing her fists on the table she rose to wrap the pie. *Where had she found such sweet, plump apricots in late May? Likely off a truck from California.*

My cell phone ringtone sang a line from the country classic, "Good-Hearted Woman." I felt a small thrill when I saw who was calling. Talk about timing.

Sonny Chief.

"Hell-oh," said his sing-song basso voice. The voice of a tall, darkly handsome and maddeningly desirable lover who might occasionally see other women—though not lately—but who also ran to me when I needed him. A long-distance affair with a freedom-loving man was risky. But somehow we'd managed to hold it together, even said the four-letter "L" word, and hinted at longevity. Well, I had hinted.

"Hey, stranger," I said, sounding more upbeat than I felt.

"Whatcha doin' on a lonesome Friday night?"

He was checking up on me. That I liked.

"You mean … other than finding a body?"

The line went silent. I watched Mom wrap the pie in foil, slide it into a bag and hand it to me. I took it and my phone into the living room.

"You're kidding," Sonny finally said as I sank into a plush, red-leather Western armchair.

"Would I kid about a thing like that? I found a dead woman in that old cabin on the farm next to my parents'."

"Tell me about it."

As I finished the story, I heard a knock on the kitchen door. Through the arch between parlor and kitchen, I saw the deputy's face in the door window. Dad cracked the door and began talking with him.

"Hold on, Sonny," I said. "The police are back."

"Wait. Where are you, Pepper?"

"At my parents'."

"Sounds like I'd better get down there."

"Where are *you*? North Dakota with the pipeline protesters? Heard there was a leak that might contaminate reservation water." Keeping order at the Water Protector camps—official and otherwise—had kept my love busy the better part of a year. Those protests, which shed a light on problems of marginalized peoples—often seemed a losing battle.

"In Seattle with my kids. And their mom. But I can come now, if you need me."

My heart thumped.

Sonny's adult children, fine. But their mom? His ex? What was up with that?

"Don't disrupt your plans, Sonny, if you're in the middle of something. I'll be fine." I tried to sound normal. I told him the rest of my tale about my discovery, and lost myself in it for a while.

When I was done, Dad motioned me to the open back door. I asked Sonny to hang on. Sheriff Welles stepped up to the deputy's side.

"Be sure to call if you have any concerns," Welles said. "The scene is secured. An OSP detective will contact you. Thanks again." With a crisp nod, he left.

I took the phone back into the living room.

"Just the police saying they'd secured the scene," I explained.

"Sure you don't need me?" Sonny said. "I might be able to slip away."

I kept a tight hold on my cool. No need to get into his Seattle situation with the ex that crazy night, and with my parents eavesdropping in the next room.

"I'll see you a week from Tuesday when I come up for the Seattle horse show, Sonny. Yes, I need you. But you need to take care of business with your... family."

"Say the word, Pepper, and I'll be there."

"Let's talk in the morning." I neatly added, "When I'm thinking straight and can think how to ask about your ex without sounding like a worried, jealous shrew."

"Go home, sleep tight. Give that beautiful body its beauty rest. I'd like to touch and taste it right now. Mmmm."

What a naughty boy. And I loved him for it, clinging tight to the idea that his desire was directed toward me exclusively, to the idea his broad white smile was all mine, and that his sexy black eyes saw only me.

However at times like this, when I was exhausted some way and other women's names or activities rose up in conversation or rumor, I slipped into a pit of worry.

After we disconnected I felt happy he'd called, offered help and told me sweet nothings. But I also felt like another bad thing was about to happen. Like the ground was collapsing under me. I hoped it was only the cumulative stress from a nightmare night. But it may've been my reporter's hunch that Sonny was loosening our bond.

Sonny and Tammy, nicknamed "Pook," had been divorced six years. He and I became an item the day after he'd filed. We'd continued our connection even after I moved to Oregon. Ours was an unconventional relationship, to say the least. Family and friends found it puzzling. But we each needed individual space and alone time, knowing we could count on each other when the chips were down.

That was the official story. However I sometimes wished we could be more.

Now his ex was back in the picture. In what way? And how much back? Sonny had his main home on the Standing Rock rez in South Dakota, working part-time as a tribal cop. But he also traveled to help Sioux people in Seattle, stayed with his young-adult kids who lived there, and visited me in Southern Oregon.

This mention of the ex wasn't what I needed to hear right now. I'd just found a murdered woman. I was, with Tulip, trying to keep my horse in training and our tack store solvent while contemplating a venture that now seemed threatened. On a lesser but similarly stressful note, I was preparing to show my Paint horse, Chocolate Waterfall, for a potentially lucrative show four hundred miles up the pike.

Now my turned-on relationship with the love of my life, Sonny Chief, might be on the brink of being permanently switched off.

4.

I shed tired tears on the way home and pounded the steering wheel. Turned the country-radio station on loud, then turned it off. Rolled down the window of my dually pickup, "Red Ryder," to let cool air blast my face. Rolled it up again.

A mile from my four-acre ranchita south of the town of Gold Hill, I wiped my eyes and cowgirled up. What a night it had been — maybe a Crown Royal kind of night. I was in a steaming pile of trouble. Had found a murdered woman. Faced an "iffy" real-estate deal. Then forced to take a look at my possibly teetering affair. I'd power through these problems one step at a time. But tonight I might be assisted by "spirits." The alcoholic kind.

Alcohol wasn't something I called upon often. I needed a darned good reason. Now there were at least three. I think I had a finger or two left in that dusty, black velvet-cloaked bottle on the fridge.

Home had never felt as good as it did that night. Oh, I know. I always say that, especially after trying times. But tonight I meant it. I replayed the scene when Welles and his deputy returned to my folks' house.

It surprised me that, upon seeing the sheriff again, I'd felt nothing. The rush I'd felt when first meeting him was gone. It was just a phantom of the night and circumstances. I wondered, though, if I'd had a premonition of Sonny's troubling call.

Welles had given me an odd look before departing. I didn't know what to make of it. Had he felt our earlier attraction, too?

Then I chided myself. He probably had just given me the look because I was the one who was fascinated with the cabin and had found the body. Along with next-of-kin, I'd likely be a person of interest in the crime and among the first to be questioned.

"Discuss the case with no one and call if you remember more," were his parting words. Strictly professional. Although I knew I'd share tidbits with Sonny and Tulip.

Therefore I was then free to move about the country, as they say. Which tonight had meant the usual feeding of the two horses at my modest acreage, checking every room in my Western-themed doublewide, and playing on the carpet with my madly licking Boston terriers.

Charlie and Shayna acted like they hadn't seen me all day, which was true. I'd gone straight to my folks' after closing the Horsehouse. My afternoon shift had run a little late. Luckily I'd left the dogs, food and water in a stall.

Charlie's popping brown eyes looked concerned when I got down on the floor to play. From under frosted brows he stared questions at me. He licked my face a long time. Soon my pretty, long-legged Shayna did the same.

What would I do without my support team?

I found a knotted towel for tug-o'-war and we set to playing. The activity soon had me sweating. But I caught myself smiling.

When I thought we'd had enough romping, I showered, jammied up and poured that finger of Crown. I settled into "Big Brown," my leather recliner with the nailhead trim and down-filled cushions, and took a warming sip. Then I switched on the TV to KMFD, the local network-affiliate station.

No surprise that my shocking discovery was among the lead stories.

"A woman's body was found a few hours ago in an abandoned shack beside the Applegate River outside Grants Pass," began the polished-looking anchorwoman. "No name or cause of death was given, pending an investigation by Oregon State Police. However we've learned a neighbor found the body. More details as they develop."

"A neighbor," indeed. Get the facts right, people. We print reporters, in our day, had never been so slack at reporting hard, breaking news. The natural animosity between us and the broadcast media was like that of cats and dogs: congenital.

A stock clip of the Applegate River and steep, close-in hills came on the screen, as well as a soundless clip of Sheriff Welles and a photo of a State Police vehicle.

That was it. I expected more. But, I reminded myself, I'd found the body around eight and it was now only eleven. Cop-suckups and ambulance-chasers like that pesky Shane Chapelle from this main Medford news station, along with other reporters and first responders, would have heard the call come over the scanner about nine. Not enough time had elapsed for police to have issued a detailed statement.

Tomorrow or Sunday, when media types had finally tracked down the so-called "neighbor" who found the body and reported her name, my phone would vibrate off the table with calls from friends and reporters craving a scoop straight from the horse, or horse-lover's, mouth.

Terrific. I couldn't wait.

Licking the last of the Crown from the rim of my glass, I gathered the Boston Nation and tumbled into bed.

Through the night, visions of hatchets in backs drifted through my mind. They awoke me once, sending me to the bathroom for a soothing glass of cold water and an aspirin. Then they troubled me no more.

* * *

Feeling more rested than I'd thought, I awoke an hour later than my usual five-thirty. I turned on Mister Coffee, let out the dogs and headed down to the barn to feed horses. That'd be Bob, my chunky bay Paint—a retired but far from retiring Western show horse—and Lucy, a brown Quarter Horse I boarded for a friend. They were up and in full cry, doing their best starving-orphan-horse-in-the-snow impression. They could have taken that act on the road.

"You guys slay me," I told them as I dumped a fat flake of grass-alfalfa-mix hay in the manger of each stall. Having galloped hard to the barn from wherever they'd been on my cross-fenced land, they panted and blew while attacking their breakfast.

Since I was down there, I set about cleaning and refilling water buckets. Then I found a ratty barn broom and swept cobwebs off the rafters, walls and hay-bale stack. Hard sweaty work gave my body something to do while my brain replayed my discovery of the body and interview with police. Coughing, I pulled my neckerchief over my nose to keep out dust.

I wondered what the woman's story was. Who she was. She might have secretly lived there, possibly growing pot out in back to make ends meet, as some did. Did she have any idea of the celebrity who long ago lived there and left a curse? Maybe she was a diehard O'Hara fan or a writer, making a pilgrimage. OK, that last was a stretch.

The burning questions were, who killed her and why. Love, money and gross disrespect were the Big

Three motives for murder. Was she killed by a rival? By a spurned lover? Or by a stranger, for some other purpose?

I had a shipload of sleuthing ahead. I was dying to know the truth, yes. Maybe a poor word choice, but appropriate. I was, after all, a born reporter. Nosy, curious, a tad pushy. I was also keen to help people, even strangers. The woman and her relatives deserved closure. And, despite all, I was still interested in the property. A side reason was that I needed to find answers and clear my name, or law enforcement and the media could make my life miserable. It's what they did.

Who knew? Maybe I myself, as discoverer of the body, was at risk. What if the killer still lived or hung out in the area, and thought that I'd seen or known something. He could even now be plotting how to "take care of" me. Considering all possibilities, here, no matter how seemingly remote.

As I wound down my work, I managed to blunt the dull pain of finding a body, of the images of her distorted face and outstretched hands. I also forgot the worry I'd felt after Sonny's call. Nothing like a physical workout to smooth out stress.

The horses were still hard at their breakfast. They pinned their ears when I approached them for pats. They took offense at being interrupted during a meal.

I noticed both horses were fat, out of shape. I needed to take Bob trail-riding in the hills outside my place. I spent most of my free time riding my current show horse, Chocolate Waterfall, a red-brown and white gelding in show training with Dutch and Donna Grandeen at Brassbottom Barn ten miles down the road. The horse I'd show in Seattle.

Which reminded me. I was due to at Brassbottom in an hour for a lesson, with Tulip working the morning shift at The Horsehouse. I had to practice show patterns with my trainer and buddies also going to the Sea-Tac Summer Classic. I'd made the final cut in prime-time amateur trail at the World Open Western Show in Texas last fall, but had fallen short of winning a *bona fide* world championship in trail. I had to work harder and smarter on that event.

Given my present situation, as finder of a body, should I still take that lesson? Was I even up to it?

Hell, yeah. I had a lot of money and time riding on the show. And stood to win some money. Money that could help support The Horsehouse for a while longer as I sorted out the death on the Applegate.

Back at the house, while I inhaled buttered artisan toast and creamed Sumatra roast, and watched turkey-bacon go 'round in the nuke box, my phone sang out.

It was Mom. I'd hoped it was Sonny Chief. Almost nine, and still no call from him. He knew I rose before six. I felt a whisper of worry, but ignored it. If he were up to something, I didn't have to know right this moment. Maybe I'd call him after a bit.

"How'd you sleep?" Mom said. "I told you to call when you got home."

Damn. I'd forgotten. I'd turned off my phone so reporters couldn't bother me if they learned my name, though I'd turned it on this morning in case Sonny called.

"Sorry, Mom. My brain was fricasseed."

"Having pie for breakfast?"

"Uh, no. Toast and bacon."

Damn!

So I'd forgotten, too, about the apricot pie she'd sent home with me. At least I still had a head on my shoulders. Too bad the brain was AWOL.

"A reporter just called. That slick, Indian-looking guy who breaks the big stories, hell bent for a national network job. Can you believe it, this early on a weekend morning?"

"Actually I can believe it, Mom. Remember, I was a reporter, once."

"I hope you didn't bother people like that."

No comment. I took the bacon from the microwave and slid it on my toast. Then I took a savory bite. I spoke while chewing with my mouth open. Sorry, Mom. What you can't see won't hurt me.

"How are you and Dad doing?"

"Well as can be expected. But on edge. State Police came early and drove their van to the Robertson place. Apparently they'll be there all weekend. Makes us feel safer. And they've assigned a detective."

"So what did you guys tell the TV guy? Shane Chapelle, I assume you mean."

"I refused to give out your name, said you don't live here, told him he'd have to look you up on his own. Or ask that handsome Sheriff Welles. Did you know he was widowed last year?"

That stopped me. So the sheriff had had an effect on Mom, too. Never mind her age. You'd never know it from how she talked—particularly when it came to the "unfair" sex.

"The media will find me eventually," I sighed. "Welles has my info, though he's not supposed to share it. But I heard somewhere he and Chapelle are pretty tight."

"I hope the killer can't access your information, and that he wasn't lurking nearby when you found the body. Be careful. Keep an eye out and a gun close."

"That'll be painful, Mom." Just trying to lighten her up.

"I beg your pardon?"

"My eye out?" I instantly regretted my tendency to joke in dire situations. A trick used in cop shops and newsrooms to make bad situations feel less personal.

As I tidied the kitchen, my mind again spun with ideas about the murder, how it made my folks and their place less safe, and how it might derail Tulip's and my guest-ranch dreams. If I could help the case, speed the investigation, I'd be more at ease and in a better position to decide whether we should buy the old farm.

Before heading out for our horse-show practice, I opened my laptop to jot notes about the night before. Then my phone rang.

"Glad I reached you, Miss Kane," said a bright, baritone voice. "Shane Chapelle, KMFD-TV News. I hope you're doing well this morning."

"Thank you."

"Can you tell us about your finding a woman's body last night at a cabin in Grants Pass? I have a cameraman, and we're just on the road outside your house."

That was a first. Now the reporter was the reported on.

"No comment. I have to be somewhere. And I found the body outside, not in, Grants Pass." Just helping him be more accurate.

"This will only take a minute. You'd be doing the community a big service."

I peeked out the front window. Yep. There was the white van with the station logo on the side and satellite dish on top. And Chapelle standing outside it.

"Please go away. I said I have no comment. Goodbye." I ended the call.

Had I been as annoying as this guy, when I was a reporter? Surely not.

I turned my attention to my laptop, created a file named "Applegate Murder," and jotted notes about last night. I closed my eyes to imagine myself back in that unhappy place and time.

As I say, I'd been to crime scenes and seen dead bodies. But this one had really gotten to me, hooked a claw under some piece of emotional armor and pried up a sharp corner. I was pretty good at keeping my feelings in check during gnarly situations, at keeping a lid on the horror until my subconscious had thrashed it enough to blunt its ability to disable.

Nevertheless, this one was especially unnerving. Worse than having super-caffeine jitters. It had occurred so close to my family home, to my parents and to my own cherished memories. I was almost like having an alien being growing inside, an alien I could only purge by solving the mystery. For solve it, I would.

I wrote about the smell. About the dark. About the ripped armchair, the scattered papers and fallen mug. But mostly I wrote about the woman—her hair, her clothes, the hatchet. I transferred my phone photos and enlarged them. I also printed some out.

There were six photos in all. The first three showed the body from different angles. The fourth and fifth were still lifes of the scattered books and papers.

The sixth was a close-up of the woman's left cheek and hand showing the fallen red-ceramic mug twelve inches from her outstretched fingers. The mug was squat, and brightly glazed with a white ring circling the bottom where the cup lacked glaze. It lay at a 45-degree upward angle, the mug bottom to the camera. The part of the left side I could see had a black half-circle, its curve faced right with a dot below. Some kind of artwork or logo.

The woman looked to be in her late forties or early fifties. The left side of her face showed her wide mouth distorted in a slight grimace, which I'd missed seeing before. Looking closer I saw a black hole where the upper left incisor should have been. Was that blood on her lip? Lipstick? And had the incisor been gone a while, or only a few days? If she'd been punched in the mouth, she could have lost it then. But I saw no bruise.

Adding these questions and the photos to my other notes, I printed and stashed everything into the large manila envelope. Then I stared at the bookcase against the wall across from the desk, massaged my eye sockets and rose. The alien was asleep.

I didn't have time to call Sonny. Maybe I would do that from work.

The Bostons bounced around my feet. I loved on them, grateful for the dogs' innocent joy, their ability to live in the moment and to share that with me. My angst slipped away. Grabbing a Honeycrisp apple from a bowl, I took a bite. Tart, sugary juice squirted into my mouth. I pinched off slivers of apple for the dogs and turned them out in the fenced yard. They'd have fun sunbathing, and chasing any ground squirrel stupid enough to invade their turf.

I put on my cowboy boots, stretch jeans and the sea green, rhinestone-collared blouse that matched my eyes. Had to look decent for working the Horsehouse after my ride. Then I shouldered my concealed-carry purse with my .38 and phone inside.

That's when a random thought noodled around my noggin. I drew out the phone and clicked on "My Music." There, staring out at me, was an album-cover photo of the country classic crooner of my ringtone. Dark tumbling hair, dimples, sexy grin and all.

Waylon Jennings. The bad-boy singer-guitarist whose tunes first put the rock in country. The naughty artist who once stood up a leading late-night talk-show host that nobody else dared stand up. The wild one who went through three wives and a jillion pills and bottles before cleaning up and finding a soulmate in Jessi Colter, a country-western star in her own right. One with a gorgeous soul and massive patience.

When I was sixteen, Mom took me to a Jennings concert in Eugene, at Autzen Stadium. She was smitten and owned all his albums. After that show where he played guitar and sang his outlaw heart out, I was smitten, too, though decades his junior.

Ahhh. So that's who Sheriff Welles reminded me of. The sheriff was toned, clean-cut, civilized and law-man proper. But he might have been Waylon's nephew.

It was a quarter to ten. Our lesson was at eleven. I grabbed my jacket. Though late, and promising afternoon heat, the morning was still too cool for my taste.

Just then Waylon sang. It was Sonny. I poured another half-cup of coffee and sat back down at the table overlooked by a painting of a fisherman hip-deep in a brooding river. This call would be interesting. Maybe I'd learn what was up with Sonny and his ex. I needed to keep my wits about me—assuming I still had some.

5

"Hey, Sonny boy," I said in what I considered a warm and sexy voice.

"Hey, yourself," he said. "And how's my lovely lady today?"

"Hot to trot," I said.

"I'll be right down."

"Hot to trot, walk and lope. I'm meeting the Brassbottom buddies soon for our Saturday lesson."

Sonny chuckled.

"*Washte*. Good. You sound pretty chipper, considering your scare last night."

"Fake it 'til you make it. No, I'm good. Wrote down a bunch of notes."

"Welles and crew turn up anything else?"

It didn't surprise me he would know our local law enforcement leader's name. Sonny had given the sheriff information he'd dug up about a sex-trafficked girl we'd helped find last fall. But it struck me as odd he'd say Welles' name in a casual chat.

"I haven't heard and I doubt they'll tell me," I said. "Of course he warned me not to discuss the case with anyone."

"Unless it's with other law enforcement," Sonny came back.

Dear, dear Sonny. Of course he'd play his tribal-police card.

"Tell me again what went down," Sonny said. "Everything you remember."

So I did. What would it hurt? I'd already told him the gist of it, anyway. And if I could trust anyone, I could trust Sonny.

"So that's my story," I concluded. "How about you tell me yours?"

"What do you mean?"

"Seattle. Your kids." I paused for several beats. "The ex."

He was silent for one millisecond too long.

"You want to know if anything's going on with Tammy and me."

"Maybe." Sassy of me, I knew. But I felt a little sassy right about then.

He laughed a long, slow, head-shaking kind of laugh. Had he done that in amused disbelief that I would even think such a thing? Or to distract me?

"Pepper. Honey. Listen. It's not what you're thinking."

"What am I thinking, Sonny?"

Oh, crap. That was shrewish. This had gone downhill quicker than I'd thought. Now I was the suspicious girlfriend. With him up north and me in Oregon. Careful. Salvage what you can. Bring it back up.

"Tammy and I have business to discuss. It involves the kids, and my will."

I sat up straighter and stared out the sliding-door window, seeing nothing.

"You're making a will? You're only forty-four."

"Something came up. I can't discuss it on the phone. But it's being handled."

"I guess it's always good to have a will. But why now?"

"Very complicated. Attorneys are involved. But it has to do with land back on the rez. All I can say right now."

Well, that fried my fern. Why wouldn't he tell me? Why couldn't he tell me?

"Give me a clue, Sonny. You don't have some terminal disease, do you?"

"No, no. Nothing like that." His chuckle sounded forced.

I wasn't going to get it out of him. It wasn't good to beg or pressure Sonny. I'd learned that lesson in the past, with heart-wounding consequences.

"Glad to hear nothing's come between us. Legal, medical or otherwise. I don't trust your ex as far as I can throw her. I just want things to be fine for us. Like always. Or like forever." Okay, that sounded needy.

"Fine, Pepper? Only fine?" He'd ignored the "forever."

"It's just been so long. I'm going crazy thinking how good we are together. I could wrap you in my arms right now."

He blew out a low whistle.

"I better not say what I could do with you."

"Go ahead, Sonny. Give me a taste."

He told me how he'd play with my hair, give it a pull, and massage my scalp. Leaning in, he'd smell my cheek, tickle my ear with his tongue. Then he'd work his tongue down my neck to spots brightly starred on the roadmap of passion.

My eyes closed. I imagined how he'd tickle me with the end of his long black braid. Or pull the red ribbon woven through it and shake that chest-length hair across my breasts. His tongue and wandering fingers would increase their pressure until my skin shivered wth want. My fingers would do some walking of their own over his hairless, iron-hard limbs and torso.

"Stop," I said, my hand sweating as I gripped the phone. I blinked hard and sat up straight. Phone sex wasn't our thing. But we'd been apart for six months, after all.

"Want me to stop?" he teased.

"No, but you need to get on with your day. And I need to get on with mine."

"Taking my kids to a Mariners game. New lefty pitcher. Front office spent some money for a change."

I felt a stab of jealousy. We had our Medford Rogues, a scrappy, successful collegiate wood-bat team to cheer for in the summer in Southern Oregon. Tulip and I, in fact, held season tickets. But it was no substitute for Major League Baseball.

"Say 'hey' to your kids, Sonny. I hope to see them when we come up for that horse show. Maybe I can take in a game. I miss my Mariners, warts and all."

"Have a good ride. Take care. Say 'hey' to Tulip and the barn buddies."

Slightly buzzed by our conversation, I took a deep breath and went down to the garage. I felt better about what Sonny was doing up in Seattle. And better about us. I had to believe that it was only business going on with him and his ex. To be realistic, what could I do if anything else was going on?

* * *

A half-dozen riding buddies' vehicles sat in the parking lot at Brassbottom Barn. The day had warmed and brightened. I so looked forward to a happy hour of riding and learning. It would be easy to put the horrors of the night and my worries about Sonny, back of the saddle.

I stepped into the long, horse-and-hay scented barn with its clean-swept aisle. Buddies prepped horses in crossties. Little Stewie Mikulski—a precocious ten-year-old redhead who, with fifteen-year-old Jeanne Allende, was one of our two under-18 riders—gave me a freckled grin while leading his buckskin horse outside.

Tulip was tacking up her gelding in an open grooming stall to my right. I wondered who, then, was working at our tack store this morning. Gracie, the rescued Rottweiler, rose on arthritic haunches and followed me to where my statuesque human buddy was tightening her saddle cinch.

The sight of Tulip's ghost-white, puffy hair—normally a believable straw blond—stopped me in my tracks. She resembled a tall Susan Sarandon. In fact she had considered working as a Sarandon "tribute" actress, at the urging of our tribute-actor pal, Tommy Lee Jaymes of Fort Worth, Texas. But that hair and the stupidly clingy yellow sweatshirt she wore were very un-Sarandon, doing her and her bouncing bosoms no favors. I snorted in disbelief.

"What?" Tulip said, salon-enhanced eyelashes a-flutter. She let her raised stirrup drop. "Stewie's mom took my Horsehouse shift. I couldn't miss this lesson."

"No, I said. "It's your hair." My best friend marched to a different drummer, always had. But sometimes her marching puzzled even me.

She patted her frothy coiffure.

"Ain't it cute? Freddie's salon got in this new product to bleach it even whiter while conditioning it. It's the latest craze all over the Southwest."

"You look like a haystack on stilts."

"I declare." She pulled a pout, and then raised her drawn-on eyebrows and smiled. "You're just jealous. And late. Better saddle up."

Our exchange put a new spin on my day. Business as usual at the barn, and I was glad. Last night almost seemed somebody else's nightmare. I wished it were.

"Donna's giving the lesson today?" I said before heading to get Choc from his stall down the aisle. "But Dutch is helping?"

"Things could get lively with too many cooks," Tulip said. "Hey. Did y'all hear on TV about the body found last night near your folks' farm?"

Every so often a "you all" slipped into Tulip's conversation. She'd lived in the South for a whole three months after the death of her ex-husband five years ago. Divorce had made them even closer, which had made it even harder to lose him.

"Heard about it, you Bozo?" I whispered, not wanting anyone else to hear. "I was the one who found the body. But I'm not going public just yet."

Her eyes grew to the size of jumbo blue-and-white marbles.

"No way! They said a neighbor found it. It was you?"

I put my finger to my lips. Luckily, no one else was near.

"Not only was it I, but it was on that property we dreamed about for our guest ranch. Dad told me at dinner it was going up for sale. I went to take a look before dark."

"Well, shoot, Pepper. Why the hell didn't y'all call or text me?"

"Too much happening. Knew I'd see you today."

"Hell of a deal. This sure throws a monkey wrench in the works."

"For whoever that poor woman was, too, don't forget." The image of the dead woman floated through in my mind.

Tulip gave me a sour look and mounted her horse. It tossed its head, eager to head to the outdoor arena where other riders had gathered. A glob of foamy green horse-spit flew past my head. I ducked in time.

"Any idea who she was?" Tulip rasped.

"Not a clue. Possibly a squatter. Looked like—or somebody—was living there. Coffee cup, papers, some furniture, a path to the door."

"So how'd she die?" Tulip scooched a step closer. I caught a whiff of jungle gardenia perfume and nearly gagged.

"Hatchet in the back, if you can believe it. But we have to wait until the autopsy, and the M.E.'s report. That can take a while."

Tulip raised her gaze skyward before giving me a look.

"Duh. A hatchet would pretty much do it, y'all."

"There's always a chance the actual cause was something else. She could have been on the way out with a medical event when she got axed. So to speak.'

"Thank you, Miss Big-City Reporter." Tulip harrumphed, mounted and rode toward the barn doors. Before reaching them, she turned in the saddle.

"I wonder how this all affects us, if we'd even want to buy the place. Of course, Ace reporter Pepper Kane is on the case."

"I kind of have to be. It did happen next to my parents'." They're in danger if the killer thinks they knew or saw something."

Tulip nodded.

"Even I could be at risk, Tule. If the media knows where I live–they called this morning–then a killer could, too."

6

Chocolate Waterfall, "Choc," for short, nickered as I approached. He hung his handsome dished head with the crooked blaze out the feed window in the barred top-half of his stall.

"That's my boy," I cooed, stroking his nose. He closed his eyes and lowered his head toward me. "Big practice today," I said. "Let's get going."

I haltered him and led him down the aisle for grooming and saddling. He stood stoically and let his lower lip hang down in relaxation mode.

Everyone at Brassbottom Barn was riding that day under the critical gaze of our trainers, Dutch and Donna, who rode clients' horses. Young Jeanne was aboard her new black-white mare, while Freddie Uffenpinscher—salon owner and champion hunt-seat rider—was atop his stocking-legged grey.

Tulip trotted her horse around the perimeter of the ring. Her breasts, a miracle of cosmetic engineering, bounced like basketballs under her yellow top. Why she'd gone up a cup size from a respectable 'D' was beyond me. She'd have to use an industrial-strength bra to keep these babies from distracting judges in the show ring. Or was distraction part of her plan?

Several ladies new to Brassbottom Barn granted us seasoned show riders the right-of-way. With horses moving along the rail and others circling or riding straight lines in the center, it was a virtual zoo under the now-blazing sun. A lively, at times annoying, but oddly endearing zoo. I loved my barn family.

Donna, in a pink top and a sparkling ball cap that set off her blonde bob, asked us to lope our horses with metronome-cadence over rows of white-and-green banded ground poles set six feet apart. Their spacing matched the lope strides of Western mounts. Done right, poetry in motion.

Next I loped Choc flawlessly over five poles lying in an arced "fan" pattern.

Jill Bennetton rode up on her 16.1-hand bay. The cute dishwater blonde ran an antique store in the Oregon Gold Rush town of Jacksonville—a store Tulip and I had been meaning to check out.

"You make it look so easy," Jill said. She didn't look that long out of high school. But then, many people looked not long out of school. Hooray for aging.

"Aim for the same color bands on each pole as you ride over them."

"Oka-a-y." Jill still looked puzzled.

"See how the distance between same-color bands on each pole is equal from pole to pole when laid out this way? While jogging, cross the greens where they're three feet apart. When loping, cross the green bands that are six feet apart."

Jill leaned forward in her saddle while Choc and I demonstrated the maneuver.

"Now I see," Jill smiled. "When you jog or lope over same-color bands in sequence, your horse's front and back hooves land between poles without a tick."

"Exactly," I smiled. "Count each stride as you lope, one-two, one-two."

"I used to ride English," she sighed. "Hunter strides are longer."

"True," I said. "Western horse strides are shorter."

I heard a clatter and "Whoa!" near the trail bridge—a low, wooden platform you ride onto and down off. Your horse should drop its head to show interest in it.

"No no NO!" Donna shouted at Freddie from where she sat a palomino-paint Quarter Horse.

Freddie reined in Dark Hellza Poppin. The horse lashed its tail, angry at being corrected. Freddie's shaved head and dozen earrings flashed in the sun.

"Why do you always do that, Freddie?" Donna yelled.

"Do what, Donna?"

"Make a full stop before the bridge? It's supposed to be a half-halt, and a slight hesitation in gait but with forward flow."

Freddie, a former small-time actor who now owned the Manes 'N Tails Salon in Grants Pass, lifted his head, obviously begging to differ. After all, he'd won himself a championship in prime-time amateur trail at the World Open Western Show in Texas last fall.

"But he *was* forward, Donna."

"Didn't look that way from where I sit," she said.

"Looked fine to me," put in Dutch Grandeen, jogging a black horse at the far end of the arena. His Italian sunglasses, sharp straw hat and cocky way of sitting his horse spoke volumes. Barn boss, cunning controller, maker of champions.

But his wife was the one giving the lesson. We swiveled our heads to study her while she glared at her husband. An awkward silence ensued.

Donna shook her head. I felt her pain. It was no picnic if students gave you lip service when you were trying to help them up their game. She was a kind, empathetic woman. But some things yanked her chain. Talking back was one of them. Don't ask me how I know.

I watched Freddie ride over the bridge again. This time it was perfect. When he moved to another obstacle, I practiced Choc on the bridge. Holding the reins loose, my left hand extending them to encourage him to drop his head, I saw that my French manicure needed repair before I headed to the show in Seattle. I would try to schedule that later in the week at his salon. I might even hear a helpful tidbit there about the murder. Manes 'N Tales was a hot spot for scuttlebutt.

In all it was a great Saturday practice. Good weather, good horses, good peeps. It looked like we just might be ready for that Seattle show.

At twelve-forty, with our mounts stashed in their stalls to enjoy feed, water and uninterrupted leisure, I was heading to my truck to go work at The Horsehouse when young Jeanne caught me. I spotted her white mini-Cooper with her aunt at the wheel.

"Hey, Jeanne," I said. "Looks like that new horse is really working out for you."

"Yup," she said. "I had a really good ride. I'm so glad we got rid of that nut case that my folks ..." Her pause reminded me how disturbed she still must be after that accident at the World Show. It was good she had stayed in the horse game.

"And I'm so happy for you," I walked her to the car she'd be driving in a few months when she turned sixteen. Her aunt's arm lay on its window ledge. "Hi, Gloria," I said. "Nice to see you. Jeanne rode quite well today."

"Excellent," said the woman, whose tan face, diamond nose-stud, fashionable sunglasses and short, upswept dark hair with blond streaks pegged her as a young-thinking fifty. That she carried a few extra pounds was no big. The best of us did.

"How's the real-estate publicity biz going? Hot market in Ashland right now."

"Always," she said. "Matter of fact, I'm studying for my real-estate license."

"Really," I said, wheels turning. Real estate. Just what I'd been thinking about. As in, what happens if a body turns up on a piece of land just before it goes on the market? Can offers still be pushed through? How long might it be encumbered?

Gloria or her attorney-husband would be able to help me sort it out. The legal and other ramifications. And maybe she could facilitate a by-owner sale. That is, if Tulip and I were still interested in the Applegate property.

I was working on that issue. Weighing the pros and cons. Evaluating my feelings. Plus I needed a whole lot more facts. I had to talk with police again and to the property owners, not to mention to my parents, Tulip and the neighbors. Now I had even more to do. But it wouldn't hurt for Gloria and I to have a little chat.

"Gloria," I said, leaning toward the car window. "Do you have time for a coffee or early dinner later today or tomorrow?"

"How about tomorrow?" said Gloria, flicking her ring-bedecked fingers through her hair. "Tons of work to do today."

"Can I come?" Jeanne looked at her aunt, with whom she lived in nearby Ashland. Jeanne's parents were out of the picture for various reasons, none good.

"Sure, honey," Gloria said, reaching through the window to pat Jeanne's arm.

"It's a date," I said. "I have some questions for you about an unlisted property Tulip and I might be interested in buying. Five o'clock Sunday, then?"

"Sounds good," said Gloria. "Jorge will be dining early at the Country Club after a tournament with his law partners. So it's perfect timing."

"Taqueria Mexico in Gold Hill okay?" I said.

"We'll be there." Gloria slipped a business card from her purse and handed it to me. It pictured her as glamorously as a Hollywood celebrity, with the words, "I have one just one plan for marketing your property: Only the best will do." Below that, in script that dripped money, were printed the words, "Brochures – videos – staging."

Gloria climbed out of the driver's seat, went around to the passenger side and slid in. Jeanne jumped behind the wheel and stroked it. She clearly was eager to exercise the privileges of her learner's permit with an adult on board.

* * *

The Best Little Horsehouse rocked with country tunes and buying clients during my shift that afternoon. I was glad of that. It was good to keep busy, keep the horror and worry outside my doors. It was, after all, Memorial Day Weekend. The annual rodeo had broken out at Jackson County Expo Center in Central Point. Everybody who was anybody, or wanted to appear so, had to have new blingy-clingy jeans, sexy shirts and barrel-racing tack studded with enough crystals to choke a horse. So to speak. The true competitors as well as the "buckle bunnies"—young women chasing cowboys with trophy buckles—were out in force.

Humming along to old and new tunes by Chris Stapleton and Blake Shelton, I practiced my Texas two-step and Western Cha-Cha to and from the cash register and card-swiper more than once. Several customers joined in.

One Brassbottom lovely, Victoria Whifield-Smith III, stopped by to see what was new in burnout tees. That sassy brunette never missed a chance to highlight her show-stopping curves. She was among my best customers.

We were out of free water bottles and powdered-sugar donut bites by three. I wished we could cash in on customers from a nearby rodeo every weekend.

I took several media phone calls. How had they found my name and number? I shouldn't have wondered. Good reporters have their ways. I did regret having to tell The (Grants Pass) Daily Courier reporter I couldn't discuss the case. The Courier had been my hometown paper growing up. It had published my very first story.

Meanwhile, the Horsehouse activity galloped on. Sarah Banks, the curvy blonde daughter of my contractor buddy, Jesse Banks, stopped by with her tightly swaddled baby girl before closing. Only a few looky-loos remained in the corners. They drifted from rack to shelf, fondling blouses and caps, only to set them down in the wrong place. I'd have to straighten up the store a lot before I left.

When Sarah pulled a corner of the blanket off the sleeping infant's pudgy pink face, I felt besotted. The tiny lips pursed and smacked with nursing movements. Who didn't love a sweet new baby?

Sarah, seventeen and unwed but as capable and determined as a Boston terrier on a mission, preened at seeing me gush over little Nell. But the minute the last looky-loo left the store, she covered Nell and got down to the probable reason for her visit.

"Did you hear about that woman found dead near your folks' place?" Sarah said, jaws working an impressive wad of bubblegum. Her breath smelled like cotton candy. "My Dad's worried. He was supposed to go there to fix fence for them this weekend."

Really?" I said. "They said nothing about it. But the fences do need attention."

"So we wonder if you guys are still hoping to buy the neighbor's place and turn it into a guest ranch. After the murder and all." She tucked a stray lock of blond hair behind an ear, and rocked the baby. Rather vigorously, I thought. "I heard the owners are really old and, thinking of selling ..."

"How did you hear all that, Sarah?"

"My dad gets around, he talks to people, has clients in the neighborhood." She looked earnestly at me while shifting her baby to her other arm and her gum to the other side of her mouth.

"Tulip and I haven't discussed it lately," I said. That Sarah would bring this up so soon after my discovery of the body mystified and unsettled me. Was she just fishing, or was something more serious afoot?

"That's a job Dad was really interested in getting," Sarah said. She looked pointedly at me. I nearly winced at her directness.

"I can imagine," I said. "But any purchase will have to be on the back burner for the time being." Hoping to distract her, I busied myself straightening displays of earrings and refrigerator magnets on the counter.

Of course Jesse would be interested. Especially if his business were slow. We'd talked of developing the ranch shortly after I'd returned to the Valley, but not since. I didn't think he'd remembered. Clearly he had. It would mean big bucks to fix up my parents' farm and reconfigure it and the Robertsons' place into a tourist destination. Jesse would stand to net a hundred thousand dollars, or more, after paying for materials and subcontracted labor.

And now here was his daughter, pressing the issue. But what a crazy time to bring it up. Were they that close to the bone, that desperate for work?

Sarah picked up a crystal-heavy earring, studied it, then returned it smartly to its display stand, where its pink and turquoise stones swung for a moment. I stared at them, as if hypnotized. My mind seemed as busy, with theories on Sarah and Jesse.

"Maybe it's not the right time," she said. "So soon after the … you know, death. But just know, Pepper, that if you do decide to buy that old place and combine it with your folks' for a guest ranch, I could help you with accounting. I've been helping Dad with that, taking courses at the college. Pretty good at it, too."

OK. Helping her father. Maybe they *were* a little hard up. There'd been a building boom in the Valley in recent years. But that had showed signs of leveling out.

I smiled, and patted Sarah's arm. She was an eager little beaver, a driven young barrel-racer with a horse habit to support and a brand new baby to feed and clothe. Of course she needed the money. Plus Sarah would be helping her dad if she found him a lucrative long-term gig.

It made me wonder. About our plans and about the Bankses'. How desperate, how on the ropes, were they? Did they know the Robertsons, the elders or the son?

If so they might know about any proposed sale. Maybe the woman in the cabin was considered a serious buyer, visiting the property as I had done. I hated myself a bit for thinking it. But what if the Bankses, having fallen on dangerously hard times, had learned that, and taken her out of the picture so Tulip and I could make our offer?

OK. That was a stretch. I could hardly believe I'd come up with it. But sometimes the most unlikely path proved to be the one leading to the heart of the maze.

7

At six that evening, after feeding the livestock and freshening up at my ranchita, I looked forward to relaxing with the Bostons and indulging in TV. But first I smeared a crusty French roll with cream cheese, added smoked-salmon, and topped it all with capers, red onion and home-grown lettuce. Ice tea with mint from my garden capped the meal.

The back deck was still bathed in sun. I sank into a patio chair in the shade. Before tucking into my sandwich I picked a dead leaf off the potted red geranium on the wrought-iron table, and took an appreciative look over the lawn, pasture with its ancient apple tree, and the forested hills tapering to a vee.

It would've been nice to have had company on this lonely Saturday night. Probably I should be doing something lively and fun, like line dancing. But I was tired from the past twenty-four hours. I needed "me" time. I sipped tea and savored my sandwich. It felt so good just to sit. I closed my eyes. They snapped open when I heard a commotion past the far fence, on Dave and Judy Days' property.

There. A blur of movement among the trees. Focusing, I saw it was a coyote, dropping to a crouch as he watched the Days' chicken pen. Most of the dozen black, gold or speckled hens pecked and burbled unconcernedly. But one raised high, rapid clucks of concern. Her head was high, turned toward the coyote.

Anger rolled through me. Nelson, my tabby cat of ten years, an outdoor feline that I kept in the garage at night because of such predators, went missing two weeks ago. I still mourned him. Several other neighbor cats and at least one dog had also vanished recently, after a coyote with no fear of humans was spotted in the area.

Where was the Days' young border collie, Alice? I hoped she hadn't fallen victim to the predator. Hopefully that skinny, restless mutt was up close to the Day house where she could poach spring peas from their garden, as my Bostons did from mine. I had a good pea crop this year and my dogs' waists showed it.

I picked up my cell phone and tapped the Days' number. The call went to their voice-mail greeting, telling callers to have a nice Day. Or two. The Days' humor was pleasantly corny, like them.

"There's a coyote after your hens," I said. "Maybe the one bothering the neighborhood lately. The one that got my cat. I'm keeping an eye on him."

In the near distance the big-eared, grey-brown critter slunk to the fence and pawed at the pen's bottom wire while panicked hens squawked and scurried.

"Hey!" I shouted. "Hey!" I clapped my hands.

The noise had no effect. The coyote dug more furiously under the fence, throwing dirt every which way, while chickens threw themselves against the far side of the pen and screamed for their life.

Tears blurred my vision. Not only at thinking about my missing cat and these panicked chickens, but at what I might have to do.

Fingers trembling, I called my next-door neighbors, the Johanssons. Their two pit bulls had run, barking wildly, to the end of the common fence where our two properties abutted the Days'. Scrappy ex-Marine Butch Johansson would know what to do.

I waited through eight rings. No answer, no voice mail.

Damn it. Why me?

I rose reluctantly, took my dogs inside and went to the rifle case in the utility room. For the distance I would need my old Henry .44, not the shotgun by the front door. I took out the seven-pound long gun. The warm, smooth wood of the stock felt good, balanced, in my hand.

Making sure the rifle held five cartridges, loaded after I'd plunked at cans in the pasture last weekend, I went back outside. The commotion from the chicken pen grew more frantic. I squatted, and braced my forearms on the deck rail. I found the coyote in my sights and levered a round into the chamber. Holding a deep breath, aiming high to compensate for distance, I squeezed the trigger.

The flash and bang knocked me backward. It knocked the coyote to kingdom come. Spurting fur and blood it flew into the air and landed yards from its launch pad. The chickens screeched in full riot and banged the henhouse and fence as feathers floated down around them.

The neighborhood got very still. Nary a bird tweet or ground-squirrel chirp to be heard. The smell of burnt gunpowder clung to my nose hairs. I saw the Bostons had left the county—or at least, the deck—for parts unknown. Likely under the bed.

Feeling numb at having killed something, but also pleased I'd sucked it up and done the right thing rather than relying on someone else, I tucked the rifle back in its case. I returned to the deck and left another voicemail for the Days.

"Wile E. Coyote's no longer a problem for your chickens," I said, trying for a light tone just beyond my grasp.

Firing the rifle had made my ears ring. But it also had temporarily rid my brain-busting fear and concern about my grim discovery of the night before. I also no longer felt tired. Justified shooting and a big dose of adrenaline apparently did that for you.

I went inside to burrow into Big Brown. I was just about to kick back with some TV—I'd see Sonny and kids in a crowd shot—when my cell phone sang.

It was not the Days, but Tulip. She sounded mad as a wet cat.

"Dammit, Pepper. Where are you? Did y'all forget?"

"Forget what?"

"To give me a million bucks. No. That we were meeting tonight at Josephine County Fairgrounds for the Memorial Weekend Wild Country Palooza. We got tickets months ago. Meant to remind you at the barn, but it purely slipped my mind."

In her background I heard chatter, laughter, and the tinny sound of recorded music. In an hour the tunes would be alive and kickin' it, first with a warmup act, then with the stellar chops of Wild Country. We'd been eager to catch this dance and concert for a year. But in all the excitement of late, the date had zinged right past me.

"Shoot." That didn't begin to cover it. I really yearned to go. But was I really up for a night of boot-scooting and camaraderie?

"Get your fanny and dancing boots over here, girl," Tulip said. "Great turnout. See some people you might want to get close to. At least for the night."

People whom *Tulip* might want to get close to, saddle tramp-in-training that she was. Then I thought, what the heck. We already had tickets. And a little partying would do me good. What was I going to do, anyway? Watch a game on TV like so many other nights? Play tug-of-war with the dogs? Big whoop. If Sonny were here, he would have gone in a flash. I was lucky he liked country tunes and dancing almost as much as I.

Well, he wasn't here. I would just have to please myself.

Tule would hold our place near the stage. I could meet her in just over an hour.

It took a while to find my ticket. It also ate up precious minutes to put together just the right outfit—not too young or old, classy yet sassy—from my colorfully crammed closet. My heart began to hammer. I felt like a teen going to Fair.

Settling on a fringed white cardigan over a sparkly, scoop-necked black top and stretch jeans, I pulled on my tall white dancing boots. I gave my face and hair a few licks, and set out for what was referred to as River City. Where town boosters often bragged, "It's the Climate" and prompted folks to "Live Rogue." Like the beautiful, fishable, raftable Rogue River itself.

Twilight was cloaking Grants Pass Parkway as I descended off Interstate 5 into the friendly town of 37,000. My cheeks flushed as I contemplated an evening of happy foot-stomping and harmless flirtation—provided there were any starched jeans and trophy buckles to flirt with. But I thought it likely. Most Western dances in G.P. drew an older crowd and the usual local bands played to them. But tonight would be different. The hot-blooded, Grammy-winning Wild Country cranked out contemporary hits as well as classics, a win for all ages.

Traffic directors in white shirts, straw hats and blue jeans swept flashlights down the narrow, crowded parking lanes on the edge of the Fairgrounds. Rolling down Red Ryder's window, I nodded to the big-bellied Sheriff's Posse member who pointed to parking in a strip mall beyond the fences. I'd have a long hike back here.

As I plodded toward my goal from where I'd parked in Timbuktu, the thump of drums and higher wails of guitar and keyboard riffs reached me from the fairgrounds social hall a quarter-mile away. A scatter of noisy teens loped past me while I walked past an older couple making their way to the eight- o'clock show—which a check of my cell phone showed was about to begin.

The exterior doors stood open. A few security uniforms were posted here and there. Once inside the bustling lobby, I dodged fans bound for the cavernous auditorium. Through the open doors where ticket takers kept busy, I spotted a short-skirted country trio shimmying and singing on stage, warming up the crowd for the main attraction. Many couples danced or swayed to the music.

I spied Tulip's haystack hair in the third row from the stage, zeroed in, and speed-walked as best I could, given the bodies, toward the auditorium doors.

Along the way I caught sight of a familiar uniformed figure striding through the door to the parking lots. My heart did a flip. Sheriff Grant Welles. Keeping an eye on things. Working overtime on a Wild Country holiday weekend at what likely was the liveliest place in or outside town.

On a whim, I whirled around and hotfooted it to the door he'd gone through. It didn't take long to catch up. He walked slowly, eyes sweeping the scene, hand on his service weapon, taking in everything near and far rather than walking purposefully.

I pushed past a couple arguing about misplaced tickets before drawing next to Welles. I touched his sleeve.

At my touch he remained composed, neither stiffening nor withdrawing his arm. But he slowly turned his head to look down at me, his eyes fixed in a confident yet approachable gaze. It took a moment for recognition to dawn.

"Oh, Miz Kane. Good evening." A small nod of his hat. His eyes looked amused, but also fixed in guarded police mode.

"Sheriff," I said. "See you're having to work overtime again." Keeping it light.

He lifted his chin and looked away, scanning pedestrians and vehicles.

"Saves the county money in the long run if we can keep the peace." He looked down at me again, clasped his hands in front and faced me. "How are you doing tonight, Miss Kane?"

I caught that I was now addressed as "Miss," not "Miz."

"Oh, I'm good," I said. Then I felt at a sudden loss for words. Almost like when I was a teen trying to make conversation with a shy boy. We stood four feet apart. His badge, stars and bars caught glints of light from lamps on the fairgrounds' power poles. A note of earthy aftershave tickled my nose.

"You a fan of country music?" he said, glancing out again over the lot and resuming his slow, watchful patrol walk.

"Oh, yeah," I said, my tongue a lump of clay as I searched for the right words. "And you?"

"About all I listen to anymore."

"Anymore?"

He hesitated, and then continued walking, looking straight ahead.

"After the wife passed," he said, in a hoarse whisper. "She wasn't a fan."

Oops. Don't even go there, I told myself. You have another reason to be engaging in this conversation with the sheriff.

"Sorry," I said.

"That's all right." He cleared his throat, turned away to key his shoulder mike and ask a question from someone likely his partner tonight. He resumed walking.

I matched Welles' steps. Then I decided to go for it.

"So, is the State Police Forensics team still working at the cabin?"

There was a slight hitch in his step.

"Last I heard. But they should be done Monday or Tuesday."

"Have they, or you, some idea of the identity of the dead woman?"

He didn't miss a beat.

"That will be coming out in good time." He said no more, and, from his faster walk and more rigid posture, appeared closed for business to too- curious witnesses. Hell, for all I knew, I might even be considered a person of interest. In fact, I was sure I was. I didn't care to add fuel to that particular fire.

"Good," I said. "My parents and I are pretty worried, the murder having happened so near their house and all."

He glanced at me sideways and stopped.

"Has the OSP lead investigator talked to you, then? Detective James, I believe? Did he call it murder?"

"No, and no. I just assumed that from what I saw last night. The hatchet?"

He looked me square in the face. He seemed to grow taller.

"We have to assume nothing. The M.E. will issue a report. As a former reporter, Miss Kane, you know that."

"Pepper," I whispered, instantly regretting it. Welles must think me an idiot. "Of course," I said, looking past him. Then I inhaled a steadying breath and looked him in the eye. "Guess I'm trying to find ways to wrap my head around this thing, identify parts of it, feel a little bit of control." I fingered the fringe of my cardigan.

Welles seemed to soften. He nodded, and rolled his shoulders, now looking at me in a non-threatening way. His gaze lingered on mine before slipping down to my white, silver-inlaid buckaroo footwear. The kind made for dancing, not riding.

"Nice boots," he said matter-of-factly, before looking back up into my eyes. "Do some serious boot-scootin' in those." His eyes crinkled at the corners.

His comment, and how he said it, surprised me. But I liked it.

"Well, that's the plan." I grinned, doing a little heel-toe step.

He gave a soft, "hmm-hmm" chuckle.

"Cupid Shuffle," I said.

Welles shifted his weight and adjusted his hat.

"Well," he said, "back to business. Take care, and enjoy the show."

"Oh, thanks…sir. Will do. One of my favorite bands."

"They're pretty good."

With that, he touched his hat brim and sauntered toward the vast reaches of the parking lot, where shouts and curses erupted in one corner. I stood there for a moment, watching him go and enjoying the view. I wondered what he really thought about me. Professionally and personally. I had the impression Welles had wanted to talk a while longer, extend the conversation. Was I thinking that because I was concerned about Sonny, because I wanted to have an ace in my pocket? Or did I think he wanted to say more about the murder because I ached to have it solved quickly?

Hurrying back to the social hall, I pushed down the unease Welles had stirred. I shut out the frustration at unanswered case questions, and about our chemistry.

Well, dammit. I was here to have fun, and fun I would have.

The loud, crowded colorful concert shook my body, cleared my mind and blasted away worry. The lights, the recorded and live music, were irresistible. You couldn't not give yourself up to them. Everyone—young, old or in between, like me—was having a ball.

The five members of Wild Country skipped and sauntered onstage. The fringed and spangled singers and musicians drew cheers, applause and raised cellphones. Immediately they launched into an ear-splitting recording of their hit, "Bad-Hearted Woman"—a modern take on Waylon Jennings' iconic "Good-Hearted Woman."

I pushed forward and found Tulip boogying her booty off near the stage. Feeling the need for extreme release, I took a breath, blew it out and did the same. I was sixteen again. My tall white boots took on a life of their own, and my sweater fringe whipped with abandon.

I might pay for this in the morning. But it was such stinkin' fun, and shoved my recent troubles to the far horizon.

As Scarlet O'Hara famously said in "Gone with the Wind," about the maddening Rhett Butler, "I'll think about it tomorrow...After all, tomorrow is another day."

8

I was home by midnight—footsore and hoarse, but with face washed, boots off and sleep-tee on. I gathered the Bostons into my chair and switched on the TV news, which I'd recorded. Surely reporters by tonight would have something new about the death on the Applegate. I'd seen a handful of media calls on my phone, likely from print and broadcast vultures seeking my take on it. But I had no intention of calling back, and deleted them all.

"Oregon State Police are still trying to learn the identity of the woman found dead Friday night in a cabin behind this house near Grants Pass," said the anchor. "Here's Shane Chapelle with an exclusive."

A video shot earlier that day showed the dapper ace reporter standing outside a yellow crime-tape barrier across the short drive of the Robertson cottage. The tiny but attractive white house stood on a lightly treed rise along the road by my parents'. The house that would be ours, if Tulip and I decided to buy the property.

The presence of crime-scene tape a thousand or more yards from the death cabin surprised me. Normally the crime scene itself, the immediate room or rooms, the structure and maybe a small surrounding area, would be secured. So had they found something inside or near the house, say, a hatchet absent from a fresh pile of kindling, or perhaps hairs, fibers or fingerprints that might tie to the crime scene? Or were police merely trying to discourage the morbidly curious from accessing the entire property while investigators processed the cabin?

I focused back on the TV screen.

"The identity of the woman and exact cause of death have not been confirmed," Chapelle said. "But the sheriff and State Police won't rule out homicide. A Gold Hill woman visiting her parents next door found the body while walking the property, reportedly evaluating it for purchase. Neither she nor the parents have responded to our calls."

There it was. The possibility of murder. At least the reporter had not mentioned my name. Stock footage of the sheriff and local OSP headquarters appeared on screen.

"The cabin was abandoned since the early 1950s," continued Chapelle, "after a famous writer, Preston O'Hara, hanged himself there. He reportedly was a victim of Hollywood blacklisting in the Communist-baiting era of the 1950s. We'll bring you more as this fascinating story develops."

So now the mention of O'Hara's death, sharing the same segment as details on the death of the mystery woman. Double jeopardy for the cabin, the property. Even if the "curse" weren't mentioned, folks might suspect one. Two shocking deaths at the same place suggested that.

Would this make the property untouchable for potential buyers? And would the sellers have to slash their price? That was good if Tulip and I decided to acquire it. We might pick it up for pennies on the dollar, and use whatever was left or could be borrowed to make upgrades, build cabins. That'd get our B, B & B off to a good start.

But the flip side didn't look as good. Maybe the property would likewise be an untouchable entity for potential customers of a guest ranch. Even if we did make an offer, even if our bank lent us more after our hefty down payment, and if we managed to transform the farm, I wondered if anyone would want to vacation there.

What if you opened a guest ranch and no one came?

* * *

Sunday morning I labored under a mild headache. Luckily it vanished after I inhaled an industrial-sized mug of coffee and got to stall cleaning. Our string of 90F-plus days was due to break. But it would still be a sweltering 85. I planned to grab a short trail ride on Bob while it was still early and relatively cool.

While enjoying a slice of Mom's apricot pie with vanilla-bean ice cream, I took a look at my phone's boatload of texts and messages. Mainly media. While deleting these, I took a call from Tulip.

"Quick," she barked. "Turn the TV on to KMFD."

"No local news Sunday mornings," I grumped, lurching to the set.

"They broke into network-show credits to tease tonight's biggie," she said as the screen lit up with a video shot Saturday. It showed reporter Shane Chapelle in front of Mountainview Manor, a retirement village near Grants Pass. Next to him stood a Harlow-haired crone in a short-sleeved purple dress that revealed ropy arms. The kind of arms that bespoke an aged owner who stayed fit.

"Mrs. Robertson has given us an exclusive, airing tonight," Chapelle said, aiming his hand mic at my parents' former neighbor.

"Preston O'Hara, that famous writer who hanged himself in the cabin?" she said in a strong, clear voice. "He put a curse on it. Awful things happened soon after we bought it. Part of why we left." She nodded with conviction.

Chapelle promised to reveal more in the evening newscast.

Oh, great. Now the whole world knew about the curse. I'd hoped it wouldn't come up so soon. I'd already planned to contact the Robertsons, and their neighbors. But this lit a fire under me.

The TV anchor came back on to say, "We have a correction. The woman who found the body is not a neighbor, but an ex-Seattle reporter residing in Gold Hill. We will continue to try to reach her for comment."

I stared dazedly at the screen, now filled with talking heads from an op-ed show. How wonderful of the local anchor to "out" me. She may as well have said my name. A lot of people here knew of my newspapering past in Seattle.

How she said, "she was an investigative reporter in Seattle," with raised eyebrows, implied I might be one inclined to investigate the case myself. Was I being paranoid, or was the anchor just adding allure to their promised story?

It was inevitable the public would figure out who I was and what I might be up to. But I hadn't wanted to be outed this soon. I wanted that "anonymous" period to do some discreet digging of my own.

It was nine. Time to hop to it. Before my trail ride, I'd call Maisie Robertson. If I did drive over to meet her, I would also canvass my folks' neighbors, see if any had heard scandal about Jesse, or seen anything odd in the area.

Before I could say "Jack Robertson," there was a knock at my door. It was Sunday morning. What now? The media again? Tulip? The impetuous Sonny Chief? I chided myself for not having locked the front gates when I returned from the concert.

The Bostons barked and took the living room in three bounds to create a ruckus at the door. Shushing them, I peeked past drapes on the left side of the window. A slim, greying black man in a yellow tee and jeans stood on the porch. He glanced around the yard, not yet seeing me. His older, navy-blue SUV was parked under a hickory tree beside the gravel drive.

My heart did a worried flip. Who was this, another reporter? I shooed away the Bostons, and opened the door as far as the safety chain allowed.

"Morning," said the fortyish man whose movie-star-handsome face was upstaged by a right eyelid tic. "Are you Pepper Kane?"

"Yes," I said, still wary.

"Detective Franklin James, Oregon State Police." He flashed his badge. "I'm here regarding the death you reported Friday? May I speak to you a minute?"

Really, I thought. The State Police, already. And Frank James. Like the old-West outlaw. Odd name for a lawman. But life did tend to toss such coincidences my way.

"I suppose so," I said, wondering why he hadn't called. Was it so he'd catch me off guard? I undid the chain, opened the door and motioned him inside. While the Bostons sniffed his jeans legs, James fondled their bat-like ears.

"If I can get past your vicious attack dogs," he grinned.

I offered him coffee, which he declined. I offered him a seat at the table, which he accepted. I poured myself another cup and took a chair.

"You're out early on a Sunday," I said. "Isn't that unusual?"

"Was in the area on other business." James took out a notebook and pen. "I won't take much time. I just need a statement about Friday at the cabin."

"Thought I was supposed to give my formal statement downtown tomorrow. Sheriff Welles said—"

James held up his hand.

"Welles got there first, but I'll be your main contact. Besides. That Grants Pass OSP office is, shall we say, cramped. I like to do interviews in the field. People are more relaxed in familiar settings."

And unprepared if you surprise them, I thought.

For the benefit of the recorder, we stated the time, date and our identities. I gave James a brief account of my discovery.

"So the deceased was unknown to you?" James said. "You know if anyone other than yourself was on the property recently?"

"Yes," I said, "and no." I knew the drill. Say as little as possible, don't invite additional questions.

"You were walking the Robertson property Friday to explore it, without the owners' knowledge or permission. Why, again?"

"Tulip–my friend and business partner–and I thought we might buy the place, add it to my parents' and combine them into a guest ranch."

I gave him Tulip's contact info. As I did so, I had the feeling I'd seen James somewhere. Maybe on TV news, regarding another case.

"Did you talk to the owners about that?" he said.

"There was no urgency. But Dad heard it might be going on the market and I decided to check it out."

James tapped his pencil on his free hand, which bore a gold wedding band.

"The cabin was clearly unsafe," he said. "Why go in?"

This now seemed less like a statement and more like an interrogation.

"Well, I ..." I looked out the back-door slider into the green-gold hills.

Oh, good, I thought. Hesitate while you think of the best answer. Why not just say you were keen on acquiring the property, but some weird lady came at you with a hatchet, which you grabbed and used to kill her?

"Why would you enter a cabin that had 'No Trespassing' signs posted?"

"I saw no signs."

"They were there. Pretty deteriorated, though. I understand."

Did he? Or was he merely trying to appear empathetic?

"The cabin was dark and empty," I said. "And that smell." I shuddered.

"You probably just should have called 911 at that point," he said, sitting back.

"No service out there."

"The property owners can prosecute you for trespassing, breaking and entering. The discovery and the attention it's received could drive down the property's price."

I stiffened. James seemed to notice. He softened his face.

"But we doubt they'll sue," he said. "They just want this thing solved."

"Them and me, both," I said.

"I am sure it was awful for you," he soothed.

"My parents are freaked, its having happened so near their place."

"That's why you need help. You didn't touch anything, did you?"

I lifted the corner of a magazine on the table, then let it flop back.

"No," I said. No need to mention the photos I'd shot of the crime scene. The OSP team would have shot their own photos.

"Why not just contact the owners if you were interested in the property? Have them or an agent show you around?"

I considered several answers. None good. Might as well go with the truth.

"As I said, it was spur-of-the-moment. No one but my folks would know."

"Did you go anywhere else on the property, in back, down to the river?"

Sheriff Welles had asked the same question. I thought that a bit odd.

"It was getting dark. I was only interested in the cabin. They didn't find anything of interest in back, did they? Or by the river?"

I guessed that question would be ignored.

"Did you kick open the door, or find it that way?"

"How do you figure it was kicked open?"

"Just answer the question, Miss Kane."

"I'm not sure what you're getting at, Detective. Do you really just want information? Or are you shaking me down in a nice way?"

James raised his hands in surrender.

"Just asking routine questions. Let me put it another way. Was the door open?"

"A few inches. I pushed it farther."

James finally thanked me and left. I stood with my back against the door. Being a bug under a microscope left me feeling raw. I needed that quick horseback ride in the hills. But not before calling Maisie Robertson.

"Hello, Mrs. Robertson," I said. "It's Pepper Kane, daughter of your former neighbors, the Kanes? You talked with my dad when you were moving last week?"

"Oh, of course," she said. "We're sorry we didn't get to know our neighbors. We've had so many problems and didn't get to know anyone well in our time there."

"I was the one who found the body in the cabin."

"*You* were the one. It must have been awful for you."

"Yes. But I'm dealing. I would like to meet you."

"And why again were you there, dear?"

"I was having dinner with my folks. My dad said you were thinking of selling the farm. A friend and I hoped to buy it if it ever came up for sale."

There was a muffled sound, as if she had put the phone to her chest. "Jack! It's the woman who found the body. She wants to talk to us. About the property."

A muffled answer, followed by unintelligible grunts that might be conversation.

"Mrs. Robertson?" I broke in.

"Yes?"

"I'm not sure we want to buy it now. But I'd still like to talk with you about pricing, the supposed curse, how it was to live there."

"You should talk to our son. We don't know what will happen. Cleve's handling the sale, if there is to be one. He's trying to find a way to buy the place, himself."

I put the phone between my jaw and shoulder while I washed and dried dishes.

"I'd like his contact info, but still want to meet you. Do you have time today?"

"We're still getting settled. This place is a mess."

"Then you need a break. Let me buy you lunch, or at least a coffee."

"Well, I suppose we need a break. Can we make it tomorrow? Maybe coffee? There's a Memorial Day lunch here at the Manor."

"I have to be at my parents' for a barbecue at noon. Pick you up at ten?"

After signing off, I took the Bostons out to spend the day in the side yard while I went for my trail ride. My cell phone sang as I entered the barn.

"Thanks for taking care of the coyote," said my back neighbor, Judy Day.

"No problem. I think it was the one that's been killing neighborhood pets. Including my Nelson. Where was that supposed guard dog of yours?"

"Alice? No idea. She's the worst watchdog. She tells the coyotes and raccoons where the chickens and rabbits are. Last rescue I'll ever take in. Wasn't raised right."

"Don't let that put you off rescues, Judy. They usually come around given enough love, time and training."

"That's just it. We don't have the time. Would you like another dog?"

I loved that busy, skinny McNab border collie. And Alice loved me, whining as if trying to say words, and offering her belly for a rub every time we met. She'd gone with me on one ride, and stayed near or come quickly when called. She'd even positioned herself between me and an aggressive wild turkey.

"Let me think about it, Judy." I sure didn't need another dog.

"Well, thanks again. The coyote hide is on the fence to warn away his buddies."

Bob and Lucy were finishing their alfalfa. Glad to have something fun to do before seeing my folks' neighbors in Grants Pass and meeting the Allendes for dinner, I led Bob to my outdoor grooming stall. He watched me with his right brown eye and spacy left blue eye crossed by a blaze. Mischief danced there. No wonder I called him "My Blue-Eyed Devil."

I brushed him and cleaned out each hoof. Then I carried my trail saddle from the tack room, swung a pad on his back and threw the saddle atop it. I tightened the girth, mounted and headed across the field to the gate to the Days' spread. My phone sat secure in a belt-holster on my left hip, and the S&W .38 revolver sat in its black nylon case behind my right.

My body rocked pleasantly to Bob's easy walk. I leaned down to open the gate, rode through it and closed it. Lucy ran back and forth in the pasture, neighing as we rode up the bank to one side of the Day house. I spied Judy in the kitchen window, waving as I rode by. She gave me a thumb up. I figured she either hadn't heard about my new notoriety or had the good grace not to mention it.

The steep, tree-lined trail edged by grasses and wildflowers leveled out a hundred feet farther. The air was cool and sweet.

Bob's ears flicked forward and back as we plodded along, eager to see what lay around the next bend. Small birds darted out from buckbrush and brambles. Jays and crows squawked in some tongue known only to them. Everything smelled of good earth, of clean greenery and of dead vegetation returning to the soil.

There was no ticking time here. No headaches or sore muscles. No tasks, no agendas, no questions needing answers. Only soft syncopated hoof beats, saddle squeaks and nature's beauty in the endless passing moment.

The first ten minutes I felt the uglier aspects of the weekend nibble at my consciousness, demanding attention. OK, I thought. I'll give you five minutes.

First the image of the dead women loomed. Well, she was dead. Probably once pretty. But now no longer hurting. I would redouble my efforts to learn her identity.

Second, how worried my parents had been for me and for themselves. Friday they heard my news and the interview with Sheriff Welles. It didn't help that they'd been hounded by reporters. I needed to remind them again that I was packing a gun, would be there in a flash if needed, and was trying to help the case along by doing hopefully discreet investigating of my own.

Third, I had to be careful not add to police suspicions that I were involved with the murder or had a serious interest in the case. Even though, regarding the latter, I did.

Finally, Tulip and I had to sit down and hash out whether we could afford to buy the Robertson place, or even wanted to. How did we feel about that damnable curse? Was there anything to it? Or was someone helping give it credence? My talking with the Robertsons and my folks' neighbors would go a long way toward answering such questions.

Satisfied I had identified my immediate challenges, I tried to put them out of mind. This hour in the woods was my time to exhale, to build strength for what lay ahead. All hell would break loose soon enough, as in most investigations. But hell would have to wait.

Before a left bend I turned to look back. Through the closing-in tree limbs, I saw the valley spread out below. My acreage looked like a toy farm with its shake-roofed, white doublewide and matching outbuildings. Similar semi-rural acreages flanked each side. Beyond those, trees marked the freeway shoulders south of the Rogue River. Distant peaks against a pale sky capped the scene.

Coming home from Seattle had been the right decision. No matter, the trauma of leaving other friends, Bridle Trails State Park and my life's love—though I could not be sure of keeping him. This was home. These surrounding hills made me feel safe, comforted, as if embraced by a plump grandma's arms.

Bob and I continued around the bend in the trail.

A sharp yelp broke my reverie. I looked back again. Bob stiffened and raised his head. Then he gazed back, too, swinging his hips around to assess the threat.

But it was only Alice, the Days' border collie, come to trot along with us. She gave me a guilty glance as she caught up. I was glad she'd come.

"Hey, girl," I said. She galloped past on a mission, nose to the ground.

In that moment, I threw back my head and laughed. If I were a dog, it would be that cute, bright-eyed but hopelessly obsessed border collie. Skinny as a rail but fat on life. Neither of us would ever give up locking onto some trail, following it ceaselessly until we found what we sought.

Or died trying.

9

I savored the air-conditioned cool of the truck cab as I drove the fifteen freeway miles north to Grants Pass. Only a little past noon, but the day already had its heat on. So much for the projected cooling trend. With five days like this in a row, no wonder the dead woman's body had smelled rank. I wrinkled my nose just thinking of it.

Parking the dually in the sparse shade of a lonely tree in the parking lot at Walmart, I made a quick call to Mom. I told her where I was and asked how she and Dad were with their meds.

"Think we're good," she said.

"You both OK otherwise? Hear anything new on the investigation?"

"Other than police cars coming and going yesterday? And some OSP officer asking us more questions about neighbors and such. How about you?"

"*De nada.* Picking up a few toiletries. Going to talk with some of those neighbors, see if they noticed any strange people or activity last week. But know that I can come over in a heartbeat if you need me."

"Stop by today, if you can. Jesse's fixing fence. Makes us feel safer with him here. And take care, baby girl. You never know if the killer was still around that night. Have your gun?"

Hmmm. My contractor buddy Jesse Banks was there. Now I'd stop by, for sure.

"Gun's locked in the glove box," I said. "Not worried, though. Talked to the State Police this morning at my house. Maybe the same guy you talked with."

"Good looking black man," she said. "Reminds me of ... who's that actor?"

I knew where this was headed.

"Jamie Lee Fox?"

"That's the one."

"I guess he did kind of look like Fox."

I had to chuckle. I was sure that's where I got my tendency to think everyone resembled someone else, usually a celebrity. My mom made me do it. When country legend Reba McEntire came into prominence forty years ago, Mom pointed out our resemblance. Though I was a good bit shorter and less well-endowed than the singer— and had no Southern twang—we had a similar saucy look. And the wild red hair.

My Walmart business done, I headed southwest to Jerome Prairie. The semi-rural community of small acreages much like my own in Gold Hill, was not a flat, sagebrush prairie as might be expected, but a miles-long reach of horse pastures, wineries, irrigation canals and homes of many styles surrounded by close-in hills.

Much as I liked Gold Hill, I would love to call this area home again.

My first stop was at the beige double-wide at the end of a short lane across from my folks'. Giant oaks stood at the road. Goats, llamas and a sway-backed brown horse grazed in a pasture. The long porch tinkled with wind chimes and bristled with herbs in colorful containers including an old iron bathtub painted aqua.

This was the home of Rosie "Pussytoes," as we'd called the genial herbalist behind her back when we were young. We'd renamed her for a native plant whose blossoms resembled the bottoms of cats' feet. Her real surname was Posselty.

I hadn't seen her in years, but the old woman hadn't changed. Cloaked in a billowing caftan, her long white hair secured with a Spanish comb, she brought two earthen mugs of tea out to the porch, set down the Chihuahua wiggling under her arm, and motioned me into an oak rocker beside hers.

"Tell me everything," she said, her blue eyes twinkling at the prospect of hot gossip. "I talked with police yesterday. They wouldn't say much, just that you found a woman's body in that old cabin by the river."

"It is as you heard," I said, taking a sip of chamomile tea.

The Chihuahua bared its teeth, uttered a growl and hopped into Rosie's lap.

As I told her the bare bones of my discovery, without mentioning the cause of death despite her prodding, she stroked the dog and adjusted her hearing aid, which produced a whistle that made me wince.

"Why I came," I said, "is to see if you can tell me if you noticed any unusual activity in the area the past few weeks."

"I'll tell you what I told the detective. Nothing unusual. Maybe more traffic. There's a new place for sale soon down the road."

"Riverfront?"

"No. My side of the road. Really ancient cottage back in the woods. But good acreage for a marijuana grow."

"So you saw nothing strange around my folks' place, or next door to theirs?"

"Just the Robertsons' son in his grey pickup with the camper, coming in and out. Figured he was helping his folks pack up. Heard they were moving."

"How well did you know him or his parents?"

"Not at all. His mother and I spoke occasionally at the mailboxes."

"What did you speak about?"

"Herbs, tea. She was interested in such things. Worked at a nursery for a while."

"Anything else? Maybe if they had visitors, or others using their driveway?"

"They had few visitors, kept to themselves," she said. "Just Cleve. A woman with him recently. Probably a wife or girlfriend. Saw kids there a few holidays. Probably grands or great-grands. Had a teenage grandson Maisie said was into some strange religion. Just mentioned it in passing. She was concerned."

"Did she say its name?"

"No, just that she hoped he'd grow out of whatever activity he was involved in."

Rosie sipped her tea and rocked while a black-and-white cat rubbed against her feet in their flip-flops. She and I talked a little longer, about family and routine neighborhood matters. Then I thanked her. I promised I'd return soon for a game of Honeymoon Bridge, or Spite and Malice. Rosie was ninety, but didn't miss a trick. Literally.

My next stop was at Walt Walters' place on the opposite side of my folks' from the Robertsons'. Old Walt was a former lumberjack whose handcrafted birdhouses, whirligigs and mailboxes with price tags were arrayed along his driveway. The skinny duffer himself sat in an Adirondack chair under a pine tree. He was smoking a corncob pipe and reading the weekend newspaper. A pile of advertising circulars had swallowed his feet.

"Well, howdy, Pepper," he said, knocking out his pipe on his boot. "Long time no see. Find any more bodies?" Accordion-pleat wrinkles popped out on his face as he gave me a grin shy a few teeth.

"Police already get to you, too?" I said, plopping onto the shaded lawn beside him. "I was just over at Rosie's. She said she got grilled."

"Told 'em I ain't seen nothin', nobody, nohow." Walt snorted.

"How long have you lived here, Walt? Weren't you one of the originals? Came here in thirty-six for the fish and the timber work, something like that?"

"Good memory," he said, louder than he needed to. "Yeah, about the same time as that author O'Hara. He and everyone else was all het up to come, after reading Zane Grey's books. Didn't know O'Hara though. I think you girls asked me that, a long time ago, when you were growing up hereabouts."

"I understand O'Hara kept to himself. He and his wife."

"But brought in a few movie stars," Walt said, with a low whistle. "Saw that good-looking blonde wife of Gable's here once," he said, eyes glazed with memory. "Riding in a big old car, longest I've ever seen."

"Carole Lombard," I said. The heat, even in shade, was getting to me. My upper lip and armpits were wet. "Know any more about O'Hara or his family?"

"Just that the one baby died. Heard somewhere O'Hara stepped out on the wife. But I never saw another woman. Even after the wife--she was Indian, you know—passed. A few years before he ... before he ..."

"Hanged himself," I said. "No one should have had to endure what he did. The haters wouldn't let up, drove him and many others to ruin or death." We sat silent, considering such matters. The times had changed, people had wised up. Hadn't they?

Walt coughed, and rubbed his chin. He looked at me with clouded eyes.

"But that's not why you came," he said. "You want to know about now. What I mighta seen or heard."

"Pretty much," I said. "Who's come or gone around here lately? Any homeless types, strangers, the past month? Walking, driving ratty vehicles, whatever?"

He wrestled with the newspaper, got it more or less folded, and let it drop.

"Well, maybe saw a few like that, can't remember the times. Don't tend to study 'em too much. But there mighta been a couple pushing a shopping cart, you know the type, week or two back. No idea where they were headed. Big older gal, darkish hair, with a little pale squirt of a man."

"Anybody unusual at the Robertsons'?"

"Well, now, come to think, there was this silver car, low slung, fancy wheels, I noticed a time or two. The one time it headed up their driveway. When I went out for my mail I saw it parked up there. Then it backed down and drove off."

"You said you noticed it a time or two."

"Well, then I noticed it parked at another house last week when I drove to the co-op. Probably just real-estate people, since property here's gone up so much."

"Did you tell this to police?"

"Didn't really remember it until you asked," he said. "Memory's about as worthless as this rag of a newspaper." He looked at the pile at his feet.

* * *

I saw Jesse Banks' maroon contractor's-pickup by my parents' garage the moment I turned onto their gravel drive. The short, sturdy jack-of-all-trades was tightening stock fence in front, along the boundary between my parents' and the Robertsons'.

His straw cowboy hat rotated in my direction. I parked by the porch, got out and walked toward him, shielding my eyes from the sun. My designer sunglasses could only block so much glare. There was no help for the sweat streaming down my back and chest. Even my hair felt wet.

"Hey, Jesse," I shouted, drawing near. His cotton-plaid shirt bore dark stains under the arms.

"Hey, beautiful." He grinned and straightened, brandishing the fence-puller. "Hot enough for you?"

"Acclimatizing myself for hell," I said.

He strode forward and gave me a hug that made my vertebrae pop. It actually felt good. Man, that little fireplug was strong.

"Long time no see, girlfriend."

"Have time for a lemonade break on the porch?"

"You got it."

We walked toward the house and were joined by a whining, tail-wagging Old Heller. Mom, who'd been watching from the house window, hobbled onto the porch bearing glasses of lemonade clinking with ice cubes.

As we climbed the steps she said she wished she could join us, but was up to her unmentionables cutting out stars-'n'-stripes quilt-squares. A huge American flag already stood in a brass holder on a porch pillar. Smaller flags fluttered in hanging baskets of geraniums and petunias.

"Don't forget our barbecue tomorrow," she said. "At noon. But be here early. Why don't you come, too, Jesse? We'll have the Boatnik races on the radio."

He nodded, and raised his glass.

"Sounds good, Mom," I said. "What can I bring?"

"Ice cream." She squinted at me while she leaned on her cane. "The neighbors say anything new? We've seen the TV, the latest on the murder and all."

"As can be expected. The newshounds still sniffing around. Pretty hot story."

"This morning we put flowers on grandma and grandpa's grave, and your brother's. Boy Scouts had flags up on every grave. Along downtown streets, too. So festive."

Ah, I thought. Memorial Day in a small town. The official beginning of summer. And we had sunny weather for it this year—not always the case.

"Thanks, Mom," I said, giving her a hug. "I'll be there. I can only stay a few minutes today, though. Meeting friends in Gold Hill for dinner."

Jesse and I settled ourselves in cushioned chairs. It felt ten degrees cooler in the porch shade. I took a drink of ice-cold lemonade and pressed the glass to my forehead.

"Any idea yet on who killed the woman, who she was?" he began, eyes sharp beneath his hat brim.

"It's a little early," I said, setting down my glass. "It was getting dark. But she didn't look like anyone I'd seen. And the police aren't releasing a description yet."

Jesse nodded and chugged some lemonade.

"My buddy Welles is playing it close to the vest," he said. He lifted his hat to wipe one hand over his brow. "Not his case, but State Police keep him in the loop."

I sat up straighter. I'd forgotten. Jesse was a member of the Josephine County Sheriff's Posse. Of course he knew the sheriff, although the posse was more of a drill team, a community-relations and search-and-rescue outfit, than an actual paid police entity. Its members had training, but not investigative or law-enforcement duties.

"Really," I said. "In the loop, huh? So what can you tell me about the case?"

"Gonna call it murder, and soon release a description of the victim," Jesse said, turning his glass around in his work-scarred hands. "But won't release the cause. Probably just call it violence with a sharp weapon."

"Is OSP still processing the scene?" I jerked my head in that direction, and took a few swallows of lemonade, sweeter where sugar had accumulated at the bottom.

"Far as I know," Jesse said. "Should be done to-morrow. Maybe by noon."

"You don't know why the front driveway is crime-taped, do you?"

"No idea. But I could ask." He eyed me with a twinkle. As if he expected some kind of payment if he delivered on my request. It was always that way with Jesse.

I ignored the look. We finished our drinks. I looked at the time on my phone. Shoot! Four o'clock. I had to meet the Allendes for dinner in Gold Hill at five.

"Sarah stopped by the shop yesterday," I said. "She indicated you are still interested in helping Tulip and me develop a guest ranch. If we decide to buy the property next door, if it's buyable, and we can afford it."

His quirky mouth went flatline. His hazel eyes looked dark. Jesse could be a tough little nut when he had to.

"Be a really good gig," he said, tapping his thumbs on his glass. He looked out over my folks' pastures. "Damn good."

Hummingbirds fluttered around the flower-shaped feeder hanging from a hook on the edge of the porch ceiling. Two of the birds screeched and battered at each other for rights to the syrup. I'd read that, pound for pound, they are the fiercest birds on earth.

"Not a good gig," I said. "Fantastic. Keep you in high cotton for most of a year. You might even be able to afford a new truck to replace your old rattletrap." I said.

Jesse nodded but said nothing. He drained his glass, stood up and stretched, giving off a strong but not unpleasant smell of honest sweat.

"Well, let me know," he said. "You know I'll treat you right, Pepper. Cost wise. Otherwise, too."

I studied him as he sauntered to the porch steps as if waiting for me to say more.

"Jesse?" I said. He halted with his back to me. "How badly do you want this job? If there is a job."

He sighed heavily, lowered his head and stared over his shoulder.

"Well, duh."

With that, he turned cockily, jumped off the porch and returned to his repairs.

10

The trip to Taqueria Mexico in Gold Hill took a lot longer than expected, what with Memorial Weekend traffic slowing my progress on the Parkway out of Grants Pass. As I crossed "Debbs" Potts Memorial Bridge over the river, I heard the roar of jet boats running qualifying heats for the big race Monday. I stole a glance over the railings, lined with spectators. White roostertails followed screaming, flat-bottomed race boats headed for two low, concrete bridges to the west.

Yes, I had to make it back to the Boatnik Races one day.

The interior of the Mexican eatery was cool and dim, with low-key décor and high-speed waiters. Gloria and Jeanne waved from a booth as I entered. I signaled that I would hit the ladies' room before joining them at the table.

Repairs to makeup and hair done, I slid in next to Jeanne and told them a bit about my day. Then I heard about theirs.

We ordered margaritas—a virgin, for Jeanne—and gorged on warm tortilla chips with hot salsa while perusing the menu. "Carne Asada Tostada" set my salivary glands working overtime. We gave our orders to a young man sporting an Elvis pompadour hairdo and colorful tattoos. He smiled and hurried away.

I turned my attention back to the Allendes.

"How's Nancy doing at the women's healing center in Ashland, Jeanne?" I ventured. We hadn't until now had a chance to discuss how her older sister was recovering from her sex-trafficking experience last year.

Jeanne took a sip on her straw, swallowed a ladylike portion of her drink and gazed at me from beneath dark lashes. She still looked too thin. By buying her this feast, I was doing my part to remedy that.

"Nancy's good. It's really pretty up there on the hillside overlooking town and Grizzly Peak. She has her own room to decorate like she wants. She's learning to be a chef. She might get to leave soon."

"A chef, eh? Nice. So do you see Nancy often?"

"Not a lot. I'm pretty busy with school and my activities."

"Well, send her my love and prayers."

"She'd like that." Jeanne rearranged her utensils. "You could call her, you know." She gave me a tentative smile.

"I might just do that." I looked over at Jeanne's aunt, dabbing her mouth with a napkin. Gloria's forehead had sprouted a worry line.

"And how have you been doing, Pepper?" she said. "We haven't had a chance to talk after the horse show in Texas last fall. Still can't believe you solved a murder there, like some paperback heroine."

"And almost died doing so," I said. "Which reminds me. Did you see the TV news about a woman finding a body in a cabin in Grants Pass?"

Gloria froze mid-sip. Her eyes grew large. She blinked rapidly.

"Yes, but ... oh, no." She looked at Jeanne, and back at me. "You're not, don't tell me ... are you the one who found it?"

I looked around. The only other customers were a noisy group of kayakers still wearing their river-running regalia, and a couple sharing a table with two bouncy toddlers by the front window.

"That would be me," I said, nodding.

Jeanne and her aunt stared at me in disbelief.

"What are the odds?" said Jeanne, quickly looking down at her placemat.

"So can you tell us about it, Pepper?" said her aunt. "I take it she didn't die of natural causes? They were pretty hush-hush on the news, but said it was suspicious."

"To tell the truth, it's partly why I asked you to dinner."

"What do you mean?" Gloria said. She lay one hand on her breast.

Our orders arrived in a cloud of fragrant steam. The waiter set them down, smiled and slipped away. Before picking up my fork, I leaned in.

"Friday, after dinner with my folks in Grants Pass, I went to walk this old farm next door that the neighbors were going to put up for sale. A dogleg fronts the Applegate. Tulip and I always hoped to buy it, to add to my folks' forty acres and create a guest ranch. It's a killer location."

Gloria narrowed her eyes.

"Sorry," I said. "Anyway, when I went into the old cabin--where the famous writer Preston O'Hara once lived—I saw the body. You've heard of O'Hara, right?"

Gloria bent forward, her eyes glancing from side to side. Her large turquoise-and-silver pendant earrings continued to swing as she stared at me.

"Who hasn't? Jill Benetton at the barn said his books are still selling quite well. She has a few in her shop in Jacksonville. If you haven't been there, you really should go." She drummed her fingernails on the table. "So, did you recognize the woman, or know how she died?"

"Sheriff warned me not to discuss it.. And no, I don't know who she was, but am trying to find out. The cabin was vacant more than sixty years. Since O'Hara hanged himself there."

Jeanne gasped, and took a gulp of water.

Gloria frowned. She picked up her fork in her left hand and prodded her burrito. Then she took a swallow of margarita. I followed suit on my side of the table.

"So." Gloria sat back, fork still in hand as if she were about to stab her entrée. "Besides your wanting to know who she was and who killed her for what reason, I imagine you're wondering if or how a sale of the property would be affected."

"Pretty much," I said. "Of course the investigation will have to proceed further as far as police are concerned. The county turned the case over to the State Police. I have a lot of thinking to do, regarding whether we still want the place."

"I am sure it could be offered for sale," Gloria said. "I can contact the owners, see if they'd list it with my broker since I don't yet have my license. But no lender would touch the deal if it's encumbered some way."

"That's what I thought. There's also the 'ick factor."

"'Ick' factor?" she said. "You mean potential buyers would be turned off because someone was murdered there?"

"Well, yes," I said. "Though they haven't officially called it a murder."

"I wouldn't worry." she said. "I'll just consult my broker and let you know. And, um, keep me informed. I'll need the owners' latest contact info."

"I'd appreciate your help, Gloria. I'll keep you informed as the case develops."

"Good." Gloria dug into her plump burrito, picking diced green onions off the top and tucking them into her mouth.

I took another long swallow of margarita. The sweet, freezing slush slid down my throat so easily. I might have a headache in the morning, because this restaurant didn't use the fancy tequila. Higher-dollar Silver Patron had a negligible after effect. However, I'd eat plenty of food to line my stomach and keep the alcohol company.

"What I'd really like to do, Gloria, is to hire you to work with Tulip and me in a by-owner sale," I said, coming up for air. "If we decide we want the property and if it's copacetic for all concerned. I'll contact the owners. But you can do the paperwork, set up escrow, do a preliminary title search and stuff. If we qualify for a big enough loan after our down payment."

She considered this and then nodded. I thought it a good sign she was halfway through her burrito. Jeanne had been daintily picking at hers, pretending she wasn't listening. But that smart little cookie missed nothing. One thing I enjoyed about her. She felt like a second daughter to me, and I knew she considered me as a second mother, though we spoke infrequently. Like my son Serrano in Seattle. But very unlike my 32-year-old Chili. She and I talked or Skyped at least once a week.

"All right," Gloria said. "Do what you need to do, Pepper. I will help you any way I can. Only charge you a thousand." She chewed and swallowed a large bite, licking her lips. "Man, this burrito is to die for." She winked. "Pun intended."

* * *

Back home and more than ready for bed, I called Tulip to remind her of my parents' Memorial Day barbecue. She coyly said she'd bring "a friend" and meet me there. She refused to say who.

"Nope, it's a surprise," she said. "Find out tomorrow."

After signing off, I sat there perplexed. Tulip had a "friend" at last? Of the male persuasion? I felt happy for her. Her long-distance affair with Tommy Lee Jaymes, the Texas lothario working as a tribute actor for film icon Tommy Lee Jones, was as frustrating as mine with Sonny Chief. Would either of us find lasting love we could live with, long term?

But then we'd have to answer the bigger question: Would we want them in our face 24/7? Being single did have its rewards.

After my call to Tulip, I caught the recorded six o'clock TV news. Sure enough, KMFD-TV had Chapelle's promised segment featuring the Robertsons. However, it didn't amount to much more than I already knew: The couple had admired Preston O'Hara's writing. Had some of his books. Known there was a curse on their place.

Maisie Robertson elaborated.

"Over the years we lived there," she said, her husband standing mute beside her, "we had tools and animals mysteriously disappear, and it wasn't cougar or coyote."

"Didn't you say a man died in a fall down the well," Chapelle said, "awhile before you lived here?"

"That's right. And our grandson fell through a rotten floorboard in the cabin. He was nearly killed. It was off limits, but he and some friends went in anyway."

Shane Chappelle moved so close they were touching. "Did you leave because of the curse? Do you believe it's still in effect?"

Jack Robertson, a thick, average-height balding man in a flannel shirt and loose tan work pants, rocked on his heels. He'd stayed in the background, letting his wife do the talking. Now he raised his thick eyebrows and gave the reporter a stern look through thick bifocals.

"Can you blame us?"

11

At nine the next morning Maisie Robertson met me in the high-ceilinged lobby of Mountainview Manor, a retirement community west of Grants Pass. Small cottages and lawns flanked a three-story building with views of the Rogue Valley, and of the Siskiyou Mountains extending into northern California.

Robertson wore huge faux-pearl earrings and a matching necklace with an aqua pantsuit of early vintage. White therapeutic sandals revealed her shiny red toenails. Bright lipstick completed the look.

"My husband is just coming," she said, turning to see him waddle our way with assistance from a cane. Under one arm he carried a photo album. Jack Robertson studied me through his coke-bottle glasses, and exhaled a breath scented with cigarette smoke and Sen-Sen.

"Pleased to make your acquaintance," he said, giving a small cough.

We discussed where to go and settled on Grandma's Cafe on the edge of Grants Pass' Old Town. The tiny brick hole-in-the wall was a block down "G" Street from the historic newspaper-and-popcorn shop, Blind George's. I'd been to Grandma's once before, when Sonny was in town and we'd taken my folks out to breakfast. It was a welcoming place adorned with old photos and redolent of savory smells.

The Robertsons and I sipped coffee, made small talk and ordered three of the restaurant's famously frosted, oversized, nut-crusted cinnamon rolls.

"We moved up here from the Sacramento area," said Maisie Robertson. "To be near Cleve, his kids, grandkids. He was a logger but now works for a car dealer." She fingered her pearls with one arthritic but capable looking hand. "We're curious what you saw in our cabin Friday. Police won't tell us much."

"I'm not supposed to discuss it. As I said, I was walking the land after dinner, and smelled an odor from the cabin. I went in to check it out."

"How'd you get in?" said Jack Robertson. "Last time we mowed that field, the porch roof looked collapsed."

"About when was that?" I said.

Stroking the photo album beside his plate., he blinked, and cleared his throat.

"Oh, some time last summer. Maybe August or September."

"Any signs of activity?" I said. "Did you try to go in?"

"No reason." He looked around. His gaze rested on a comely blonde entering the cafe with a towheaded toddler, and then travelled up the wall to black-and-white photos of Grants Pass in the early twentieth century.

A Filipina waitress who looked to be in junior high brought our pastries. I took my first sweet, flaky bite and rolled my eyes with delight before swallowing.

"So," I said to the Robertsons, dabbing my lips with a paper napkin. "When did you two move to the house?"

"Almost three years ago," said Maisie. "Not long after, the trouble started."

"What trouble?" I said.

"Things would break or disappear. Tools, Canning jars full of fruit. Animals."

I stopped chewing.

"Animals?"

"We had a goat that disappeared. Jack said it was killed by a cougar, but it disappeared in daylight. We locked the goats up at night."

I took another bite of cinnamon roll, licking frosting off one finger. I watched the Robertsons for signs of emotion, for overthought answers. But they ate calmly.

"Anything else?" I said.

"We had a fire in the barn," said Maisie. "Got it out pretty quick. Then we started having health problems."

"We'd been pretty healthy before," Jack put in. "Old age ain't for sissies."

"Your smoking didn't help," Maisie snapped.

He rolled his eyes.

"We had some beef cows," Maisie continued. "And chickens. One time a rooster went missing after a loud party down at the river. We thought someone took it to roast. Or sacrifice." She forked a chunk of roll into her mouth and chewed fast.

Her words made me sit up straighter.

"What do you mean?" I thought of what Rosie Pussytoes had told me about the Robertson grandson's alleged involvement in a fringe religious group.

Jack blinked, tucked a stray pastry flake into his mouth, and shifted in his seat.

"Always had cults in this neck of the woods," he said, with a dismissive wave. "You know how it is." He glanced at his wife, now picking daintily at her cinnamon roll. "Or it coulda been tweakers, druggies, all the above."

I had the impression he had more to say.

"The kind that sacrificed animals?" I whispered.

He raised his eyebrows.

"Well, we did find that headless rooster carcass." He looked away and coughed.

"Any weird stuff ever go on out at the cabin?" I said.

"Not that we knew," Maisie replied. "Could have been. But we don't know, do we, Jack, since we never went there and wouldn't let anyone else go there. It was overgrown and unsafe."

Jack nodded.

I took a few swallows of coffee that, surprisingly, was still hot. Quality stoneware did that for beverages.

"So, down to brass tacks," I said. "Do you still want to sell your place?"

Jack coughed into his fist.

"Cleve wants it pretty bad," he said. "Just can't quite come up with the money."

"Says he's working on it," said Maisie. "We'd drop the price a bit to help him. He must sell his place first, though. And we can't wait too long. We plan on being around a while, and have our own expenses."

"Like you wouldn't believe," Jack sighed, shaking his head.

I fiddled with my paper napkin. I had a pretty good origami horse going on. I'd had just figured wrong on one corner, and refolded it.

"What's your best price?" I said.

"Maybe seven-, eight-hundred thousand," Jack put it. "By the river and all. Lotta vineyards nearby. Be good for a pot farm, too."

"Fair price," I said.

"This murder and that so-called curse, didn't do us any favors," Maisie said. "A realtor we talked to said under normal circumstances it should it be worth a million."

"We still hope our son can find a way to buy it," Maisie said. "Even if Cleve can't come up with the money, he still has final say on price."

I pressed my lips together and nodded.

"Probably a hard sell, at least until this trouble blows over," I said. "My friend and I might still be interested, though. Let's stay in touch."

Before I requested the check, I asked if they knew my friend, Jesse Banks. If the Robertsons were the "neighbors" Jesse's daughter said he heard gossip from.

"Jesse did do some work for us," said Maisie. "When Jack's health got worse last year." She looked at him, and he frowned. She offered no more.

"On TV last night," I said, "you said someone died in a fall down your well."

"Before we moved there," Jack Roberston said. "Was in all the papers."

"I was working in Seattle," I said. "But I did hear something like that."

He handed me the photo album.

"The clipping's at the back," he said.

I opened the album with its cracked leather cover and snapshots held in place with old-style corner stickers. There were photos of Jack and Maisie in younger days with kids ranging from babies to teenagers, shot in California. Fishing, playing on swing sets, riding trikes and ponies. Maisie said they'd had three children including the ruggedly attractive Cleve, whose dark brows nearly met above wary eyes. But the other two had stayed in California, one a teacher, the other a land surveyor. Neither was interested in then Applegate property. Unless they inherited it.

When I came to the pictures of the Robertsons' local cottage, I paused. An aged Jack and Maisie stood with thumbs up in front of a "For Sale" sign, and picnicked with a middle-aged Cleve, his two adult children and his teenaged, "late-life surprise" smiling under a fruit tree near the handsome old barn. A pony peeked into the frame while Cleve, silver at the temples, offered it an apple. No partner or wife, though the presence of offspring indicated he'd had a partner.

The clipping about the previous owner who fell down the well told how the property was rumored to carry a curse.

"Tell the truth, I'm not convinced about that curse," Jack said, "Don't have no truck with superstition. But find it kinda interesting."

"Jack likes weird things," said Maisie, giving me a look.

There was only one photo of the cabin, shot from a distance, blurry and undated, showing the sagging roof, climbing vines and leaning power pole. It could have been shot a half-century ago, or just last year.

"We told the grandkids to stay away," Jack said. "Or the ghost would get them. But you know how well teenagers mind."

I did, indeed. I was still one, in some ways.

"Cleve's youngest son went inside the cabin a few years ago," Maisie said matter-of-factly. He almost got killed falling through the floor."

* * *

It was nearing eleven when I dropped the Robertsons back at their new home. On the way to my parents', I stopped at the downtown supermarket to buy ice cream. One vanilla, one chocolate. Plus apples for the horses.

Mom looked up when I rounded the house. She was ensconced in a padded cedar swing on the patio, shaded by oaks. I went over to give her a kiss.

Dad snoozed in a chair and ottoman. Old Heller lifted his head and thumped his tail at my approach. I leaned down to pet him as I took in the holiday scene.

Near the house stood a redwood picnic table covered with a red-checkered cloth and set with Western-print dinnerware. At its center was a white-tin pitcher sprouting an American flag, red and white roses, and lavender-blue sweet peas. A radio on one side of the steps poured out vintage tunes from a country-classics station.

I jogged up the steps to put my ice cream in the fridge freezer-drawer. Peeking into the main compartment to check out the array of edibles, I felt a gush of saliva fill my mouth at the sight of two enormous pies heaped with huge, syrup-glazed strawberries. Nearby stood a huge bowl of satiny whipped cream shaped into Swiss-Alp peaks.

Back on the patio I complimented Mom on all her hard work.

"Hope you brought your appetite," Mom grinned. "Dad went nuts at the meat store, and I decided we needed three different salads – fruit, coleslaw and potato."

"Are you feeding an army?" I said. "Who else is coming besides Tulip?" I sank into a comfy chair.

"Jesse and his daughter might stop by," Mom said. "He wanted to fix some electrical problem in the covered arena. I told him not to bother, but he needs the work."

I got up to grab a bottle of lemonade from the cooler by the steps, and a handful of mixed nuts from a bowl on the table, then sank back into my chair.

"That tiny homes for the homeless project that he was counting on fell through," Dad said, startling me. I'd thought he was napping. "Cities like Ashland have the tourist and tax revenue to pay for projects like that. But Grants Pass doesn't, although they're working to change that. The revamped fairgrounds with restaurants and condos will bring in tons of revenue."

"How's it going, Dad?" I said, blowing him a kiss. "Can I get you a beer or something?"

"Can get my own."

While he got his brew, the radio broadcast switched from recorded music to live programming from

Riverside Park. The roar of race-boat engines competed with the announcer's voice as he told of an imminent fly-over by an F-16, marking the official start of the Memorial Day Boatnik Races.

"You guys hear any more about the investigation?" I said, raising my voice.

"No," said Mom. "Thought we'd be kept informed. Being neighbors and all. We're a little nervous. Like another shoe's about to drop."

"I get that feeling, too," I said. Despite the heat, a shiver coursed through me as I recalled the scene at the cabin, the sight and smell of the dead woman. It was difficult to catch the holiday spirit, with that memory popping up in random moments.

"Maybe we should say a memorial prayer for the woman who died," I said.

"That would be nice," said Mom. "Dad! Turn down the radio and bow your head. We're saying a prayer."

Dad, who'd grabbed a cold Rainier from the cooler, folded his hands, beer and all, and bowed his head.

"Dear Lord," said Mom, "thank you for this day, for this food we are about to enjoy, and for loved ones coming to enjoy your gifts with us. Bless those, too, here in spirit. Especially the lady in the cabin. Amen."

I took a moment to dab a napkin with a drop of lemonade, a dot of fruit salad and a slice of salami, and set it on the rim of a birdbath beside the patio.

"Spirit offering," I told my parents. They knew I referred to a practice Sonny Chief observed, honoring the departed with a bit of one's own meal, believing they could smell and taste, though not eat. Somehow it felt right and calmed me.

We ate snacks, remembered past Memorial Days and listened to the race for a while. Where were the others? Were they even coming? At one o'clock, Dad fired up the grill. Mom and I bustled about setting out tableware and side dishes.

Heller suddenly jumped up and trotted toward the front. Company had arrived.

First around the corner strode Jesse Banks and his daughter Sarah. He carried a bottle of wine, and she carried her fussing baby wrapped in a pale pink blanket with white lambs on it. We cooed over Nell, while Jesse and Dad discussed barn work.

A few minutes later came Tulip, all carefully tousled hair, pink Lolita sunglasses and endless legs in lace-trimmed jeans shorts. Jesse whispered, a tad unkindly, I thought, "Mutton masquerading as lamb."

She popped a pickle into her thickly glossed mouth, sucked on it and tilted her head to gaze at me through her heart-shaped lenses. You could never be unhappy or serious for long, with Tulip around.

"Just me today," she pouted. "Tommy Lee's tribute show in Portland last night apparently turned into an all-nighter. And not with yours truly. I'm bummed."

"That dog," I said. "I told you not to pin your hopes on those Hollywood types."

"Like you have it any better," she snapped, clearly in no mood to joke.

I felt stung by her remark, her reference to my long-distance lover. It was uncalled for and uncharacteristic. But then I relaxed. We did share an unluckiness in love of the eternal-bliss kind.

"Is Mr. Jaymes still coming down to see you, though?" I said, touching her arm.

"Maybe later," she said. "He's on his way to the opening of a Tommy Lee Jones movie in San Francisco. They're having a contest to see who can tell them apart— the famous actor and his official lookalike."

"Does he want you to ride along as a Susan Sarandon lookalike? " I said.

"I wish." Tulip sniffed dramatically and eyeballed the picnic spread. "The barbecue smells fabulous, Mr. Kane. Anger makes me hungry enough to eat a horse."

"Sorry," Dad grinned. "Only beef and pork on the menu today."

We laughed, bringing Mom into our embrace. Then I pulled in Sarah, who had been settling her baby on a blanket on the lawn. We'd party hearty. Worries about the dead and the absent could wait.

We enjoyed our meal, each other and the race broadcasts. Watched little Nell crawl about the lawn and bob her head at dandelions. I was put pleasantly in mind of when my children were babies, all squishy little arms and legs, curious eyes, bouncy heads and grasping fingers. It was sweet being so near a tiny one, smelling her skin, hearing her delighted squeals. I wished Chili or Serrano would give me a grandbaby one of these days. But they didn't seem partial to long term relationships, so I wasn't holding my breath.

"Gonna put Nell on a horse soon?" I joked.

"Probably when she turns one," Sarah laughed. "That's when Dad started me out, in front of him in the saddle."

"Earlier the better," I said, remembering the day Mom sat me up on one of her barrel-racing horses when I was three. From then on I was hooked.

After we'd talked about the latest political scandals, our neighbors, our lovers, the upcoming horse show and what the media were saying about the murder case, we fell on dessert: the afore-spied strawberry pie nestled in a buttery crust and topped with mounds of airy whipped cream. No words.

Somewhere along the afternoon, after the talk-stopping pie, Tulip and I found time to discuss our guest ranch and where we were with it.

"So you and I will sell or rent our houses," she said, "and each take a hundred thousand or more from our 401Ks, and your folks will put in their hundred grand for the down payment on the property. Then get a loan for the rest."

"We not only bring our tack store here," I said, "but also live in the Robertson cottage, and build housing for a dozen guests between here and there."

"Yes, and have dude horses or let guests bring their own," Tulip said. "I just love our idea of calling in a 'B, B & B—bed, barn and breakfast. Maybe I can talk Tommy Lee into appearing at the grand opening. We could screen one of the real Tommy Lee's Western-theme movies. Like 'No Country for Old Men.'"

"Oh, that'd be cheery," I said, my voice dripping sarcasm.

Mom, who'd been eavesdropping as we voiced our dream, now leaned forward.

"I don't know how you two can fail," she said. "Guests will have city amenities nearby, fishing and jet boat trips on the river, visits to clubs and shops in Medford, and galleries and plays in Ashland."

"Don't forget the wineries," Tulip put in. "And we're exactly halfway between Seattle and San Francisco."

It sure sounded like a winner. A low-key ranch that was Western in flavor, but with other attractions an hour or two away—the Coast, the Redwoods, Crater Lake.

We beamed at each other, warming once more to the possibility of making this thing work. We not only had a great plan, but family and loved ones offering support.

"Jesse's hot to develop it," I said, glancing at him and his daughter. "Building six tiny homes to start, for guests. Plus a tipi." I was on a roll. "Maybe even rehab

O'Hara's cabin as a museum with books, posters, décor …" My voice trailed off.

A small cloud drifted over the sun. Then another cloud. The hot, humid air turned slightly cool. Even the birds in the trees fell silent.

Tulip looked up and fixed me with a concerned gaze.

"So. What did you learn from the Robertsons today? You met them, right?"

I sighed. Dreaming was fun. Facing hard reality, not so much.

"Got some good history," I said. "He kind of believes in the curse, but she doesn't." I filled her in on what the couple had shared, including the photos.

"Whoa," Tulip said when I told her about the previous owner who fell down the well, and about the Robertson boy who nearly died falling through the cabin floor.

"I declare," she breathed. "I'd forgotten that well thing. There was talk about it for weeks. I did wonder about the curse, then. I don't believe in curses. Do you?"

I didn't know if I believed in curses, despite having incurred one once myself, from an ex-husband. But I was about to find out.

12

It was just past five when the company left and I piled into my dually, ready to head for home. Sated with ribs, potato salad and epic strawberry dessert, I buckled up and turned on the AC.

Then I hesitated. Tapped my fingers on the steering wheel. Looked around the yard and back to the road. My mind, though dulled with food, drink and merriment, ticked with a not-so-random, not-too-surprising idea.

I was in the area. Surely the OSP forensics team was finished at the Robertsons' by now. Should I go take another look at the cabin, and at the cottage, as well?

The answer was clear. It was an itch I absolutely had to scratch.

I drove around to the entrance to the Robertson place and up the short, forested drive to the cottage. There were no police units in sight. But remnants of crime tape stretched between columns on the front porch. A paper was taped to the front door, warning readers not to trespass.

Parking the truck by the detached garage, I stuck my phone in a hip pocket and the .38 in my waistband, and stepped out into jungle humidity and blazing heat. A raucous cawing of jays accompanied my steps to the cottage door. Standing on the porch, I craned to see through a split between drapes over the window. I saw only a small slice of the vacant room.

The tiny yard was seriously overgrown. Irises pointed their spear-shaped leaves toward a hazy white sky. A red azalea labored to sustain a few star-shaped blooms in a side yard under the apple tree I'd seen in the photo album. A corner of the barn was visible about two hundred feet from the left side of the house. The ill-fated well must lay under that decrepit roof on posts to the left of the house.

I walked toward the red barn. I eased into it through a partly open sliding door. The inside was a memory tethered by cobwebs, a bit of passing time immobilized like prey in a spider's shroud. It was hot, still and dust-scented. To my left stood a vintage tractor and other farm tools and equipment. I wondered if the Robertsons were selling these with the property, or if they were no longer of value. A wooden ladder led to a hayloft on the structure's second story.

To my right was a door with a rusted knob. I opened it. Empty saddle and bridle racks lined the wall of the small, stale-smelling windowless room. A bucket of cobweb-covered grooming tools stood forlornly in the corner. A sparrow flew in through the open door, battered itself along the ceiling, and then flew out again.

I lingered in the aisle a moment longer, taking in the four horse stalls on either side and the open loafing-shed seen through the open top half of a Dutch door at the rear. Old barns turn me on. Just the thought of the life, healthful work and country peace they suggest makes me feel more at home than almost anywhere else.

My parents' barn and covered arena were like that, too. Just more spread out.

I'd spent a night or three in barns—awaiting the birth of a foal, sharing a sleepover with a friend, listening for hoots of owls and calls of nighthawks. Being afraid bats would tangle in my hair. Having my sleeping bag invaded by a mouse.

But I had no time to linger. I went out the back and into a long, narrow pasture leading up toward trees that lined the riverbank and sheltered the old cabin. A track of crushed weeds, likely made by incident responders and forensics people, led that way.

As I trudged in the growing heat, sweat streamed down my back and between my breasts. The sun scorched my jaws and neck below the brim of my ball cap. Tall grass rustled as I walked through it. Poison oak showed its shiny three-leaf clusters, while hidden rocks tripped my stride.

Soon I faced the woods along the river. Passing a torn "No Trespassing" sign that hung catawampus from a rotted post, I stepped over the freshly cut wires of a barbed-wire fence, and saw the cabin among trees two hundred feet away.

That fence was likely as near the cabin as the Robertsons had allowed their stock and grandkids to go. They would have other river access nearer the house.

Staying in the track of crushed vegetation, but still dodging saplings and thorny vines, I inched toward the cabin. A feeling of danger grew with each step. I halted fifty feet away and weighed my options. Yellow tape was on the cabin door, but some ends dangled down. The forensics team was done. If anyone with sinister motives were around, they would've seen me by now, and acted.

May as well go all the way.

I had no idea what I was looking for or what I might see. But if I found even a hint of a clue that would help solve the case, Tulip and I could proceed with our plans. And then I could consider my parents safe.

Evidence of the scene processing was everywhere, outside and inside the cabin. Smashed and chopped foliage, a wide-open door, fingerprint dust, footprints, a plastic booty. The body was gone, of course, with the floorboards still bearing dark stains. The front of the kitchen counter and one wall also bore stains.

The papers and books were gone, too. Even the mug with the odd logo. Only the vintage armchair and little table remained, moved into a corner by the rock fireplace flanked on one side by a modest pile of kindling. Had that kindling been split by the hatchet that had served as a murder weapon?

Hot though the day was, it felt cool in the cabin. In fact, downright chilly. And there was still the faint odor of death, which wasn't helping with digestion of my holiday lunch.

I again glanced right to where the pine kitchen-counter and cupboards ran along the wall. Cabinet doors and drawers gaped open, insides bare. An old steel sink, and spaces where a stove and refrigerator once stood, were vacant. I imagined squatters would have used a propane stovetop for cooking and a cooler for perishable food.

The little scarred table still stood by the window. It held nothing of interest, just a few moisture rings from glasses or mugs. Next I studied the armchair, feeling inside the gaps and holes for hidden objects. I came up empty.

Finally I examined the fireplace. Charred chunks of firewood remained. But who knew how long they'd been there? I ran my hand along the cool river-rocks in shades of blue, green and pink. The mortar binding them was dusty and cracked. A few stones jiggled when I rubbed them. Not much prevented this beauty from crumbling.

I felt down each side of the firebox, along the redwood mantel and up both sides of the chimney. What a beautiful thing this must have been once, what a comfort in cold weather. I could clearly imagine what it would have felt like to read, write and reflect there. It had been someone's beloved home. Preston O'Hara's home.

I looked up at the cobwebbed ceiling with its hefty, hand-hewn beam running from one side of the space to another, and at the warped, dark vault above. I wondered where exactly O'Hara had wound his rope, fashioned his knot, suspended the noose for his final chapter.

A breeze fingered my arms. I moved out from under the beam.

I took out my cell phone and shot half-a-dozen photos of the room.

That's when a faint shout punctuated the cabin's stillness. A shout as if heard through blankets, though it was only through trees. Then laughter. Another couple of shouts, followed by a crackling fusillade that sounded like fireworks. Or automatic weapon fire.

I held my breath. Were the sounds coming from the riverbank? It sounded so. I craned my head to look out the cracked window above the chair, and saw nothing but trees. I waited a few moments until the noise subsided. Touching the gun at my hip, I told myself it was only young people partying at the river. It was a holiday, after all.

Now I was on edge. I knew I shouldn't tarry, and tempt fate to produce a worse-case scenario. But I wanted to give the cabin a better look than I'd had before. I was sure forensics had gone over it with the proverbial fine-toothed comb. But what if they'd overlooked a subtle clue? Knowing the cabin somewhat from the old days, I might see something that looked wrong, out of place.

I walked quickly into the short hall at the back. A tiny bathroom with a stained clawfoot tub, ancient sink and toilet lay at the hall's end. A pair of ten-by-twelve bedrooms flanked either side. The one on the right was empty. The one on the left also looked empty, although in a corner lay feathers like those from bed pillows, and dust mice with fabric nuclei that likely came from blankets. I occasionally came across similar "clues" in my own house.

The floor bore scuff marks such as would have been made by a heavy bed moved a time or two.

It struck me as odd that overall, even though recently processed and walked on, the sides and corners of the floors were not terribly dusty. But, I reasoned, if someone had lived there recently, they might not be. That gave more credence to my squatter theory. Had it been the woman living there? Or her killer?

Creeping to the window of the room on the left, I stepped on one old foot-wide, deeply cracked floorboard that creaked and gave slightly under my weight. I jumped back. The twelve-foot plank bearing a yards-long center split was held in place with nailheads protruding an inch or more each along what must be joist lines. It had to be the plank that the Robertson boy had fallen through. Each half would have collapsed down when stepped on, opening a narrow slot that would accommodate a thin body.

I stared at the damaged plank. Police may have ignored it. Or they may have pried it up, peeked into the crawlspace, and, seeing nothing that concerned them, repaired it haphazardly.

The buzz of rising blood pressure filled my head. I knew what I had to do.

Sitting down on the floor, I drew my boot heels to my buttocks and kicked repeatedly as hard as I could at the protruding nails. They bent and loosened. I kicked harder. One by one the nails popped up. I yanked them out. Then I stomped on the lengthy split, which screeched like an angry cat when both halves angled down.

I jerked at the sound. I was on the edge of sanity, anyway. I shone my phone's flashlight beam into the dark crawlspace. The smell of dirt, mold and animal debris filled my nostrils. Breathing through my mouth, I lay at right angles to the foot-wide opening and peered deeper into it.

Nothing was visible straight down the three feet to the ground. But by swinging the light around, I made out rows of masonry blocks holding the floor joists, plus something the same general shape, but smaller and with a round top, ten feet deeper into the cavity. It sat behind joists under where the cabin's hall floor would be. And that odd "block" appeared to support nothing.

I wiggled forward and lowered my head sideways into the hole. Now a row of blocks hid the freestanding block, whatever it was. Below me lay only dirt and torn, rodent-feces encrusted tarpaper. I coughed, swallowed and coughed again. Not the healthiest environment.

As I prepared to lower my body into the crawlspace for a better look at the boxy object under the hall floor, I froze. The shouting I'd heard earlier coming from the river seemed louder. And closer. I made out voices of at least two men and one woman. They sounded upset. Angry, even.

"Don't do that," yelled a woman.

"We have to," boomed a male voice.

More loud words, this time, unintelligible, as if traveling from farther away. Then the sound of snapping twigs. Or a crackling fire.

Hell. Who were they? More important, were they headed toward the cabin?

My mouth went dry. I drew back, banged my head on one edge of the opening, saw stars but jumped to my feet. Hands shaking, I pulled the halves of the split plank back up and scrambled for the door.

While leaping off the porch onto solid ground, my revolver bouncing at my hip, I glanced around. There was no one in sight, and no more shouting. But I wasted no time galloping through the overgrown fields, past the trees and across the Robertson lawn to my truck.

I climbed in Red Ryder and set a new land-speed record for Gold Hill.

My body was a sweaty mess, my lungs taxed to the max. I cursed myself for returning to the murder scene. What was I thinking? Assuming I'd been thinking?

Hell. I could have been heard or even seen. Maybe by the murderer. Or at very least by the people shouting and setting off fireworks or guns down at the river. Was it just party people? Or somebodies more sinister?

At any rate, no one should know where I had just been.

I drove in shock, on autopilot, for a while. Then I turned on the country tunes and tried to calm down. I lowered my speed and swung off the freeway at Gold Hill. Before going home I stopped at the market to stock up on breakfast fixings. And on staples like ribeye.

Sure, I wanted my troubles over, my mystery solved, my ranch dreams to start coming true, yesterday. But in my experience, patience was not always a virtue. Some of my best times came about when I could not or would not wait for answers.

Back home by six-thirty, I parked the hot truck outside the garage, went to feed the horses, let the Bostons out of the side yard and hauled myself up the deck steps.

Cool house air whooshed over me as I slid open the back door and took my tired body into the dining room. A shower would be heaven. I headed for the bathroom.

But the Bostons barked, sniffed and had a conniption fit at the front door. Their raking claws on fiberglass sent shivers through me. Like fingernails on a chalkboard.

Now what, I thought, as I trotted to the door. Just to be on the safe side, I pulled aside a drape and looked out the window. Nothing. No one. The dogs kept barking. Charlie clawed harder at the door. Shayna cocked her head as she stared at it.

I unlocked and pulled the door open an inch. Nobody on the porch or lawn.

Then I looked down. My heart dropped. My eyelids wouldn't close.

Through the crack I stared at what lay against the base of the door: a bloodied and smoke-charred white Leghorn chicken. A chicken in possession of most of its feathers, but missing a head.

13

Nausea swept me as I starred at the carcass. I choked back bitter bile when my gaze slid to where the bloodied neck stump ending with hacked-off vertebrae and red stringy tissue lay against the kick plate. A silver Post-It note with black writing lay beneath the severed neck.

Heart racing, I cocked my head to decipher its message:

"Wind up like him, you stick your neck where it don't belong," read thick letters penned in shiny ink. A chunky exclamation point followed the last word.

What the hell? Was someone really threatening me? I tried to convince myself it was some kind of prank, or even a warning from neighborhood tweakers who guessed I'd tattled on them for cooking meth. But it had been weeks ago when the Jackson County sheriff paid that couple a little visit.

No, this was far more serious. It amounted to a death threat. Somebody wanted me to stop investigating the killing on the Applegate.

But who wanted me to stop? If I could answer that, I would know the killer. And that might give me a start on learning who had been killed. And why.

The dogs snuffled and whined around my ankles, eager to be let out and have at the chicken. I herded them into the utility room, closed the door, put on plastic gloves and took a black garbage bag and clear sandwich sack onto the porch.

That chicken was heavier and floppier than I'd thought. Probably eight pounds. I fumbled around and dropped it twice, repeatedly losing control of the wings. But I finally got it in the bag and twist-tied, sans Post-It. The latter got a new home in the sandwich sack.

I toted the bagged bird to the kitchen. After moving frozen lasagna, vegetables, ice cream and coconut cake around, I compacted its bag with twine and stuffed it in there. Evidence. But I had no idea what to do with it.

What I really needed now was that shower, a warm cup of white tea with lavender honey, and an early bedtime for a change. In that frazzled moment I thought of Sonny, my best friend in times of crisis. And a whole lotta other times.

I sat on the edge of my bed and pulled out my cell phone.

"Hell-oh," drawled Sonny, sounding as if he'd expected my call.

"Oh, Sonny," I sighed, not knowing where to begin. "I'm in big trouble."

"Uh-huh."

"I got what amounts to a death threat." My voice quavered, but I kept it low, to show him I was somewhat *washte,* or all right. "And I'm pretty sure it's from whoever killed the woman in the cabin."

"Talk to me."

I filled him in on my activities of the past two days. My interview with Detective Frank James. About the Robertsons, Gloria Allende, Jesse Banks. I may have left out my visit to the cabin. But I brought him up to speed on the chicken I'd just found. And the warning note.

"Takes this thing to a whole new level," I said, mentally sweating.

"Until now there's been no trouble on a personal level since the murder."

"Right."

"I wonder what's different now."

Not a direct question. It was his Indian way not to attach suspicion or blame, put another person in a negative light. Asians might call that approach of letting someone else answer obliquely, thereby "saving face."

But I was busted. I took a deep breath and blew it out slowly.

"OK. I went to the cabin today after the barbecue," I said, suddenly feeling relieved to unburden myself. I braced for the hell I was sure to catch. "Forensics was done, there were no warnings around, I was in the area —"

"Whoa whoa whoa. Some would say that was not the wisest move."

"Damn it, Sonny," I rasped. "I know that. But I had my gun. There was no one around. And I kicked in a split floorboard and saw something that might help the case. A box or something hidden way back in the crawlspace. I thought I heard people coming, so I got the hell out."

He said nothing. But I heard him breathing rhythmically. He may even have chuckled. At least one of us was getting something from this conversation.

"Sonny?"

"Cages have been rattled. The investigative reporter has been investigating."

"What's that supposed to mean?"

Silence.

I let go of a sigh and lowered my hunched shoulders. I went to the sink. With my free hand, I splashed water on my hot face.

"You OK, Pepper?"

"Yeah, yeah," I said. "Just trying to cool off. Guess I'd better call OSP. Detective Frank James was put on the case. Can you believe that name?"

"Good dude."

"Jees, Sonny. Is there anyone in local law enforcement you don't know?"

"Just know James by reputation. He'll do a good job for you. Let him do it."

"Yeah." I crossed my fingers as I said that, knowing it would be a tall order for a determined ex-reporter with a heavy-duty rescuing gene.

"Concentrate on preparing for your horse show. Let it be known you're off the case, are leaving it to police."

"Good ideas, Sonny. But I can't help obsessing over who she was, who killed her. I'm sending you my crime-scene photos. You might see something I don't."

I sat down, found my Friday photos and texted them to him.

"Got them," he said a moment later. "Lady looks Indian. Not much indication of a struggle. I'll have a closer look when we hang up."

The photos were pretty grainy. They didn't show the nearest walls or the rest of the cabin floor, where I'd seen some blood spatter this evening.

"Right," I said. "So I am thinking she was either homeless, a squatter, or else a writer, or a crazy fan of O'Hara, making a pilgrimage to his place or something."

"Best to keep an open mind."

"Like I don't? Thanks, Sonny."

"Just sayin'."

"Wouldn't police release her description? To help locate next of kin?"

"In good time."

"I can't help thinking the Robertsons are involved, Sonny. They strike me as over-protective of Cleve. He wants to buy the place, can't afford it, but his folks need money from a sale. Old age with health problems is not for the light of wallet."

Sonny clicked his tongue. He was either agreeing with me, or else judging me for being so gung-ho to solve the mystery.

"Lightening up isn't always bad, Pepper. In police work, I've found that appearing to back off allows more details to come out, while keeping me safe."

"I'll consider that. Thanks. But I have to pursue my reporter's hunches."

"I know your hunches," he said. His voice took on a more affectionate tone. "Quite often they're right. Take care. Sleep tight. Dream of me."

"That's an assignment I love to take. Dreaming of you."

After we signed off, I called Detective James to report the dead chicken and the warning note. My call went to voice mail, but he picked up partway through. I repeated my message, but left out my visit to the cabin. He asked me to photograph the note and text it to him. He'd pick up the note to add to his file, when he got a chance.

I showered, slipped into my sleep tee and poured a fresh cup of creamed tea. The honeyed brown liquid caressed my innards all the way down, and in a few moments brought a warm buzz to body and brain.

Switching on the bedroom TV to catch the top of the local news, I perched on the end of the bed. They had nothing new on the murder. Therefore the Bostons and I burrowed between the bed linens. After a full and occasionally frightening day, horizontal had never seemed more appealing.

* * *

Waylon's deep-throated tones jolted me awake at five in the morning. A tad early and pitch dark, but showing signs of brightening.

Half asleep, I fumbled for the phone on the nightstand and knocked over my water glass. Jamming the phone between shoulder and ear, I yanked a wad of tissues from their box and mopped up the mess. Sudden awakenings weren't my thing.

"Pepper! You awake?" Mom shrilled.

"I am now."

"Someone set fires in the garbage cans by the back porch last night. Scorched the grass and part of the steps."

My heart thudded. I jimmied myself up on one elbow, dropped the sodden tissues on the floor and brushed the hair away from my eyes.

"You think they were set? Are they completely out? Did you call 911?"

"Yes, yes and yes. "

"And you're OK?"

"Yes, but we got a damned good scare. Rural Fire's been and gone. I waited as long as I could to call. you." She paused. "We could've lost the house, or died in our sleep. I shudder to think."

"How did you wake up?"

"Heller started barking. We thought it was at raccoons. Dad went downstairs, saw the blaze, hosed it out. Soaked his PJ's, tracked in soot, but got it out."

"Why do you think they were set? Maybe you had something combustible in the cans. Like, from the barbecue."

"Oh, no. We are very careful. This was no accident. Your dad found part of an oily rag in the debris. Rural Fire reported it to OSP and is investigating it as arson."

Dad was shouting in the background.

"They're getting back at us," he yelled. "Pepper never should have gone there."

"He thinks somebody knows we were kind of in on finding the body," Mom said. "Police were here Friday night. It's been all over the news. A killer might think that we saw something, and said something incriminating, or were about to."

"Possible. Well, hang tight, Mom. I'll drop by later and check it out for myself."

With the timing, the events of the past few hours, things were definitely heating up for me and my family.

I lay back down and tried to sleep for another hour. A futile effort. My mind ran like a hamster on a wheel. About six I dragged my carcass out of bed. I let out the dogs and tended to the horses. Then I grabbed my cell phone, filled a mug with creamed Colombian and took it onto the deck. The day was cool, bright and perfumed with essence of pine and roses. All of which would help wake me up for what promised to be another helter-skelter day.

I tapped my folks' number while gazing out at the hills and listening to birds chattering in the garden. With the automatic sprinkler running, they pecked about the damp earth, looking for grubs. Down the lane a neighbor's miniature donkeys began their "Donkey Serenade"—a goofy chorus of brays and honks that made me grin.

If I did buy the farm neighboring my parents', and move, I would miss this little piece of paradise, though not its aging accoutrements that needed constant attention. I would just have a new piece of paradise. And attendant projects.

"Hi, honey," Mom said, sounding fresh despite her early-morning scare.

"Sorry if I sounded a tad out of it earlier," I said. "Everything still okay? Anything new?"

"As can be expected. But we want you to come over and look at our shots from the security camera. You know, the one you had Sonny put on the garage last year? We forgot we even had it until Dad and I started talking over breakfast."

"I'd forgotten about that camera, too, since there was never anything to worry about after you thought your lawnmower was stolen, and Dad later remembered he'd taken it in for repairs. What did the video show?"

"It was night-vision, pretty rough. Shot from forty feet. But we made out a person by the trash cans near our back porch."

"Did you call Rural Fire about the video?"

"I was just going to."

"What else did you see?"

"Someone in a raincoat. Very blurry, couldn't tell if it was man or woman. But we thought the face had heavy eyebrows, almost like they were grown together."

I knew who it might be: One of the Robertson men. Father, son or even grandson. They all had those trademark eyebrows. A shiver ran up my spine. Whoever this was, he wouldn't bother my parents unless he meant the fires to serve as warning to them and a certain nosy daughter not to meddle in the murder investigation. He had threatened my parents. Therefore he'd threatened me. Maybe twice, now.

The question was, would he stop at threats or warnings? And were the warnings enough to stop me from investigating the murder? I'd already talked with the old man. Now, more than ever, I needed to talk with Cleve, and not only about a possible purchase of the Robertson place. Maybe talk to his grandson, too. As soon as possible.

"I really hate this," I told Mom. "But it almost sounds like one of the Robertson men. Possibly Cleve, as the old man's pretty shaky. I saw Cleve pictured in the album they showed me. His teenage son, too."

The elder Robertsons needed to know that I knew about the fires, and had video, though I wouldn't say I suspected them or a family member. I'd just let them ponder what I thought or suspected.

At very least, the way they responded to my information might shed more light on what was a rapidly escalating danger. Hopefully they weren't somehow in collusion with their son. Or grandson. With the murder or the fires.

"But why would they be involved?" Mom said.

"That's what I am trying to work out," I said. "Call it a reporter's hunch. Maybe Cleve was trying to evict a squatter, or convince her to leave, when things took a bad turn. His parents learned of it and are trying to protect him."

"Maybe."

"Or he wants so bad to buy the place that he's trying to give credence to the idea of a deadly curse, to turn off potential buyers. Sorry. Just blue-skying, here."

Mom was silent. But her skepticism was palpable. So I changed subjects.

"I had a scare last night at my place, too," I said. I told her about the chicken and the warning note.

"No," she gasped so loudly that I had to hold the phone away from my ear. "I don't believe it. We had one of our best laying Leghorns go missing last night. Right out of the henhouse. I went to gather eggs about an hour ago and she was gone."

The realization that our troubling events were connected, and represented a concerted effort to shut us up or put us off the case, hit me like a slap across the face. I was sure the realization was terrifying for my parents. For me, too. Would it be enough to deter me? Hell no. It merely added fuel to my desire to solve.

After we hung up, I poured myself more coffee. I held my mug with both hands, feeling the soothing warmth seep through the ceramic, letting my jangled feelings subside. Had the dead woman held her mug this way? If it had really been her mug?

Then a sadness coursed through me. I took a deep breath. I needed to be held in this way, with both arms and warming pressure. I thought again about Preston O'Hara, all he'd loved and lost, and his curse on his property. Did the present trouble really relate to the curse? Was it possible?

I remembered something Sonny had told me six years ago, right after we'd met at some horrific crime scene. At a time in Seattle when my last husband was enraged that I'd dared to serve him with divorce papers. In a drunken rage, that husband had placed a curse on me, saying I'd die before age fifty and never again know love.

Death had come alarmingly close several times the past year. It might be stalking me now.

But age fifty was in my rearview mirror.

And I did know love again.

"A curse is nothing to mess with," Sonny had said. "One grandfather was a holy man. So is my uncle in Mount Shasta City. They saw horrors happen to people who don't respect a curse or do ceremony to reverse it. Things you can't imagine in your worst nightmare."

14

The twenty-five minute drive to my folks' gave me a welcome break. I put Red Ryder in cruise-control at 72 mph on the I-5, and let my thoughts wander. As with my worries, there seemed no end to the green-gold hills cut by the river and folded upon each other in receding ranks to the horizon. They represented both liberty and steep challenge, concerns as sharp in memory as in the passing moment.

The dead woman's image was a given in such thoughts. It rose up when I least expected it. Like a karate chop to the back of the knees whether I was riding, cooking or driving. She would never again experience such things.

Did she leave family behind? Adult children, a lover or husband, riddled with questions about her disappearance? Or was she a loner, pursuing some life-and-death goal known only to herself?

I was through Grants Pass and at my parents' place before I knew it. Mom was on the porch, watering new hanging baskets she'd found at Greenleaf Industries' store, proudly employing the disabled. She was adamant about helping persons to whom life threw curves. I had inherited that trait, as well.

We hugged and went inside. The house smelled like baking pie. I wasn't surprised. Having supplied me with my quota, she now was fixing to supply neighbors such as Rosie Pussytoes and upscale cafes. Her towering lemon-meringues brought twenty dollars apiece. She used only the freshet Meyer lemons, and folded zest and marshmallow fluff into the filling. And she never over-whipped the topping, which seemed poised to levitate any moment.

We walked through the kitchen to the back porch. Mom was using the walker again. Although it had been her constant companion after the strokes a few years ago, this clunky appliance hadn't seen much use in the past few months.

"Having balance problems again, Mom?"

"Stress seems to affect it," she said, holding open the screen door for me. "And we've had plenty of that lately."

I followed her gaze down to the left side of the porch, where stood the two steel garbage cans with blackened lids near the scorched edge of the bottom steps. They all still emitted a faint odor of smoke. Trampled grass surrounded them. Bare patches of dirt appeared damp from the previous night's hosing.

We went back into the kitchen, Mom carefully using her walker. With all the excitement the past few days, I had forgotten how at risk she still was for a fall.

"Here's what we got for security video," she said, leading me to a cluttered desk in a kitchen corner. She fiddled with the monitor switches. I knew I shouldn't help her because it would make her cross. Like me, she preferred doing things for herself, even if it took forever. Heaven help you if you offered. Kane pride rang strong and deep.

"Where's Dad?" I said.

"Out in the garden," she said. "Got some more new chili starts to add to these he grew from seed saved from last year. Okay. Look here."

We leaned in toward the dim, grainy screen. Someone of medium height wearing a long raincoat and tall knit cap stepped into the frame that showed the back porch. The person, who I guessed might be male, looked left and right while hurrying with a herky-jerky step toward the cans. His age and features were unclear, but it did appear his dark eyebrows grew together.

He lifted the lids off the trash cans and set them on the ground. Then he pulled rags from a pocket, stuffed one in each can, dragged debris out so it hung over the can edges and touched a lighter to them. A sudden flare leaped above the can rims.

The man jumped back. He slapped one raincoat sleeve with his hand as if he'd been burned. Then, looking around, he shuffled away toward the back fence as flames grew from the trash-can tops and burning debris dropped onto the steps.

We replayed the video several times. It was shadowed black, grey and white. We still could not make out the face. Looking closer, I now wondered about the eyebrows. Were they really eyebrows, or something conjured up by a mind desperate for clues? I realized my imagination might be in overdrive again. The "eyebrows" could have been a shadow created by the garage security light shining over the arsonist's tall cap.

But the video made clear one thing: The fires had been intentionally set. I needed to share the video with authorities. Have staff copy it. A home and three lives had been threatened.

Feeling a twinge of nausea, I pulled out my phone and tapped Rural Fire's non-emergency number. The call went to voice mail so I left a message about the security video. Next I called the sheriff's office non-emergency number. It flipped my call to a phone tree with about ten choices—anything to avoid paying a real human to answer the phone. I chose "administration." Of course that went to a voice mailbox, too.

I even called the back number Sheriff Welles had written on the card he gave me at my folks' Friday night.

Same thing. A recorded greeting. It was nice to hear Welles' voice, though. Pleasingly deep, warm yet businesslike. That took skill and practice.

Mom hovered at my side as I reported the video's existence to Welles's voice mail, said I was at my folks', and asked for a callback as soon as possible.

Next I called the Robertsons. Maisie answered. I politely asked after their health and then got to the point.

"Mrs. Robertson, someone set fires in my parents' garbage cans last night, and they caught it on a security cam. Did you hear if there was similar trouble at your old place?" I omitted saying it might be a man with features like their son and grandson.

"No," she said. "Did they put it out? Know who did it? Is everyone all right?"

"Yes, no, and yes, thank you. Nothing like that at your place, then?"

The phone went semi-silent as she muffled its speaker and held a short conversation with a man who mumbled back, probably her husband.

"We haven't...heard." There was a catch in her voice. "Could you, your parents, tell who it was? From the video, I mean?"

What did that catch in her voice mean? Could she and her husband possibly be involved? I heard Jack hacking in the background.

"Not really," I said. "The images were pretty grainy."

"Oh," she said. "Well, then. Could have been kids, looking for thrills. About what time did this happen?"

Why was she so quick to suggest it might have been kids? Either she was involved, or she knew someone who was. Like Cleve.

"The video recorded it at two-thirty a.m."

"I see. Here, my husband wants to say something." There was a pause.

"We were always pretty skittish about fire," he said, clearing his throat. "People get careless. You know how hot and dry it gets in the summer. I worked as a volunteer fireman. My son, too. Saw some bad ones. Biscuit Complex in '02 was the worst. Lasted for months."

And now here was Jack Robertson, implying my folks had been careless.

His wife was on the phone again.

"So you think the fire at your folks' was arson? I don't suppose it was a kind of warning for your family about the murder? We know you've been looking into things, and are eager to get answers so you can go forward with your plans ..."

Hearing her words raised the hair follicles on the back of my neck. I thought that an odd thing for her to say. As if she had been reading my thoughts.

"Well, I suppose that's possible," I said, "coming so soon after, and there being no reports of similar vandalism in the neighborhood. At least, not yet."

"Have you talked with our son, Cleve? He's supposed to look after our place now. I just hope nothing like that happens out there."

"Oh, is Cleve living at your old house?" I almost said it looked empty when I went there yesterday, but caught myself. If she were protecting her son, why would she suggest I call him? Maybe that was a conscious effort to throw me off

"He still has his own place," she said. "But he plans to stop by our house several times a week. Mowing grass, turning lights on and off, that sort of thing. We don't want it to appear vacant. We're worried since the sheriff thinks transients were in the cabin."

My pulse quickened at hearing that piece of news.

"Welles said that, Mrs. Robertson? When did he say that?"

"Actually I guess it was the State Police who interviewed us yesterday. I can't say for sure they think that, but I got the impression they're considering that."

I relaxed a little and asked her to call me if she learned more. But after disconnecting I felt unease settle over my shoulders. Nothing I could pin down, just the impression I was being strung along.

Having fulfilled my phone duties, I said goodbye to Mom and stopped by Dad's chili patch on my way out. He wore a beater straw hat and a plaid Western shirt that I'd given him a few Christmases ago. His face wreathed in a broad grin and his bent form straightened, with difficulty, at my approach.

"Got 'er all solved, Miss Marple?" he said, referencing the sleuth in the Agatha Christie paperbacks on his office shelves. The Christies were Mom's. Dad had read some. But he cottoned more to books of the Louis L'Amour ilk.

"Not solved by a long shot," I said. "Still not sure I wanted to be that involved. Look where it's got us so far. Stress City in the middle of nowhere."

"Oh, come on, Pep. Never saw a mystery you didn't want to dig into. It's in your blood. Why you became a reporter."

I patted his shoulder and looked into his lovable rheumy eyes.

"And now I have more reason than ever to solve. The property may have an active curse, or people believe it does, so I need to get to the bottom of that. The fires last night. Hate all of it but I'm involved whether I like it or not."

"I guess." He shrugged. "Just you take care."

"Chili patch looking good, Dad. They'll love this heat spell."

"And I love their heat," he joked, stooping to examine a row of new specimens with narrow heart-shaped leaves and tiny white buds.

After driving out the long drive from the house and garage—it seemed longer than its eighth-of-a-mile, today—I stopped at the road and called Cleve Robertson.

"Cleve," said a high wispy voice. It reminded me a bit of Clint Eastwood's.

I introduced myself and asked if he had been by to check on his parents' place since the police were there over the weekend.

"Planned to do that after work today," he said. "Now the smoke's blown over."

I thought that an unusual phrase for him to use, considering.

"Did you hear about the fires set at my parents' house?"

There was a pause. It sounded as if he were fiddling with papers. A dog barked repeatedly in the background.

"Princess! Shut up," he shouted. More barking. "I said, 'Shut up!' Sorry. Did you say there was a fire at your folks'."

"Yes." I left a space for him to fill in.

There was a quick inhale at the other end of the line.

"How bad was the fire? Do any damage? Your folks OK?"

"They put it out before it did damage. Yes, thanks, they're fine." I left space for him to add or ask something more.

"Where was it? Do they know what caused it?"

He sure had a lot of questions. Probably the volunteer fireman in him.

"In the garbage cans by the back porch. It looked intentionally set."

"Is that so?" he said. "Why would it be arson? Who'd do something like that?"

"We wonder the same things. After the murder and all. My folks called it in."

"What was the response?"

"Fire sent someone," I said.

"You're calling to see if there was any activity like that at my parents'," he said.

"I would appreciate if you'd check. Or we could meet there, as I'm near."

Another pause.

"Don't bother," he said. "I'll stop by there later."

"Let me know if you find anything."

"No problem."

"Hopefully we'll meet soon. I'd like to hear your take on the property, its history, anything you know about previous owners. The curse."

"Police are on it. Not sure I understand your involvement."

"My interest in a possible purchase? Or the fire at my folks?"

"Sure. That makes sense. Let you know if there was trouble at my folks."

As I turned Red Ryder toward town, I glanced at my watch. Only nine-twenty. I had time to drive to Brassbottom Barn for a quick practice ride on Chocolate Waterfall before starting my afternoon shift at The Best Little Horsehouse. Maybe a few minutes to stop by the Farm Co-op on the way. I needed salt for my horses at home, and some answers about a certain lady who'd visited the Co-op last week.

The parking lot was nearly empty. I piled out of the truck and hurried past outdoor displays of wheelbarrows, wading pools and flowers. Inside I refused to let my gaze drift to the Western fashions or the ice-cream freezer, and headed straight for the service counter.

Sam Jenkins, a square-jawed middle-aged cowboy in starched jeans and crisp cotton shirt, smiled when he looked up from the computer screen and recognized me.

"How's it going, Pepper?" he said, adjusting his bifocals. "Long time no see. Too bad about the trouble near your folks' place."

"That's kind of related to why I came, Sam. Other than picking up a few mineral blocks. Horses are licking a lot of salt in this heat."

"For sure. So to what other reason do I owe the pleasure?"

"My dad ran into a woman here last week who struck him as out of place, odd, as if dressed up for square dancing. Or rather, she ran her cart into him. They had words. Do you remember the incident, or her?"

Jenkins drew back and rubbed his chin. At the sound of a child's laughter and frenzied cheeps, he glanced to where steel troughs held baby chickens and ducks near the front doors. Then he leaned forward, elbows on the counter.

"I do. Short, heavy older lady dressed real fancy with long black hair. He leaned in farther. "You think she's connected somehow with the murder?"

"Can't say, Sam. Just looking into possibilities, people or incidents that seemed out of place. Seen the woman before? Know anything about her?"

He took a deep breath and shook his head.

"Sorry. Never seen her before. Not from around here. Had kind of that big-city air, you know, pushy, entitled, in a hurry."

"Huh. Did she buy anything?"

"She was in the women's area. Then used the restroom. But she did ask one of our younger clerks something, which they came over to ask me."

"And what was that, Sam?"

Jenkins' face suddenly drained of color as he seemed to put two and two together. He gripped the edge of the counter.

"Wanted to know where that famous writer had lived, was it open to the public."

15

That gave me something to chew on while I drove back toward Gold Hill and Brassbottom Barn to ride Choc. A ride that would make me focus on other things for an hour. Cure my building anxiety. Or give it the temporary appearance of being cured.

Because the morning was warming, with a touch of humidity from thunderstorms gathering in the mountains, I rode Choc in the indoor arena. The shade of the roof was welcome, and the hint of a breeze over the gate tops helped our sweat evaporate. Somewhat.

Choc seemed in good spirits. He kept his red-brown ears tipped happily forward as we stretched muscles and joints in jog circles this way and that. I was in good spirits, accordingly. Even the usually annoying chatter of sparrows courting in the rafters didn't bother me. A dusty radio on a shelf in one corner played a mix of old and new country tunes, adding to the calming ambiance.

For the moment I had the whole arena to myself. I crossed ground poles at a walk, jog and lope, gently schooling. I wanted a pleasant ride, reviewing established maneuvers. The pressure of an imminent show would come soon enough, next week, when we really put the spur to the ribcage.

My heart skipped when I thought about showing in Seattle. Well, about twenty miles outside Seattle in a new horse park halfway between my old town and the state capitol, Olympia. It would be fabulous to see my riding friends from there and enjoy the forested scenery with its postcard-worthy rivers, lakes and saltwater bays. Although I wouldn't have a whole lot of time to visit and see the sights.

Mainly I'd be showing or preparing my horse and myself to show.

And seeing my dear Sonny Chief, of course. I felt calmer about him and whatever was happening between him and his ex-wife. Maybe it was because I now felt a little closer to getting answers on my own heart-stopping mystery. Usable clues were emerging. I was taking action, however small. Rattling cages, as he said. Developing some plan, however hazy. The flip side was that a killer was crafting a plan for me.

I had to keep that glow on. Sonny and I had a good, solid relationship – though one challenged by distance–and great memories to draw upon. I would just go north and enjoy my time with my lover while keeping my eyes and ears open for clues that our affair might be at risk.

While I mused on such matters and schooled Choc with perfection-seeking hand and leg cues, Dutch Grandeen rode Jeanne Allende's new black-and-white mare into the arena. He and I said "Hey" and continued working our horses.

About ten minutes in, Dutch rode the mare at a walk along the rail with me. His flirty hazel eyes were shaded by the bill of his Chicago Cubs World Champions cap. But there was no mistaking the intention behind the cocky lurch of his shoulders and snake-lean body in the saddle, or back of the teasing lilt in his voice.

"How's our cowgirl sleuth today?" he winked, watching my face but letting his eyes drift down and back up my body.

"Dandy," I said with a noncommittal smile, riding on.

"In what way?" he pressed, tilting his head.

The guy never gave up. A born hound-dog, much to his wife Donna's consternation. Such behavior in horse trainers was common. Much of it was just to make their customers feel welcome and flattered. Much was harmless. Except when it wasn't. I took care not to give out flirt vibes myself. It's fun to dance around a fire. But not so great when you dance close enough to get burned.

"I'm dandy in every way," I said, keeping my eyes on Choc's flax-frosted mane while we ambled along. "Horse, family, love life." I instantly regretted that last statement, which would provide Dutch an opening. "I see you've got Jeanne's new horse really dialed in. Bet you like riding this one better than the nut job she had before."

"Nice mare," he said, adjusting his seat in the Western saddle, the better to appraise me in profile. "So how're you doing with your murder investigation?"

Staring at the far arena wall, I felt Dutch's gaze boring a hole in my right cheek.

"Okay," I sighed. No use pretending I wasn't looking into it with every cell of my body. Dutch and my other buddies saw through me as if I were cheesecloth.

"Any idea who the lady was?"

"I ...they are working on it. Nothing yet."

I picked up the reins and legged Choc into a jog, which was like gliding on air.

"Well, I know you'll get to the bottom of it," Dutch said.

"How do you know that?"

"You and Tulip are keen on buying that ranch. But it's obviously cursed. Next to your parents'. And, it's your nature." He paused, and turned to look over his shoulder at something past the arena gate.

"What?" I said, following his gaze.

"Plus because Gloria wants you to solve it quick so she can facilitate your deal."

Gloria Allende's silver Mercedes glided to a dust-raising stop in the stable yard.

I rode into the barn near the end of the aisle just as Gloria came into view hip-lugging a 40-pound bag of horse-treats toward the feed room up front. I wanted to hear what Jeanne's aunt knew about buying a piece of property encumbered by a slight case of death. I dismounted, led Choc forward and halted outside the feed room's open door.

Gloria looked up while setting down her bag beside a steel mini-can marked "Allende." Taking care not to ruin her "arrest-me-red" manicure, she ripped open the thick paper bag, hefted it with a grunt, and filled the can.

"Treats for the sweet," she grinned. "Jeanne texted me she ran out of apple-molasses chunks after her ride yesterday and asked me pick up a bag. She says her new horse works for praise, and treats. I was nearby for an open house, so why not?"

"Did you stop by Sunny's Corner?" That four-corners complex was a town unto itself. In addition to having a farm-and-garden store, it had a gas station, grocery, car-repair shop, beauty salon and realty office. Also The Doubletree Restaurant/Lounge where Tulip and I often showed off our dance moves. All the Corner lacked was a church and doctor, though there were a few of those within a mile or two.

"Naturally," said Gloria. "I love stopping by to see what's new in the gift shop."

"I get a kick out of their cowboy mugs and funny cards," I said.

Choc pulled at the reins to go back to his stall. I steadied him with a neck stroke. Well-broke dude that he was, he dropped a hip, rested one hind leg on its toe and settled in for a horse nap. Who knew how long humans would take in a chat session?

"Are you and Tulip ready to make an offer on that Applegate property?" Gloria said. "I have paperwork. Just fill it out and I'll submit it to the owners. Better hurry, or face some hot competition that will up the price."

"Talking to our banker soon," I said. "But I doubt there's any rush, with the murder investigation underway."

"I ran comps. You should start at six hundred thousand. More, if you can swing it. It's the hot real-estate season. Likely be multiple offers once buyers get wind of it."

Whoa. I hadn't expected such answers or pressure. Tulip and I were motivated, but Gloria seemed to be a giant leap ahead of us.

"So you can facilitate our sale, Gloria, even if you're not yet licensed?"

"My broker will look over the offer and be your formal representative. My husband will verify everything as to legality. I am doing paperwork and legwork."

"Does it have to be that complicated, Gloria? So many involved?"

"Takes the worry out of it. We might convince the sellers to kick in a bit more for eliminating potential complications. I'll present the offer as your representative."

"But the sale might not go through until the police officially are done. Right?"

"I doubt there will be a problem. And, if you and Tulip are first in line with a nice offer, anyone else has to match or exceed that. It's still up to the sellers. You should write a note telling them why you want it. I can deliver it with your purchase offer."

I leaned against Choc's shoulder.

"So, Gloria. Do you really think there will be anyone else right now? With what's gone on? The murder, the alleged curse?"

She blew out a breath and ran a hand through her hair.

"Listen, Pepper. There will be buyers, maybe from out of state, once it becomes known that the property is available. Are you kidding? Riverfront with full water rights? Prime growing land? Close to the highway and town? A view to die for?"

I rolled my eyes.

"Nice word choice, Gloria."

"Sorry." She made an exaggerated "sorry" face.

"How would anyone else know it's available?" I pressed. "It's not been listed."

"The owners could have told friends, relatives, neighbors," she said. "I have their name from Josephine County records. I'll call them and see."

My mind was doing a slow spin. Gloria's aggressive plan to help me was quite the surprise. I had asked her to find out whether the property could be purchased, what hoops may have to be jumped through. Was she more interested in listing the property, or in helping me and Tulip?

I also wondered, under this pressure, if Tulip and I were really ready to take this plunge so soon. I felt my gut constrict, my whole being resist making a formal offer before more headway was made on the murder. Yet, as Gloria suggested, if we didn't act now we might lose our chance.

"If we do this, it will have to be a contingency offer," I said. "Contingent on the murder's being solved, and that there are no encumbrances on the property."

"Most offers are contingent. But not sure I'd advise you make it contingent on the murder's being solved, Pepper. That would be risky. Being more definite, showing the sellers how passionately you feel about a place, carries much more weight."

"Surely in this case they'd understand even a passionate buyer's concerns."

Gloria looked away, and then set her lips and gave me a hard stare. Something back of her eyes chilled me. It was a side of her I'd not seen.

"Depends how bad they want to sell, their situation, any relatives' interest in it."

Relatives. That would be Cleve, as far as I knew. But possibly a wife or his own adult kids, as well. Almost anyone could poison the stew.

I sighed, and ran my hand along the steel sheath lining the feed room door. It cooled my sweating palm.

"Let me talk to Tulip," I finally said. "Can I take an offer form for us to discuss? This isn't something we can rush into, no matter how urgent it may seem. Plus we have to pin down our financing."

Choc and I backed aside as Gloria left the feed room and slid shut the door.

"Well, of course," said Gloria, giving me an apologetic smile. "I'm only trying to help. As I say, we think the property will price in the high six figures, maybe more. So line up your ducks ASAP. Let's get the bullet in the chamber."

Bullet in the chamber? That wasn't any realtor-talk that I knew of. Who was this woman, really? This sale would be a big score for her, even if she only facilitated, and one certain to impress her broker. And maybe earn her a fat kickback on the side.

As I watched her head for the barn doors, I knew my speculation about her was sparked by one of my last stories for the newspaper, blowing the whistle on a broker who'd worked behind the scenes to force the sale of Lake Washington Gold-Coast land next to Microsoft co-founder Bill Gates III's sprawling compound.

Something like that surely would not happen in our own little Rogue Valley, I thought facetiously. Not in our sweet vale of pears, wine and roses—Harry & David started here a century ago, wineries abounded, and roses adorned lattice arches held by juniors for seniors to walk under at high-school graduation ceremonies.

Surely not. Yet, pigs did fly—albeit crated, and inside airplane cargo holds.

"Hey, Gloria," I said, leading Choc as I followed her to get the purchase-offer forms. "Can Tulip and I get back to you in a few days?"

"Absolutely," Gloria said over her shoulder. She opened her car door, reached in and handed me a sheaf of papers topped by her business brochure. "Just don't wait too long. Once word gets out, you won't believe the offers that will materialize."

* * *

On the way to The Horsehouse I picked up Italian submarine sandwiches and iced sweet tea at the Sunny's Corner store.

I breezed through our tack store's back door to a country-Western concert and floor-show starring a six-foot-tall blondie named Tulip wearing white boots, hot pink blouse and tight jeans-skirt cut up to here. Luckily there were no customers to witness this. If there had been any of the male persuasion, it would only have encouraged her.

She was dancing to an old hit by country heart-throb Luke Bryan. A clean cut but still dangerous Southern boy in painted-on jeans. No Waylon, but sexy just the same.

"Hey!" I shouted. I hurried to the console that pushed music out the corner-mount speakers, and jammed the volume down to a whimper.

"What?" said Tulip, frozen in mid-kick. "Got your old-lady knickers in a twist? Better practice up on that 'Footloose' routine we learned." She gave a few flutters of her shorty boots. Which needed whitening, I saw.

"You learned it," I said. "I don't think I'll ever get that ankle-buster. I limped for a week after that lesson. Maybe longer."

Tulip pushed her pink-manicured fingers through her hair.

"Well, I declay-er, girl. You showed Saturday you're not dead yet. Live a little."

"Had lunch?" I set my bulging paper bag on the counter.

"You gotta be faster and meaner than whatever's chasing you," she said, still on the "Live-Like-You're-Dying" theme. She ambled to the counter, flounced down on a stool and unwrapped a sandwich. What had shaken her cage?

"Did Tommy Lee make it down?" I ventured. "That why you're so jazzed up?"

"Oh, honey, he made it down, up and sideways," she said, wiggling her eyebrows. "On his way to San Fran, but coming back to mama's arms on Saturday."

I sat down next to her, took out my sandwich, and saw my chance while she was involved touching a napkin in an exaggerated ladylike fashion to her lips.

"I saw Gloria at the barn," I began.

"And?" Tulip said through a mouthful of sandwich.

"She wants us to figure out an offer on the Robertson property ASAP. She thinks it's gonna be a hot one, and doesn't want someone else to come in first, and higher."

Tulip swiveled her chair to face me.

"But it's not even listed," she said. She gulped down the last remnant of pickle. "How would anyone know it might be for sale?"

"Word gets out," I said. "Relatives, and others with loose lips." I shrugged, and bit a chunk off my own spicy repast.

"They're not listing it right away, are they?" she said. "And who on earth would be interested, with the curse, the murder, and all?"

"Details, details. That's prime real estate, Tulip. A huge potential score. Gloria or her broker might convince the Robertsons to list anyway, no matter what she has us believing about a private, by-owner sale."

Tulip harrumphed.

"That's not the most logical or elegant way for her to get started in the real-estate biz. Or keep friends and influence people. What the hell."

Now Tulip was into her sub sandwich in a big way. Her energy never ceased to amaze—nor did her zest for food and men, in that order. Like her idol, Dolly Parton.

"What the hell, indeed," I said. "The first thing is for us to decide if we for sure want the property."

I told Tulip about the dead chicken and warning note at my door, and the arson fires at my parents'. Hearing the news, she nearly fell off her stool.

"No way." She readjusted her seat and fixed me with a shocked gaze.

"Someone was warning us to stay out of it all." I took another bite of sandwich. Olive oil and vinegar trickled down my hand. I licked it off.

"Why wouldn't they just let it go at warning *you*, Pep?"

"Because they know I care deeply for my parents, and also because they think Mom and Dad know or saw something Friday."

"Hope your folks have the law on speed-dial."

"The second thing, Tule, is to find out from our banker if we can really afford to buy and develop the place."

A thin line appeared above the bridge of Tulip's nose. She chewed, considered my words and swallowed. The fingers on her left hand moved as if counting.

"Like we talked yesterday," she said, "we should be good. Of course we'd incur penalties withdrawing money from our 401Ks since we're under 59."

"Right," I said. "There is that."

She finished her sandwich, licked her fingers and patted her lips with a napkin.

"A lot to think about," she said. "If we are still gonna try to do this deal."

"You have reservations, Tulip?"

"I've begun to think the universe doesn't want us to."

"You've got a point," I said. "A big one. I think we can swing a purchase financially. But I'm beginning to wonder if it's worth risking our lives for."

16

Tulip tossed her sandwich wrapper in the trash can by the counter and slung her crystal-studded white purse over her shoulder.

"Hope you have some live bodies at the store. My morning was beyond slow. Landlord called wanting to know where this month's rent is. I made up some excuse."

"Hope it was a good one, Tule. We gotta hold onto this baby as long as we can. The future's iffy, to say the least."

After Tulip left I freshened up in the store's bathroom. Spending a hot afternoon in the cool Horsehouse was a blessing. I cranked the tunes up high, dusted shelves like a dervish and moved displays of tops and jeans around so they'd be seen by customers who'd missed them on a prior visit.

I paid special attention to my daughter's silver-and-stone earrings, brooches and bracelets. Pulling them to the front of the display, I reminded myself to call Chili soon. I didn't want to worry her, but I also didn't want her to hear from my folks about our recent troubles. I should call my son, Serrano, too. See how his art was doing.

Halfway through the shift I sat down to review my new photos and take a run at The Daily Courier archives. Nothing helpful from the day's pictures. But in the online archives, I found a 2003 story marking the 50th anniversary of O'Hara's death. It took up the entire inside back-page of the A section, with photos—the kind of feature provided weekly by Josephine County Historical Society.

There was a retelling of O'Hara's life in Grants Pass, his reclusive ways, his book and movie successes. How his home and possessions were sold for back taxes.

But there was also the stunning "rumor' that there were thought to be relatives to contact after his death, and that he may have left some kind of "legacy."

Relatives? Surely there had to be some, though the article and my online search had mentioned none.

A legacy, or rumors of one? If it were something of value such as a lost O'Hara manuscript or stash of valuables, this might explain the murder. Someone might have learned or discovered O'Hara's legacy in the cabin, or been looking for them.

His cabin attracted occasional visitors, I'd heard, over the years. It even once had been nominated as a state landmark. But the latter move, initiated in the 1970s, died when a newer property owner and near neighbors objected.

I raced through the article, skimming and searching for keywords to the end. But then I felt let down. There was nothing more on the subject of a legacy. If I had written the story, I at least would have speculated more on that fascinating angle.

As of that writing, in September 2003, though searches were conducted, neither relatives nor legacy were ever found. The idea apparently was permanently dropped, buried. I called the Society, but they were no help. A nice lady said she had no idea where the legacy rumor originated, but would ask around when she found time.

"Maybe a neighbor or friend of O'Hara's just supposed there would be a legacy, or relatives," she told me. "Usually someone can be found, eventually."

"Where did they bury O'Hara?" I asked.

"I believe he would be at Pioneer Cemetery," she said. "Out Upper River Road. But you also could call around the funeral homes for family information."

"They may not have records going back that far," I said. "But worth a try."

I called, and they didn't. At least not the main funeral homes. No records going back that far, at least that they could lay hands on. No mention of O'Hara relatives in county or state obituaries online, either.

Back to the drawing board.

I re-read the article. Slowly and thoughtfully, with no agenda. This time an eerie feeling crept over me. Maybe it was because the reporter, in punchy or lyrical passages, sunk me deep into O'Hara's happy times of writing and fishing by the Applegate. How it looked and sounded and smelled. What O'Hara must have felt, as told in his books. His delight in his increasing acclaim. His joy at finding his second wife, Rose, calling her "a miracle conjured by Creator."

The plummy times were balanced by an account of his descent into the depths.

"My God," I found myself whispering. And, simply, "No."

Unaware of time, praying no customers would disturb me, I read that O'Hara's stormy first marriage and divorce had precipitated his "escape from Hollywood madness" to Southern Oregon. That his dead-honest depictions of Indians after 1924, the year they won the right to vote, drew heated criticism. That the loss of his child and second wife precipitated his decline. Finally that crushing lawsuits and the vitriolic McCarthy hearings shoved him to the bottom.

The story made O'Hara seem more human than any other account I'd come across. The polio he'd contracted as a child, keeping him from playing male-dominated sports such as football. My son had suffered from asthma, and was devastated by being excluded from sports. Serrano was branded a "sissy" for turning to art, though he was quite good at it.

I sat back and rubbed my eyes. Opened them again, stretched, sipped what was left of my now-warm lemonade, and stared unseeing out the front widow.

How could anyone have endured, let alone thrived, battling such demons? I had barely survived myself, being criticized and temporarily fired because I sided with Indian people in a story about minority activism.

What really struck me, what lingered in shadow as I read but finally pushed to the forefront again, were the words "legacy" and "relatives." These were given short shrift in the story, added almost as an afterthought. But to me they were the 36-point, above-the-fold headline.

Now I had something new to pursue. Something major. Likely key to unlocking the mystery. But how on earth to start?

Maybe with the newer ancestry websites and adoption sites. Yes, certainly those. I had thought about checking them before, then found no time, or had forgotten. I had little time to spare now. Yet I needed any information they might provide.

I called Chili. Not only was she a whiz-bang jewelry designer, but also a wizard at negotiating the Internet and a dizzying host of social-media platforms. She'd even been known to do a little hacking. Just to see if she could., not for evil purposes. Always pushing the envelope. Her mother's daughter.

"Hi. Mom," she said, a lilt in her voice. Things must be going well for her.

"You sound happy," I said. "Is there a new love in your life?"

"Maybe."

Hmm. That got my attention. My tall, gorgeous carrot-topped baby girl, finding a mate at last? What mother didn't love that? But I had no time to go there now.

"Listen, Chills. I need your tech savvy. Help on with genealogy. And adoption."

"Hmm. Anybody I know?"

Her end of the phone line erupted with jangling-bracelet sounds. She wore a wrist full of her creations on each arm, and baubles in each ear peeking out from her choppy hair.

"Maybe you know him by reputation." I gave her the CliffsNotes version of recent disturbing events in the Valley. And told her as much about O'Hara as I knew, including that at his death he was rumored to have had relatives still living.

"Wow, Preston O'Hara," she said. "Who hasn't heard of him? Remember that super-hyped remake of one of his movies a few years ago? Totally bombed?"

I sighed, and ran my fingers through my hair.

"Maybe the world wasn't ready for a blockbuster Western right then, Chili. John Wayne's dead. But I still faint when I think of that kiss he gave me when I interviewed him for the newspaper. Before you were born."

"Whatever. Anyway, Mom, I'm on it. May take a few days. So you still need me down to house sit when you're in Seattle? Make more sense for you to use somebody there so we can see each other here. Plus I have a big craft expo to prepare for."

"Anything you can do, Chills. But I don't want to know, if it involves a hack."

I returned to tidying up the Horsehouse and rotating stock. The jewelry displays stopped me. We carried only a few samples of Chili's chunky North-by-Southwest ear baubles, bracelets and brooches. What was I thinking? We should feature CK Designs in a big way here. And even bigger when we relocated the shop to our hoped-for guest ranch. Jewelry mixing turquoise and coral in silver with local lava stone and marble-like granite were sure to delight souvenir seeking tourists.

Before closing time, the Horsehouse door finally banged open. Customers? I hurried over, visions of dollar signs dancing in my head.

But, oddly, it was Brassbottom buddy Stewie Mikulski—our ten-year-old rider with a huge grin and a flaming red buzz-cut—and his mom. Karen Mikulski was the physical therapist who'd done wonders helping my own mom regain strength and mobility after the stroke. Karen's occasional help at our store was a godsend.

Stewie headed straight for the cut-crystal bowl of mini Mars bars on the checkout counter. He unpeeled one and stuffed it whole into his mouth.

"You oughtta keep these in the freezer," he mumbled while chewing. "They're really good that way."

"I should," I said. "And what brings you in this fine day, Karen?" I asked his mom, looking good in her shoulder-cutout peach top and black capri-leggings with crystals down each leg. She'd bought the togs at our shop. "Love your outfit."

"Only the best will do," she winked. "So, Stewie got this burr under his saddle. We ran into Jeanne Allende and her aunt minutes ago at Trader Joe's, and Jeanne said you were the one who found the body in that writer's cabin. Now Stewie's obsessed with doing a project on O'Hara for his school. They have a reporting contest."

"Yeah," said Stewie, eyes dancing. "There's a fifty-dollar prize. "I've read some books of his. Westerns and everything. I want to be a writer like him."

"Really?" I said, impressed.

"So I need to interview you about his cabin and stuff." Stewie's voice dropped to a whisper. "And about that dead lady you found."

"I am not supposed to talk about the death, you know."

Stewie was not to be deterred.

"Was there really a curse on the cabin?"

His mother slid her gaze sideways.

"Once he gets an idea, Pepper, there's no stopping him."

"Like me," I said. "Not such a bad thing. We get things done. So, Stewie. How did you hear about the curse?"

"Jeanne told me. And it was on TV." He dumped his backpack on the counter and pulled out a reporter's note pad. "Do you have any coke?"

When I brought bottles of lemonade from the back room, the boy already was seated on a stool at the counter, his pen poised. He gulped juice, set down the bottle, and wrote the date and my name at the top of the first page of his pad.

"What do you know already?" I said.

"The names of his books and his movies. That his real first name was Sidney, but he went by his middle name, Preston. Probably because it wasn't sissy?"

"Uh-huh," I said. "What else?"

"When he died and stuff. He had this cabin on the Applegate River that the pioneers from California followed to come up to the Rogue Valley. The Applegate Trail."

"O-kaaay." I said, amazed he'd already done that much research. "What else?"

Stewie ran one hand through hair that seemed perpetually startled.

"Then he got sued or something for plage … plage …"

"Plagiarism," I said, "which means copying another author's stories."

"Mm-hmm. He got depressed and couldn't work because he lost all his money," Stewie continued. "And he was attacked for being a ... community?" Stewie raised his eyebrows and shot me a puzzled look.

Man, I thought. If they ever consider a remake of the Andy Griffith sitcom, "Mayberry," this kid would be a shoo-in for young Opie. He even had a cowlick.

"Communist," I said. "People who want the government to rule everyone, make them work hard but not keep much money in exchange for having all their needs met. Health care, education, housing. There supposedly would be no rich or poor."

"Huh." His forehead creased. "Why would he get in trouble for thinking that?"

Uh-oh. How to answer that one? I plunged ahead.

"Long before you were born," I said, "in the United States, people were afraid Russians and other dictator-run countries would conquer us. Take away our rights, the freedom to be and do what we want."

"Hmm. So they thought O'Hara was one of the bad guys. Like a spy, or something? I've read about spies."

"Something like that, Stewie. So, powerful people blacklisted him, refused to buy his books or movies or let others buy them. And spread bad rumors about him."

Stewie stopped writing and looked up. His eyes widened.

"Oh, I get it. Like bullying. They made O'Hara poor, and sad, so he killed himself. I've heard that happen to kids who're bullied online."

I sighed. I used to think children grew up too fast and too hard with the influence of movies and TV. Nowadays we had all that plus the Internet and cell phones.

"Yes, Stewie," I said. "Sadly."

"Some kids at school, sports guys, bully me because I write, and wear fancy clothes to ride in horse shows. They say that's sissy stuff."

I looked at him. I had no good answer. Karen Mikulski stepped in.

"You have to be who you are, honey," she said, stroking his back. Those who criticize others are the weak ones." She turned imploring eyes on me.

I nodded.

"So before he died," I said, "O'Hara left the curse, saying anyone who owned the place after him would come to grief. The newspaper archives have stories of a drowning nearby, a fall down a well ..."

Stewie scribbled furiously in his notepad. The tip of his tongue stuck out from one side of his mouth as he worked. After a few minutes he looked at me again.

"But his family could have helped Mr. O'Hara. Why didn't they?"

"No family was found. This was before the Internet, you know." I thought of Chili, and how she'd now be trying to access some of that information if it had been transferred digitally. If anyone could find that, she could.

"Tell me about this dead lady," Stewie said. "What she was like, how she died?"

Boy, he was a pit bull in training.

"Not supposed to say, Stewie. But I'm sure her description will be made public soon. Police are trying to learn her identity, why she was there."

"You're doing that, too, right?" His eyes searched mine. He knew I'd been a reporter and helped solve crimes in the Valley. I may have blushed under his gaze.

"A little," I said. "It did happen next door to my parent's place. And Tulip and I were thinking of buying the property to turn it into a guest ranch."

"I know," he said, excitement flickering across his features. "Jeanne told me. And now you have the perfect name for it."

I grinned at his mom, and then back at him.

"And what's that, Stewie?"

"Ghost Ranch."

Before the Mikulskis left, I asked Karen if she could house sit and also work The Horseshouse while Tulip and I were in Seattle. Stewie couldn't go because of school. He would stay home with his father. Karen happily agreed. She loved my Bostons and could use the extra cash.

I was preparing to leave for the day when I saw a familiar white TV van parked out front. I hurried to the back of the shop and slipped through the door. I hoped to escape sight unseen.

But Red Ryder's starting roar likely gave me away. I'd almost made it to out of the back lot and onto the street when the van nosed around the corner and braked at the driveway, blocking the way.

Go ahead, Universe. Stick the leeches on me. Get it over with.

Shane Chapelle, all slicked-back hair and professionally whitened smile, sprang from the van, a stout cameraman in tow. He strode toward my truck with a bulletproof confidence. He smoothed his black-stripe grey necktie against his blue shirt, gestured for me to open my window, and moved in for the kill.

"Miss Kane? Shane Chapelle, KMFD-TV," he said. "We have met before, I believe." He extended a soft white hand through my open window. "I have just a few questions about your finding the body. My cameraman, Trent Galvin."

I nodded, but frowned. The hand retreated.

"I have no comment, Mr. Chapelle. You're blocking my way. Don't make me call Sheriff Henning." When the red light began flashing on the shoulder camera, I raised my hand to block my face. "Kill that camera. You're invading my privacy."

"Is it true you were on the Robertsons' land because you are interested in buying the place?" Chapelle pressed. "Or were you trespassing for some other reason?"

"No comment." I shut the window and looked for a way around the van, possibly through the opening between it and the big horse-chestnut tree on the right.

Chapelle hammered his fist on my window. The camera's red light was still on. I rolled the window back down and picked up my cell phone.

"Did you know," Chapelle shouted, "if transients may have been living in the cabin? I understand there were marijuana plants out back?"

"No, but it's always a possibility." My cheeks warmed as my anger increased. "Look Mr. Chapelle. I have the sheriff on speed dial. This is my last warning. Move out of my way. You're holding me against my will. It's called kidnapping?"

The smile vanished from Chapelle's face. He shook his head and raised his hand, nicely manicured, I saw, with a sheen of what looked like clear polish. The lengths to which an upwardly mobile TV personality will go. No mistaking that Chapelle had pinned his hopes on working in a major TV-network market.

"No need for drama, Miss Kane," he said. "I am just trying to do my job, get a few facts, for the public. You, as a reporter, surely can empathize."

I dropped my tight shoulders.

"You already know I found the body. And, with your rumored and highly unethical connections to Sheriff Welles, I am sure you know everything else there is to know. If so, I would appreciate your telling me something. What clues have they as to the woman's identity?"

Chapelle was silent a moment as he continued to stare me down.

"That is confidential," he said.

"So they do have clues," I said. "Tell you what. You give me something, I will give you something. Professional courtesy."

"You didn't hear this from me," he whispered. "But she may have ties to Seattle. You have to dig up the rest on your own."

"Why do they think she had ties to Seattle?" I said.

"Give me your something," he said.

"My father *may* have seen that woman in the feed store last week," I said, mocking his earlier words.

"May have?" he snorted. "Shit. That's not a something." He shook his head.

"Then here's something. Bugger off. Don't let my see your arrogant ass again."

I rolled up the window, leaving him gape-mouthed as a landed trout. I wrenched the steering wheel right, bumped over a dirt mound and dropped over the curb, missing the van by centimeters. I gunned the engine and didn't look back. If I never saw Shane Chapelle again, it would be too soon.

17

The "something" he'd shared niggled my mind until I got home. I fed and watered the horses, wrestled with the Bostons and prepared a huge salad with garden greens, slivered almonds and leftover chicken smothered in bleu cheese.

Grabbing the folder of case notes from my office, I laid the photos of the murder scene near my plate. Then I sat down to feed belly and brain.

I looked closely at images of the scattered books and papers in the cabin. None of the printing on them was clear enough to decipher, even with my magnifying glass. But when I focused on the "mug" shot, the black half-circle and dot on the left wall of that cup seemed familiar. Goosebumps of recognition popped out on my arms.

Still chewing a wad of salad, I went to the cupboard and peered into its depths. There, sitting innocently at the back of my mug collection, was a twin of the red-and-black mug in the photo. I reached up and lifted it out, turning it around in my hands.

One side of the mug bore the full black question-mark. My photo had shown the mug a quarter-turn around, displaying only the right half of the question-mark's curve, with a half-dot displayed below it.

Slowly I rotated the mug, admiring its glossy black rim and white interior. Sure enough. The black front logo with red print looked like a blob of old-fashioned sealing wax—or blood. Inside the blob was a tiny Sherlock Holmes-pipe image above the words, SEATTLE MYSTERY BOOKSHOP.

Was this the basis for Josephine County Sheriff's Office—and hence, Shane Chapelle's—purported belief that the dead woman, or her killer had ties to my old town? If so, I wondered if the ties were familial, or professional.

Of course, this might merely be a random bit of evidence, not even related to the killing. The mug could belong to someone else. Or even have been purchased in a thrift shop. But I suspected not.

Seattle Mystery Bookshop had been one of my favorite haunts during my time in that city. The curious little below-street brick store, lined floor-to-ceiling with every manner of crime book, and related tomes, was a Pioneer Square fixture since 1990. It had thousands of books, many by Northwest authors.

It also had tens of thousands of customers from around the world. What would one middle-aged, Indian-looking woman in flowing skirts and vintage boots be to them? Maybe I was back at square one.

But this mug photo was the first real evidence I had in my possession. Let's face it, just about the only evidence. I wasn't going to let it go until I learned what it meant.

* * *

The anchorman of the six-thirty TV news looked somber as he spoke.

"Oregon State Police and Josephine County Sheriff 's Office seek the public's help identifying a woman whose body was found Friday in a cabin south of Grants Pass. Officials won't say the cause of death, but are investigating it as a homicide. However our reporters have learned she may have ties to Seattle."

Indeed. Now they were saying so publicly. Both about the murder, and that the victim had possible ties to Seattle. Surely the bookshop mug was one thing they were going on. But was there another reason?

"She was about five-feet-two inches tall, a hundred-sixty pounds, in her late forties or early fifties, with long dark hair and a Celtic tattoo around her upper left arm. Anyone knowing of such a person should call OSP." A number flashed on the screen.

There. More clues to her identity. Her long-sleeved blouse had hidden the tattoo from my sight. But I would add all this information to my notes, along with her Seattle ties, if there really were any.

I was relieved the evening news had shown nothing of my impromptu chat with Chapelle, though the camera had been rolling. Our so-called interview probably was shot too late in the day, and had offered nothing of interest.

While getting ready for bed, I recalled the visit Stewie and his mom paid me at the Horsehouse that day. What a pleasant surprise not only to learn he wanted to be a writer, but also that at his tender age, he'd read books by the likes of Zane Grey and Preston O'Hara. I had done the same in my horse-mad youth.

He'd asked if I knew anything about O'Hara's family, which, I was sorry to admit, I did not. But that would soon to be remedied if Chili hit the jackpot with her ancestry "research."

Maybe I could help it along. I tucked into bed with the Bostons around me and powered up my iPad. A pen, paper notebook and the manila folder sat nearby on the nightstand, along with a warm mug of sweetened white tea. It had been such a crazy two days, I needed comfort that wouldn't numb my mind.

I searched for more info about O'Hara's life and published works. I ran through websites until my eyeballs burned. He was born to a salesman and a teacher in California, no names given. He'd contracted the polio as a teen, leaving him with the crippled leg that prevented his playing sports or joining the military when World War II loomed.

But I reflected on how he'd been active anyway, enjoying the outdoors and writing yarns about cowboys, woodsmen and other colorful characters.

"He lived what he loved," I muttered to myself. One of the dogs stirred at my feet. "Just like us, you guys."

I got up, poured myself another cup of tea and resumed my search.

Photographs showed a tall dark-haired man with sad yet oddly attractive Bassett-hound eyes, a silvered dark mustache and a tailored leather jacket over a flannel shirt. Sometimes only with the flannel shirt, which had elbow patches as well as the traditional gun patch on the left shoulder. Professionally shot, for back book covers.

One photo showed him on a chestnut horse, both of them gazing toward the hills and mountains girdling the Valley. Others showed him panning for gold, or proudly holding a yard-long steelhead he'd snagged. No photos of family, that I could see.

As The Daily Courier had stated, O'Hara had spent two years studying English at UCLA, worked as an assistant scriptwriter. Then, lured north by tales of wild rivers, lush scenery and abundant fish and game, settled in the Rogue Valley, a two-day-drive from Hollywood. Built his rustic retreat and wrote most of his magazine stories, novels and movie scripts within a stone's throw of the Applegate.

I looked up at my vintage oil painting of the Rogue tributary on my dining-room wall. Similar to one owned by my parents, the picture featured a lone fisherman in hip-waders posed in dark, glinting water as an osprey glided overhead.

"That man could have been O'Hara," I told my dogs. They were not impressed.

O'Hara divorced one wife in California, moved to the Rogue River Valley in 1935, and in 1945 married a Lakota woman said to have local Takilma Indian blood. That would have shocked his fans. But the mixed-race marriage also silenced rivals who circulated rumors that he was homosexual—a crime then in many places.

That made me wonder if all O'Hara's supermanly activities were also an effort to prove rivals and critics wrong about his sexual leanings.

Again, I read how he and his second wife had a boy who died at age one. There was no mention of other children. Rose died in 1946, leaving O'Hara a widower. But his last book, "Rogue Princess," about Indian struggles in health and work in the '30s and '40s, had an Indian heroine named Marguerite.

I found "Rogue Princess" and "River's Run" at online booksellers, and downloaded eBook copies. I'd call Seattle Mystery Bookshop tomorrow, and try to contact our new barn buddy, antiques dealer Jill Benetton, to see what she knew about O'Hara.

A peek into "Rogue Princess" on my eBook reader told in terse but lyrical language how a local Indian woman, pressured to give up her child to a white boarding school, founded a standout school featuring Native American studies along with the mainstream America teachings.

"A beauty as commanding as a ponderosa, yet unassuming as a shoot," he'd written of his heroine. "A home to friend and enemy, bird and beetle. Gifted with a sight discerning Past in Present. A heart that knew the life-and-death paradox of fire."

This resonated. Both the words, and the reminder that fire can wipe out everything in its path but also create opportunities for new life.

I read on, about the difficulties of founding her school despite opposition by establishment education, and about her joy at seeing the most recalcitrant students graduate to lives that had a positive impact on people of all cultures.

I came up for air hours later, fatigue weighting my bones but satisfaction somewhat lightening my concerns. Where does time go, when you read like you're dying?

* * *

After a wonderful night's rest, I had a light breakfast, called Tulip for the OK, and phoned our banker to set up a Friday meeting about financing. I also tended to yard and house work, long neglected.

At nine-thirty I pulled out my cell phone and found Seattle Mystery Bookshop's number. I tapped "Call." A male voice answered. The owner, J.T., a knowledgable and affable but occasionally brusque individual.

"Seattle Mystery Bookshop."

I identified myself, reminding him I was a former byline reporter of Washington's leading newspaper, and a past SMB client. He recognized me at once.

"How's retirement?" he asked amiably.

I gave him the light version, then got right to the purpose of my call.

"I'm pursuing a freelance story here," I said, feeling no shame for the white lie. "I wonder if you might know a woman I'm writing about, if she visited the store. You have a ton of customers, but sometimes one stands out."

"Go ahead."

I gave him the woman's description, adding, "Her mug looked fairly new." Of course I left out the about her acquiring a hatchet in her back.

"Well, I don't recall anyone of that description," J.T. said. "But I'll ask around. I have your number now. Can I help with anything else?"

I asked if he carried any of O'Hara's books, as I had discovered that a number of them were out of print.

"Preston O'Hara? Didn't he used to live down your way?"

"Bingo."

"I will check that, too, when I get a chance," he said. "Pretty slammed right now. Tourists are out early, and there's a Mariners game today."

"One more thing."

"That would be?"

"What's the rarest O'Hara first-edition title, and how much would it bring?"

There was a brief silence. I could hear keyboard tapping on his end of the lune.

"That would be 'Rogue Renegade,' his first novel, the Pulitzer winner right out of the gate. You remember the movie. Clark Gable. That book, signed, in that special first edition his publisher brought out, would command the high four figures today, from at least one serious collector I know."

I took a flyer on that last statement.

"What about an unpublished manuscript?"

"High five figures, from the right publisher. Know where I can find one?"

"Sorry, J.T.," I said. "Not today."

I thanked him, reminded him to ask his employees about the woman I described, and hung up. I had to hurry to Brassbottom Barn for another practice. We'd leave for Seattle in less than one week. I hoped like hell to have my mystery solved by then. If not, I'd have one giant weight to drag as I tried to win thousand-dollar jackpots.

It was cooler that morning in Sam's Valley, the last stronghold of local Indians before the Army rounded up Chief Sam and his relatives for a forced march to a reservation up North the winter of 1853. I wondered if

O'Hara's second wife, with her alleged Rogue Valley ties, had been related to Sam.

When I entered the barn, I saw Choc's head hanging out his feed widow toward the end of the aisle.

"Hey, boy," I called, but got no welcoming nicker. In fact, he pointedly looked away. Several days of intense show-schooling in a row by me, and by the Grandeens, meant only one thing to him: horse show coming up. I think he enjoyed showing as much as I did. But it was just so much stinking work. For me, there also was the expense — over a thousand dollars just for one weekend including hauling, trainer, stalling and entry fees.

I patted my handsome chestnut with the high stockings and crooked blaze, and led him back up front to the grooming stall.

"Let's take it easy today," I told him. " We don't want to peak too soon."

He ponied up and did his best for me, without fussing, as we jogged and loped in the dim but still warm indoor arena. I stroked the top of his neck with every perfect sequence. The physical movements and our emotional connection did me worlds of good, after my recent crazy days and nights. Horse therapy: the best kind. It fed body, mind and soul.

I grabbed a French-dip sandwich at Katie's Kitchen in Gold Hill, and headed for my shift at the Horsehouse. Tulip had already left. My afternoon started smoothly. I almost felt relaxed — a novelty these days. Early on I texted Tule to confirm our Friday morning appointment with the banker who'd helped us get the Horsehouse and tack trailer on their feet and occasionally stepped in with funds to keep them trotting.

Next I turned off the country music, to keep my head clear for linear tasks such as catching up on bookwork and filling online orders for tack or clothes. We had to tend to business no matter what else was going down. A few customers came in for grooming supplies or a new halter. But in general, business was slow — a bad sign for May, when rodeo and show season was just getting its groove on.

We were behind in the rent yet again. Part of that was because our landlord had just raised the rent for the second time in a year, when we had trouble keeping up with the old rate. A big saddle-sale had filled our coffers last month. But that was just one month. There simply was too much overhead and not enough steady income.

We'd already cut back on stocking cheap, border-line-profitable items like horse treats, hoof polish and fly masks, which farm stores carried by the bushel. Our main job was to provide standout tack and apparel for the competitive crowd, special bling jeans and fancy bridles that caught a judge's eye and generated envy in other competitors.

I made a list of more loss leaders we could do without. And dreamed of the day when, if all went as it should, we might pay no rent at all because we had downsized, retooled and relocated The Horsehouse to our guest ranch on the Applegate. We must clear the way for that to happen. It was a great investment and a potential livelihood.

I did a little figuring of my debt-to-income ratio, of what I could sensibly spare from my beleaguered 401K, of what Tulip and what the folks indicated they'd kick in. Less penalties and taxes. I checked it several times, playing with numbers.

Then I started getting excited. Really excited. I was putting real numbers together, and thinking in concrete terms about our heretofore blue-sky dream.

Now I had to revisit the Robertsons, including Cleve. Pin them down about the price. Put off Gloria Allende's involvement as long as possible. Hey. No worse than juggling cats. I'd done some of that in my day, and had the scars to prove it.

I took a moment to hit the PC to learn more about the alleged curse, wondering how it might affect a sale or a price. I visited Josephine County Property Records site. A long string of owner names, some two-dozen dating to the 1950s, displayed on the screen. Average length of ownership was three years. Some had owned the place less than a year, others had owned it up to six.

But never more than six. It lined up with what the Robertsons and my folks had said, that strange happenings and accidents prompted people to get out. Either there really was something to that curse levied by O'Hara, or someone wanted it to appear so. Who could that be? A person related to him, or with another stake in keeping the land from having a longtime owner?

I printed out names with last known addresses and other information. I managed to get information numbers for most. Then I researched phone numbers and began calling. Several numbers had been changed. But I hit pay dirt on three names—people who had sold the property to the Robertsons, and two people who'd owned it in the 1960s and 1970s.

The owner before the Robertsons, a Dwight Cumberland, sounded wary despite my attempts to sound convivial and "just curious" as a potential buyer of the property. He still lived in the area and had heard about the murder.

"Didn't surprise me," he said in a gruff voice.

"And why is that, Mr. Cumberland?" I said. "We need to know all the facts, even rumors, before laying down money."

He rose to my bait

"That place really is cursed. We had fires set, pets missing, it became too much. And then my brother fell down the old well. They called it an accident. But still a terrible thing that gives me nightmares today. Got out while we could. Place took a year to sell because of that, and the curse."

He also mentioned the drowning on the Applegate during his ownership.

"Was the it on, or near, your river frontage?" I said.

"Across the river," he said. "But they found signs of a party, maybe a religious ritual, not far from where our land borders the river."

"What made it seem a ritual?"

He cleared his throat elaborately, as if having trouble forming his answer. His voice lowered a notch.

"Well, there was this hatchet. That was not in the newspaper story. And some kind of bird, burned, beheaded. Likely by the hatchet. Sorry. You wanted to know."

"Yes. It must have been a frightening time for you, Mr. Cumberland." I thought of the headless chicken in my freezer. I had to get rid of it, burn it on a trash heap. Oregon Department of Forestry had not yet imposed its summer limits on outdoor burning.

"You got that right," said Cumberland. "As I mentioned, we had a hard time selling the place. Took more than a year. Had to really slash the price."

I considered this. This might happen in our case. Yet not if Gloria were right, or had her way.

"I talked with the couple you sold it to. Guess the reported curse didn't bother them when they bought the place from you."

"Oh, no, they seemed real practical. Good Christian people. Didn't believe in curses. If I remember right, though my memory's gone a little hazy, I thought one might've said they were distantly related to the writer. Guy who hanged himself."

"Really?" I sat up straighter. "Can you elaborate?"

Why hadn't that they might be related to O'Hara come up in my talks with the Robertsons? Was it true, or had Cumberland indeed mixed his memories?

"Well, now, I really don't know if they said that, or I just dreamed it," he said. "I had nightmares after the wife and I moved out. Lots of reason to."

I thanked Cumberland for his time, and disconnected.

The other two prior owners I contacted owned the property four years each. The one from the '60s lived with her daughter in town but was too frail to speak. However her daughter, now her caregiver, spoke for her. She recalled little about the property, having lived "back east" at the time. But she'd heard neighbors like Rosie Pussytoes whisper tales of strange happenings.

The owner from the '70s never lived on the property, only rented it out. It was bought as a future retirement residence, but sold when renters trashed it, and then left with the appliances.

I checked the wooden Horsehouse clock over the door. The clock with the horseshoe-nail numbers that Sonny had given me three Christmases ago.

"Four," I exclaimed to no one in particular. "Where does the time go when you're having fun?" I prepared the store for closing.

It had been an afternoon of hard work, true. But also a strangely pleasant way to pass time—planning how to make your dreams, minus the romantic one, come true. A guest ranch and horse facility on the river. The folks nearby–they might even help with bookkeeping or cooking. And my best friend working with me. Everything consolidated, with room to grow as the money flowed in.

All that was lacking was that bedrock thing: a steady man, an on-site, reliable partner to share the love, work, disappointment and triumphs. Sonny might never be that. And I was getting no younger. If that were what I really craved to complete my dreams, I'd better get cracking. As long as I was reaching for one gold ring, I might consider reaching for the whole basket. Helping Tulip and me develop a guest ranch might be the elbow-in-the-ribs Sonny needed.

I wondered if the specter of a rift between my lover and me, this idea of his going back with his ex-wife for whatever reason—business, illness—might be a wakeup. Was I being prompted to consider what I honestly needed or expected from a relationship. Guided to consider finding someone new. Like Sheriff Welles?

Or was I just getting a nudge to recommit to the love and relationship dear Sonny and I did have, to our "floating affair," odd as it sometimes seemed.

I looked again at the clock, tapped my fingers on the counter, and thought, why not? I needed a break. Since there had been no customers all afternoon—the Wednesday doldrums—I'd close up early, and have a for-once leisurely grocery shop before heading home. There was a special on Northwest-caught jumbo prawns downtown.

But then I had another idea. I had enough time and energy to head south on Old Stage Road to Jacksonville, twenty minutes away. I'd wanted to check out Jill's store, and hadn't visited the historic Gold Rush town all year. It would be fun. And I might learn something. I could pick up groceries on my way home.

Bits of forest, lazy farmlands or wineries and well-tended homes—some on the National Register, and repurposed as beds and breakfasts—dotted the east-facing hillside as I rolled south. After some 90-degree turns, I was in J-ville, as locals called it.

Tourists and townies still roamed the sidewalks in front of low brick shops and eateries. Jacksonville Inn, where presidents like Teddy Roosevelt had tarried, loomed prestigiously on the central downtown block.

Store windows displayed custom clothing, unique kitchenware and imaginative furnishings, somewhat like a smaller-scale Ashland farther south. An old man looked down at a sidewalk inset with thick glass squares allowing views of a well that served the town before the reservoir was built.

I found a parking spot, consulted my phone for the shop address, got out and started walking. Two bubbly teens licking ice-cream cones nearly ran into me, so lost were they in conversation. I swerved in time, but felt a sudden craving for sweets.

An ice-cream parlor with a barbershop pole out front drew my eye on the next block. Would a peanut-crusted, vanilla and chocolate cone provide most of the elements of the major food groups?

"Pepper," exclaimed a woman's voice from the doorway of a shop I'd passed.

"Oh, Jill, hi. I was just looking for your shop. You're still open?"

I scanned the window displays on either side of the ancient, polished oak door. A small horse-cart was filled with old kitchen and farm implements in one window. A parlor tableau with antique furniture, clothes and books, filled the other.

"About to close," Jill said. "But come on in. Making headway on your case?"

"Not my case," I said, entering her store, Antiques 'N More. "But I am seeking information on Preston O'Hara. Do you have any of his books? Or know anything about his family?"

"Wow," said Jill shaking her short, dark blonde hair. "I just got something in today you might like. And several of his books. Can't help about the family, though."

She led me to a wall containing floor-to-ceiling bookshelves, some with chicken-wire gates with locks.

Rare books, first editions. She plucked a key from her pants pocket, unlocked that section and stood back.

I found four O'Hara books, hefty hardbacks with brightly colored dust covers, in varied condition. I pulled out "Rogue Princess" and flipped it open. It was signed, but a second edition, released in 1953, the year of O'Hara's death.

"How much?" I asked. But when I turned, Jill was gone. "Jill?"

"In back. But you just have to see this."

She returned carrying a framed picture with its brown-paper-covered back facing me. Slowly she rotated the piece. She grinned. I gasped.

It was a two-by-three, full-color movie poster for O'Hara's 1950 blockbuster, "Ghost of the Applegate."

"No way," I said, taking in the vivid black words, and dramatic cameo photos of a wild-eyed actor and actress, dressed in Old Hollywood's idea of proper white-settler attire, being haunted by the specter of an Indian warrior. Stereotypical, stupidly overstated, but still well designed and completely captivating.

I turned to Jill, who waited expectantly.

"No way. On so many levels, Jill. Where did you get this?"

"Saw it on my last buying trip to L.A. It was at a swap meet outside town, if you can believe that. Pretty dirty, and the frame is banged up, but quite the find."

"I'll say." Although the store was air-conditioned, I felt slightly feverish. I couldn't take my eyes off the poster. It would be perfect for our dreamed-of ranch.

Jill set it down against the bookcase and stepped beside me. I ran a forefinger over the wide, black wooden frame. It looked like it had been polished recently. The glass over the poster gleamed. Jill clearly was as geared to presenting her wares to their best advantage as she was to showing her horse.

"How much?" I whispered.

"I only paid fifty," she said. "They didn't know what they had. So … I was going to ask a thousand. At least. But I think for you … if you tell everyone where you got it but don't mention the price, maybe, five? Ish?"

"Done. I can give you a hundred down. Pay the rest at the end of next month, if that's OK?"

"I trust you. Plus, I know where your horse lives," she grinned.

I touched the frame and leaned in for a better look. "Is that his signature in the lower left corner?"

"Sharp eye."

"Wow."

I pulled out my wallet and wrote a check. While Jill wrapped the picture, I carefully looked through the O'Hara books with their thick, soft pages. The biographical information was much the same as I'd read. I was disappointed. But what did I expect, really? A stunning denouement that would crack the murder case?

Anyway, I'd spent a lovely hour in Jacksonville, finally seen Jill's wonderful store—worth another visit—and scored an amazing picture. If we renovated O'Hara's cabin, it would be the first thing to go up on the wall.

"See you at the barn," I said, before leaving. "Your shop is great. And thank you so much. I think this poster will bring me luck."

Jill moved close to me as we lingered in the doorway. She put a finger beside her mouth.

"Don't tell anyone," she said. "But I found it a little creepy. That's just me. If you love it, that's all that matters. And who knows. Maybe it will bring you luck."

* * *

Back at the ranchita by six, stocked up on prawns but not the ice-cream cone, I put the poster in the guest bedroom closet. There I could look at it often, but not put it at risk. I still couldn't believe this find. It seemed meant to be. I'd call Tulip in a little while. Maybe she'd help me with the cost. Our first real investment in the ranch.

Then I fed, watered and otherwise tended to the critters. I hurried because I wanted to hear the TV news, recorded a short time before.

The latest on the murder investigation wasn't the lead story. And what there was offered little new information. But I sat at attention when they showed Sheriff Welles saying there'd been a suspected arson fire at the residence neighboring the murder scene.

So he had checked into that, and confirmed my parents' and my belief that it was intentionally set. Why hadn't Welles or his staff returned my calls? Why, indeed. The answer was obvious. They were too busy doing their own investigation, and had neither time nor staff for extras. I understood. Didn't I?

Now on screen, Shane Chapelle sporting a royal-blue windbreaker whipped by a breeze but a black coiffure frozen by spray, stood with Welles in front of the Josephine County Sheriff's Office. Chapelle looked smugger than usual. That was saying a lot.

"So, Sheriff, do you believe the fires at a neighbor's house may have been set to warn possible witnesses near the murder scene on Friday?"

I again was struck by how different this sheriff in the county next door was from Sheriff Jack Henning, the grizzly-bear lawman in charge of my own Jackson County. Night and day.

"We have not determined that," said Welles. "But have referred it to the Oregon State Police, the investigating agency for the murder. I have no further comment."

The sheriff's handsome face flickered almost imperceptibly with what looked like annoyance, though he had composed it to look impartially stony. I could imagine his pique at his alleged favorite reporter's having again gone too far. "Favorite," according to my Daily Courier friend who'd hinted about favoritism some time back, regarding another case about which Chapelle seemed to have privileged information.

I wondered again about the relationship, though I might never know. Why was Welles even remotely close to such a snake? Could Chapelle have something on him? Or was it professional back scratching, a dubious relationship in which each benefitted in ways that counted. That had been known to happen with a Seattle reporter or two, when Pulitzers shimmered on the horizon.

After watching a few more stories and the weather, I killed the TV and rounded up the Bostons. Their smiling faces, bouncy moves and popping eyes brought me a measure of balance, and ease. I play-boxed with Charlie, ruffling his bat-wing ears, to his delight. Then I rolled long-legged Shayna over and rubbed her plump pink tummy. A Boston Buddha. When she licked my face, her mouth smelled like spring violets.

I sat on the deck and savored Caesar salad with prawns, followed by a slice of Mom's apricot pie. Yep. She definitely could help cook at the ranch, if we bought it. Maybe I'd see if Nancy, Jeanne's older sister in Ashland, could cook, too. She was training for food work.

Sated and relaxed, I reviewed my day's labors. Maybe I would hear from Cleve Robertson soon. I'd left another message. Things seemed to be moving along. There were major hurdles to leap before we realized our guest-ranch dreams. But we were giving it our best shot.

Before preparing for bed I wrote notes about the day and tucked them into the manila folder. I called Tulip to tell her about my day, and the movie poster.

"I'm dying to see it," she said. "I might kick in a dollar or two. And I do hope it brings us luck."

Then I called Sonny to see how his battles were going. I needed to hear my lover's voice, hear his input on what was happening with the case—and with us.

But his cell phone rang and rang, never going to voice mail. I left a short text for him to call me. Was he out of range somewhere, or had Sonny turned off his phone? If so, why? That was very unlike him. I hoped he hadn't been called back to his Standing Rock rez on some emergency.

I had heard there were complications on the proposed pipeline. Drilling had begun again after the owners had pugged a leak, avoided major hurdles in court, gained presidential permission and taken over the land in question. New camps were up.

But a more personal fear arose, that he might be avoiding me. There was still this mysterious thing with the ex. I'd push it back, only to have it resurface when I was overtired, or otherwise let down my guard.

In the shower I tried to let all that go while jets of soothing hot water pummeled my back and shoulders. The French lavender-scented soap, applied with a plush washcloth, took me to another place physically and emotionally. A good wash, and the prospect of a good night's sleep, would bring peace.

As I slid into bed and envisioned my lover—tall, bronze and strong in black jeans and a muscle tee, his shiny black hair braided and fallen over one shoulder. His full lips parted as he moved in for a kiss, and I moved into him like a nesting dove. Slowly we'd kiss and lift each other's shirts so there was only hot skin between us. Mine silky, his more so save for the tiny sun dance scars where eagle-talon skewers once had pierced his skin. He'd prayed, and sought visions for the People, while he pulled bleached buffalo skulls around the sun-washed circle.

I admired him for that sacrifice, done many years in a row. What had I ever done for a people, for their healing, for answers to life's great mysteries?

I sighed and rolled over, cradling my cool oversized pillow. That would have to do for now.

Sleep was coming. My tired limbs melted into the mattress, my mind felt clean and restored. My worries about Sonny once more were put to bed. As always, if I were patient enough and tended to my own business, Sonny eventually would resurface and at the perfect time, making everything wonderful between us again.

18

Upon waking at five-thirty Thursday I saw the text on my cell phone. The number was not Sonny Chief's, but Cleve Robertson's.

"Fire in plastic trash can by my folks garage. Melted it. No other damage."

It was too early to call him. But I wasted no time texting him to call me.

I went into the guest bedroom and gazed at my newest artwork. The sight of it filled my heart. A piece of our guest-ranch dreams fallen into place, though I couldn't remember dreaming it. I still felt amazed at finding a signed Preston O'Hara movie poster. And at such an amazing price. I owed Jill Benetton. Big time.

Keeping my phone nearby as I did horse and house chores, I felt antsy as the hours crawled by. I was in some kind of dead zone figuratively and literally where loved ones were in limbo and the dead weren't talking. I felt adrift, waiting for something I couldn't identify. I didn't know if I needed permission to act or permission to stop acting. Keeping busy was the only way to keep my thoughts from burrowing further into a dangerous hole.

Donning my garden hat and gloves, I weeded the vegetable garden for fifteen minutes, and then watched the sprinklers come on. Chickadees, sparrows and juncos darted in and out, relishing the trickles and sprays. Watching them cheered me. So did glimpsing the glistening leaves of newly planted tomatoes, squash and sweet-peppers. Life went on despite unpleasantness elsewhere. I took comfort and strength in that. It was something I called Animal Truth. Nature's way. The only way, really.

About nine, as the heat began to build, I took a call from my daughter.

"Chili, hey," I said. "Find anything yet on O'Hara's family?"

"Not yet, Mom. But I wanted to share the good news. I got an interview about my jewelry in the paper. And I have news about Serrano. He probably hasn't had time to call. He's got a contract to do paintings for a show at the Mariners' Diamond Club."

"Wow. Good news all around. Thanks. I needed some about now."

I was thrilled that my baby girl was finally being recognized for her designs. Maybe she'd be an overnight success after trying internet work and other pursuits for half her thirty-two years. Might even attract a nice, steady man and settle down. I fingered the sandblasted sterling Celtic cross with lava stone on a black rawhide thong around my neck. One of her best pieces.

"Email the clip, Chills, or a link to the page," I said. "And I'll call your brother and congratulate him."

"Good luck. Serrano's working like a maniac to finish the paintings. They took a long time getting back to him but were crazy about his portfolio. They're featuring him and another artist there next month."

It figured. Both my offspring finally showing promise of making it, of finally giving a mother some lasting pride and peace after years of fits and starts, emotional problems, disappointing relationships. Maybe I could exhale. At least about them.

I tapped Serrano's number. It went to voice mail limbo. He probably was too busy to call back. So I texted, "Congratulations on the Diamond Club Show. Call or text if you can. See you in Seattle next week."

When I was set to go for a quick ride at Brassbottom Barn, Waylon's deep voice sang out. If only it were real. But it was Cleve Robertson. About time.

"Yeah," he said in his high, breathy voice. "I did a check at my folks' place last night. There was a fire in the plastic garbage can. Melted it and scorched some grass. No real damage, though."

My heart jumped with concern.

"Good about no damage, not so good to hear about the fire. Were any other neighbors hit, do you know? Did you call Rural Metro Fire and the sheriff?"

"Don't know about the neighbors. But guess I could call the sheriff. The fire burned itself out before doing any damage. I'll let Rural Metro know."

"Any idea how the fire started?"

"Not sure. Probably same as at your folks'."

"Investigators will sort it out."

"I was a firefighter. Know the protocol."

"You probably want to stop by their property more often, now, if possible."

"Sure. Gotta protect their investment."

Still holding the phone to my ear, I fiddled with my car keys, entered my garage and shut the door against my dogs in the yard.

"You know that my friend Tulip and I are thinking of making your parents an offer for a by-owner sale, right? They said I should talk to you about price and such."

There was a pause. One of the Bostons barked, then clawed the garage door. A whine indicated the dogs' opinion of my action. Or inaction.

"I heard you were interested," said Robertson. "What were you thinking, in the way of an offer?"

"What were you or they thinking as to price?" I climbed in Red Ryder, hit the remote to open the garage door and waited.

"Have to be close to a mill," said Robertson with a cough. "Riverfront and all."

"A realtor friend of mine did some comps," I said. "Bit more than half-a-mill was what she came up with. Six-ish."

"Pretty damn low. Nothing compares with it."

"That's true," I said. "No other properties come with an apparently still-active curse. Not even sure if we want to touch it. But we at least want to see what it may price out at, if it were available, if we still wanted it."

Another cough, followed by a phlegmy spit which I hoped was into a tissue. Was he a chronic smoker like his father?

"So. Are you still looking into that murder?" he said, sounding if he already knew the answer.

"A little," I said. "Don't you want to know who it was, and who did it, too? And their motive? Maybe you're in danger." It was bold, but I wouldn't get any-where by being timid.

"Oh. for sure," he said, a little too quickly, I thought. "That curse thing is nothing to mess with. I didn't go in for it before. Neither did Dad. But Mom is pretty sure about it. 'Specially now."

I wasn't sure he was telling the truth, but I wouldn't let on. I had to keep him talking so I could get a better idea.

"The fires did happen right after the murder, at both our folks' places," I said. "Unless we hear they were started by bored kids, it's possible someone is warning us about messing with the property."

I cast that line out to see if I might snag some-thing. Cleve wanted his parent's property. But he couldn't come up with the money. Did he want it badly enough to commit arson and murder to force down their price to him? And then tell prospects about an exorbitant price, to keep them at bay?

"Well, remember," he said. "I had a fire. So I need this thing solved, too."

Good answer. But was he telling the truth? I had to meet this guy face to face. That way I could read body movements, facial expressions, eye shifts.

"We need to talk in person," I said. "How about after work today? Sixish?"

"Sure. That'd work. I need to check something else at the property anyway."

"Meet you at their house at six, then."

Maybe Tulip could go with me. I was sure she'd like another look at the place before meeting with our financial officer. I texted her.

I ended the conversation not much wiser than when I'd started it. But I began to develop a tentative theory about those trashcan fires and who may have set them. Cleve Robertson was beginning to come into focus as a suspect. Perhaps he had set my folks' fires as a warning, and then set his own to deflect suspicion off him. It was possible he wanted the property, or the money for it, enough to kill. And if so, how had the dead woman figured into his scheme?

* * *

Brassbottom Barn was a bright, calming place that morning. Few people were there. Only the stall cleaners, singing while they worked inside the stable, and Dutch and Donna riding clients' horses in the outdoor arena. I caught their attention and waved as I strolled through the barn's open doors.

Grace ambled up to me, her glossy black butt wagging. I patted her and we walked side by side down the aisle.

Opening the stall door, I embraced Choc's slick furry head. He closed his eyes in contentment, letting me hug his warm strength to me as long as I needed. One of the many things I loved about my horse. A haven in a stormy sea.

If only a man were as reliable as a good horse, as our resident barn vixen sometimes said. She claimed horses were loving, trusting, always trying to please, yet showed enough spirit and independence to keep everything interesting.

I didn't tell Victoria Whitfield-Smith III that horses were reliable because you kept them in a stall or pen so you knew where they were, what they were doing, whom they were with at all times. I wondered if Victoria kept that tight of a leash on her wealthy, trusting husband. Although Victoria occasionally went off-leash herself.

Choc gave me a short but splendid ride. I merely had to think what direction or speed we'd go, and he complied. He hated micro-management. His gaits were smooth, forward, cadenced as a well-wound metronome. And his ears pricked happily forward, or rotated back to listen for a gait-changing cluck or kiss from me. Cluck to trot, kiss to lope, a soft "whoa" combined with a leg-squeeze to halt. A language many modern Western show-trainers and riders spoke fluently.

We both worked up a little sweat doing long trots, gallops, jog-circles and diagonals in the day's skyrocketing heat. But it was good sweat. I'd be sure to wash off the horse smell before heading to work at The Horsehouse. But, hey, it gave me a certain authenticity with clients.

As I put Choc away, his sleek body hosed down and squeegeed semi-dry, my cell phone sang. I slid the stall-door bolt, blew Choc a kiss and strode down the aisle toward the parking lot.

"Pepper!" Mom's normally well-modulated voice rose an octave with alarm.

"Mom, what?" I paused beside Red Ryder's door.

"I can't find Dad. He said this morning he wanted to walk the Robertson property, see if it really would be okay for you and Tulip to buy. I told him to stay away, that we didn't need more trouble. But when I turned my back he was gone."

"How long ago?"

"Almost two hours now. He said he was going out to the chili patch. But when I looked out the window a while ago he was nowhere in sight. His phone's still here."

"Did you check the workshop, the barn? Did he take the truck?"

"It's in the garage. He has to be at the Robertsons'. Maybe disoriented or even injured. God, I hope he's okay."

"Did he take the dog?"

"No, Heller's still here. But he's been whining. He knows something's wrong."

"Damn," I said. "Dad's so stubborn. I can't even imagine why he thought he should go, after what happened."

"Wasn't thinking. Just worried sick about you girls wanting to buy the place."

"Well, freakin' hell, Mom. Why did he ...? Never mind. I'll be right over."

My chest compressed so tightly I could barely breathe. My pulse shot up.

Why did my father have to get involved, going over to the Robertsons'? What did he think he could accomplish while endangering himself? Tulip and I were grown women, perfectly able to scope out the property and everything that went along with it. He knew that. Yet he still felt it was up to him to look out for his baby girl's best interests.

He should be looking out for his own.

19

I called Tulip to let her know I was heading back to my folks' to try to find my father. She wanted to come help look, but someone had to work The Horsehouse. Dad had been practically a second father to her, while we were growing up in that Jerome Prairie neighborhood. He'd saved her hide a time or two along with mine, say, when we'd once gotten lost after dark in the tangled woods along the river. That's the last time we ventured out without our horses. They always knew the way home even if their riders didn't. Even in the dark.

A rooster tail of gravel sprayed from the truck's tires as I left the Brassbottom parking lot. I stopped at the road and called 911. I said who I was and that my father had gone missing, likely to explore the Robertson property. Where the murder took place, I emphasized. Next door to my parents' place.

"When did you notice him missing?" said the dispatcher.

"My mother just called and told me," I said. I gave the man my mother's name, phone number and address.

"Did your mother say how long he had been gone?"

"Two hours."

"I see. Did she check everywhere in the home and vicinity? Neighbors? We usually wait twenty-four hours before we declare someone officially missing."

My pulse pounded in my temples and my cheeks burned with anger. I knew that, but vehemently disagreed with it.

"My father has memory issues," I shouted. "He could be in danger."

A slight pause in the conversation.

"I will check with your mother and pass this along to the proper authorities."

"You need to send someone out there now!" I said.

"Ma'am? Calm down. I understand your concern. We are very short staffed, as you know. But I will notify the sheriff. Someone will contact your mother."

My heart thudded. I knew a stiff-arm when I felt it. And I certainly knew where they'd find my father if they stopped dithering and started looking. But that could take who knew how long. Twenty-four hours? Really? With what had happened next door?

Keeping one eye on the rear-view and the other barely on the road—my brain-TV was working overtime imagining a worst-case scenario—I barely touched tires to pavement as I raced toward Grants Pass. The world was in slo-mo but I was in hyperdrive.

Every driver I encountered on the northbound I-5, every semi and sedan I came upon at an almost-safe eighty miles an hour, seemed to be traveling in some kind of funeral procession. They were that slow. They pulled out in front of me and then slammed on the brakes, subsequently slowing to a crawl.

More than a few curses flew out open windows as I swung out around them and back into the so-called fast lane. More than a few middle fingers were hoisted in my wake. May the bird of paradise fly up their clueless noses.

Every traffic light on the Grants Pass Parkway and southbound 199 flashed to red at my approach. Even the low-slung NASCAR wannabes crept sleepily forward from the green lights.

I tried to calm my rattling heart by breathing deep, letting the air out slowly and lowering my hunched shoulders. To little avail. A twenty-minute trip had turned into what seemed an hour-long nightmare. I was a wreck when I finally rolled down my parents' long gravel drive.

Mom, using her bull-pizzle cane, stepped off the front porch as I rolled up and parked under the oak that shaded part of the yellow two-story farmhouse.

"Dad's still gone, I take it," I said as she pulled me into a desperate hug.

"He's disappeared before," she said, stepping back, her rouged lips trembling. "But never to where I couldn't find him. He's not on the farm. Checked everywhere. 'Course I can't make it out to the Robertson back acreage."

"I called the 911. Did anyone contact you?"

"No," she said.

"That figures," I said, settling my cowboy straw hat on my head and tucking my .38 into its belt holster on my right hip. I stuffed my cell phone in a back pocket.

"I can go with you as far as the back fence," she said. "Oh, honey, be careful. I wouldn't want to lose both of you."

I slanted Mom a grim smile.

"You've done enough. Go inside, cool off, have an iced tea, maybe with a little shot of Dutch courage. I'll be okay. I'll be back with Dad in a New York minute."

"New York minute? When your Aunt Connie and I visited New York to ride in a rodeo in Madison Square Garden, our truck got stuck in traffic. That New York minute took us thirty. Some crazy had thrown himself off a skyscraper."

I looked at her as she shook her head and ran a hand over her thick white hair, now in a braid trailing down her back. I could see how she'd once been a glamorous cowgirl out to beat the world, a distant cousin of Annie Oakley. Their same fearless streak ran strong in me, as well.

With a kiss on her cheek, I was off around the house and through the back yard. It would be quicker this way than getting back in my truck, driving to the Robertson house and slogging through their back forty to the woods with the cabin.

As I crawled through the barbed-wire fence, now sagging even more with all the recent action, I swept my gaze around the meadow. I searched not only for a familiar figure, but for lines of bent weeds and grass that indicated a recent passage.

Thinking I saw one to my left, angling away from the cabin and toward trees lining the river, I took it. Sweat moistened my skin, and biting flies worried my face and arms. Swatting as I went, blowing them off my lips and eyes, I felt annoyance build.

"Dad?" I called as I hurried through brush. "Dad! Where in hell are you? Dad?"

Silence. I kept walking, finally entering a thick stand of pine, oak, alder and willow that crowded in on me. The ground was uneven, studded with protruding roots and rocks. I had to be careful not to twist an ankle. My boots weren't the best for walking, but I hadn't had time to change after leaving Brassbottom Barn.

Voices. I heard voices, rumbling and trilling, coming to me in broken and blurry snatches from the vicinity of the riverbank I guessed to be a couple hundred feet ahead. I hadn't been this far on the property since I was a teenager, sneaking a swim on my horse with Tulip. We were forbidden to ride the area let alone take a cooling dip in the river. But we didn't let that stop us.

In fact a dip would feel pretty good about now. The temperature was nearing ninety. So much for the forecasted cool-down.

A woman's high voice trilled through the trees.

"Shoot me, shoot me," she teased, following her order with a bubbling laugh.

Another woman laughed, as well. Then a third.

I stopped. Did these people, whoever they were, have a gun? I touched my Smith & Wesson for reassurance, pushing away saplings with the other hand as I pressed forward, heart in mouth.

I heard splashing, and then a man's deeper voice.

"You can't go back to work like that," he said.

Finally I saw them—three girls and two young men—from my hiding place behind the checkered trunk of a ponderosa pine that had to be at least eighty years old. As old at Preston O'Hara would be, if he'd lived. Perhaps he had planted it. At least it would have been a sapling during his years living by the river.

The women were standing or swimming in dresses, screaming and giggling as they splashed each other. Their colorful clothing clung to their curvy forms. The two men, one shooting photos or video with a phone camera, watched silently. I only saw the men's backs. But they wore jeans and tees that each bore a strange pyramid symbol containing a fierce, winged creature. Some kind of dragon?

Already primed with knowledge of strange happenings of the past, as told by newspapers and former owners, my mind registered "cult." I moved from behind the pine and made for an oak fifty feet from the action. There came a loud crack! As I stepped on a dead branch and stumbled sideways.

"Oh!" Shoot. I'd forgotten to engage the safety on my voice.

The men turned and stared. The women stopped splashing and also looked over.

"Hey," I said, my voice doing its best to approximate a casual tone. I added a shrug to impart authenticity. "Nice day for a swim."

"Hey," said the taller young man, his dark brows colliding over his long Roman nose. I couldn't help but notice a resemblance to the Cleve Robertson pictured in his parents' photo album. Could this this be his grandson?

"Um, I'm Pepper Kane. My parents live next door?" I swept one arm behind me. "I was looking for my dad, who has memory issues and just walked away. We think he headed back here. Have you seen an older man, wiry, balding?"

The taller man nodded, looked at his friends and shook his head.

"Are you by any chance related to this property's owners?" I ventured.

"Why do you care?" He folded his arms across his chest and glared at me.

A plump older teen in a purple dress whose full skirt billowed up to her waist, took a few steps forward on the rocky river bottom. She teetered in the swift current, shaking her wet black hair over her shoulders. It looked like wriggling snakes.

"Haven't seen a soul," she said. "We're not supposed to. This is private property. There are signs everywhere. Your father would've known that."

What was this attitude all about? An old man was missing and his daughter was simply out looking for him. No reason for her to be defensive. Or was there?

"So you are related to the Robertsons, then, or have permission to swim here?"

"Lady, you got some nerve," she said. "It's none of your business."

"Nosy bitch," muttered a thinner girl wearing wall-to-wall tattoos and a clingy red dress. The third girl, a fireplug dressed in blue, nodded.

Purple Dress jammed her fists on her hips and glared at me.

"Better get your ass out of here," she snapped. "There was a murder nearby, you know. Not that far from where you're standing." It almost sounded like a threat.

"I heard. I was just leaving. Do me a favor? If you see my dad call 911." I half-turned to go, but then turned back. "Are you shooting a movie, or video?"

The taller man took a few steps toward me up the slanted, rocky bank. His boots slipped on the stones and his hands formed fists as he held out his arms for balance. He stopped and narrowed his eyes.

"Listen, Lady." He took a hip-shot stance. "You're asking, like, way too many questions. You a cop or somethin'?"

"Like I said, just a neighbor. Who is looking for her father. And also looking at this property, maybe to buy." I wasn't sure why I added that. To show I had an extra reason to be here? The first reason would have been enough.

"Shut up," said Purple Dress looking at her female companions as if for support.

"You a millionaire?" said the shorter man. "Want to fund a movie?"

"Johnny Depp filmed his first movie on the Applegate River," I said. "Not far from here, in fact. Upriver a mile or two. An old black-and-white about river pirates."

"Huh," said the short man. "Never knew that about Johnny. Ol' Jack Sparrow himself. When was that?"

"About 1995," I said. "Google it. Say. What does the pyramid on your shirts stand for? And the bird thingy. Or dragon." Nothing ventured, nothing gained.

The men and women looked at each other. The short man turned his back to me. His tall friend spoke again.

"Just some logo from work," he muttered. "Not that unique."

It didn't look like any local logo I'd ever seen.

"Where do you work?"

That brought Purple Dress briskly from the water. As briskly as the river rocks, swift water and her two-hundred pounds would allow. Godzilla/Venus emerging from the sea. I broke and ran, or rather, threw my feet into reverse, and scrambled.

"I was just leaving," I shouted back over my shoulder as I crashed back through the jungle, legs pumping furiously. "Never saw a thing."

"A thing, a thing," reverberated in my brain.

I flailed my arms as I ran, skinning one elbow the taking a stinging snap to one eyelid. Blinking back pain, lungs straining, I took as straight a route as I could back to the open field in front of the cabin. I stubbed my toe on an exposed root, doubled over, caught myself with one hand and bullied on.

At the edge of the field I paused to listen. I could hear muffled yelling and arguing down at the river. But no sounds of pursuit. Then quiet. I exhaled.

I saw my phone had one bar of service. I immediately called Mom.

"Nothing yet," I said. "But I saw some sketchy people swimming down at the river, shooting pictures or something."

"Oh, dear. You went that far?"

"Saw a little trail and thought Dad might have wandered that way. Then I heard voices. They were just kids shooting a movie for YouTube or something. They said I was trespassing, so they might know the Robertsons. But they hadn't seen Dad."

Mom didn't need to know they'd virtually threatened me.

"Okay," said Mom. "Thanks for letting me know you're okay. You've been gone a half hour. I was beginning to worry something had happened to you, too."

"Oh, Mom, don't do that. It'll be all right. I'll just check the cabin and the area behind, and come right back." We clicked off.

Standing about a hundred feet from the cabin, I looked around once more. From that vantage point I could see more of the collapsed pole-barn and also what looked like a half-dozen marijuana plants standing in dirt mounds in front of the pole barn. I pushed through honeysuckle and blackberry vines to inspect it. What was another scratch or two?

Sure enough. Someone was, or had been, growing dope. I spotted a drip-irrigation setup, complete with propane bottles and generator, connected to a PVC pipe running back into the woods along the river. Not a big grow, but a huge clue. The soil looked fairly fresh, and held new footprints here and there. The police surely had snapped photos and otherwise were all over it. A two-foot-wide hole gaped where a rootball had been. Evidence.

So someone had been squatting in the cabin, after all. And why not? They had all the water and privacy in the world, here. Not to mention a shelter of sorts. Was it the homeless couple old Walt Walters had seen a week ago? Or the kids down by the river?

I walked to the front of the cabin. The door was still ajar. Yellow crime tape still hung or lay along the porch and door. I ducked under the roof and slipped inside. The great room was the same as a few days earlier, nearly empty and refreshingly cool.

But it wasn't the front room that interested me.

"Dad?" I called. "Dad? You here?"

Chilling silence. It felt as if the spirit of the dead woman were still there. A low branch scraped the roof and I flinched. Then I relaxed as much as I dared. The afternoon breeze must have come up early.

Aware of time ticking away, of every minute Dad was missing and I was at the murder scene, I raced into the bedroom on the left. My eyes shot to the split-pine plank. Its long halves were pushed down, the repair nails scattered, as if someone had been down there.

My heart skipped. Who could have been here since Tuesday? The river revelers? The killer or killers? Someone else, even my Dad?

"Dad?" I called. "Dad?"

Nothing. Maybe he'd gone in, and gotten hurt. Or was unconscious.

I dropped to my knees and pushed the split board open as much as I could so I could climb down into the dank crawlspace that held the odd blocky object I had seen in dim shadow before, behind the hall floor joist-support blocks.

Sitting on my bottom beside the long, foot-wide hole, and breathing through my mouth because of the awful scent down there, I lowered myself in and stuck one foot down until it hit bottom. Then the other. Slowly, carefully, making sure my phone and gun were still with me, I scrunched down through the long, narrow opening, scraping my ribs and back as I went, until I was on my knees on the hard, scratchy dirt. Then, leaning down, supported by my forearms on the ground, I pushed my legs back and until I lay on my stomach on the cold, rock-strewn surface in the foul-smelling gloom.

"Dad?"

Silence.

Well, I thought, as long as I'm down here I may as well so some recon.

Pulling my phone from my right hip pocket, I pushed the flashlight feature and saw the crawlspace ahead light up. No Dad, that I could see.

But there. Not seven feet ahead, partly hidden behind two big rocks, was a square-looking edge of that blocky object that a few days ago seemed out of place.

I dragged myself closer and angled my head to the side as I continued shining the light toward the joist-support blocks and what lay behind them. Then I saw the object was some kind of small box. A little chest, maybe ten inches long, with shorter sides. I inched further, reached out my arm and ran one hand over it. Wood, covered in stiff leather, with metal edges, a hasp and a domed lid. The whole thing crawled with ants and centipedes, plus a cobweb remnant. I brushed them off.

Feeling goosebumps stand up on my arms, I wondered why I had encountered no cobwebs on my earlier look into the crawlspace and my present entry. Had someone been this far in here before me? It couldn't have been police. They would've taken the box. The thought that it wasn't police did not thrill me.

Fumbling with my phone, using what light had filtered into the small-windowed room and through the slot in the floor, I found the camera app and shot four flash photos of the box. I set down the phone for a moment. Carefully positioning my forearms and hands, I pulled and clawed my way forward, avoiding the huge joists. I dragged my body over gravel and dirt until my face was inches from the trunk.

Something slimy wriggled under one hand. With an involuntary "Oh," I jerked the hand away. A cobweb dropped its thick veil across my eyes and drifted into my open mouth. I noisily spat it out.

No matter. Pulse quickening, I reached out and extended my fingers. I had to see what was in that little casket. But my exploring fingers found the hasp locked.

While I lay helpless on my belly in the dank, soundless dark, I heard a creak from above. <u>Squeee.</u> Then another. And another. Footsteps. <u>Thump, thump.</u> Slow. Heavy. Coming closer. They stopped almost directly overhead.

I froze. My eyes locked on nothing. I held my breath and listened. The next moment there was a long screech as both sides of the split plank were yanked back up to floor level, plunging my crawlspace into inky blackness. Scrabbling sounds immediately followed, and then the ear-splitting ring of big nails being hammered into wood.

My breath caught in my throat.

"Shit," I yelled. "Who's there? What the hell are you doing?"

The hammering intensified. Hard-breathing sounds filled the silence between blows Then all went silent. More creaks above, and heavy footsteps receding. They were going away. I held my breath, and waited.

But a minute later the footfalls returned, growing louder. With them came the count of something heavy screeching across the floor above, as if being pushed or dragged. There was nothing in the cabin that could make that noise, unless … of course. The ancient heavy arm-chair.

There was a grunt like that of an animal. Another creak. A slight pause. Then the sound of receding foot-falls. Lighter footfalls. Hurried footfalls. Would they be the last footfalls I ever heard?

20

"Hey!" I shouted into the dark of my makeshift grave. "Hey! You won't get away with this. People will be looking for me."

Only silence and the rapid beating of my heart met my cries. When I caught my breath, the crawlspace went quiet as a tomb. Or how I imagined a tomb would be, since I'd only seen the outside of one until now. As quiet, and as final. I shivered.

Taking short, shallow breaths, I lay on my belly in what might be my next-to-last resting place, if I were not found or did not figure a way out. Surely Mom would call 911 in a while, activate a search party for me—and for Dad, wherever he was. I hoped that whoever it was who hoped to dispose of me, hadn't gotten to him, too.

Heavy gloom weighted my bones. Why on Earth had I crawled inside this hole? In a cabin I shouldn't have entered, that I'd been warned not to enter, that might be the death of me and my family. But I knew why. Once more I'd let my curiosity lead me to dangerous people and places. Once more I stared death in the eye. Once more I could not afford to blink.

Breathing through my mouth because of the nauseating smell of mold, animal feces and a decaying critter carcass, I focused on my surroundings. I felt for my phone, but couldn't find it. If there were a way out, any feature might be the key to it. If no one thought to look here for me, even a microscopic detail could mean the difference between life and death.

The air of the shallow black space felt cool on my cheek and bare arms. That seemed normal because the space was below grade, carved out by a small dozer, or even hacked out by pick and shovel back in the day. The uneven, pocked and ridged, claylike dirt under my hands suggested that. Maybe the famous author had even dug it himself before laying river rocks for the foundation.

The second thing was, as my sight adjusted to the velvety dark, pinpricks and coin spots of daylight pierced the river-rock foundation maybe eight feet ahead. They let me see faint outline of rocks surrounding them – angular stones about the size of a human head. That meant they would weigh as much as twenty to thirty ponds each. Granite, feldspar, travertine. Good foundation rock meant to last.

I craned my neck around to look overhead, at the underside of the floorboards, trying to assess the ancient slabs that held me prisoner. Reaching up my right hand, braced on my left elbow, I felt the thick, rough-hewn support joists running at right angles to the boards.

Still solid.

My mouth felt dry, and tasted foul. I spat to one side, licking my dry and tacky lips. A growing thirst bid for my attention but I pushed it back. At the sun dance that long-ago August with Sonny Chief in South Dakota, I'd gone waterless for a day, in sympathy for his going without food or water for four days. I'd have no problem now.

I pushed at the overhead plank. Then pushed harder. Not even a slight give. Next I juggled my torso and limbs around and rolled onto my back directly under the floorboard with the long crack. Scraping one supporting joist with my shins, I folded both legs, booted soles up, on my stomach. I placed each sole against the board, and pushed with all my might. No movement of the board. I held my breath and this time delivered a sharp double kick. The result was the same as before.

Trying one more thing, I wriggled back onto my stomach, raised up, ducked my head and pushed the base of my neck and shoulder against the floorboards. I grunted like a Sumo wrestler and pushing harder, redoubling my efforts. I winced at a twinge in my back. I collapsed onto my stomach again, weakened and sore. Whatever was holding down that floorboard and its nearby mates, was going nowhere. I had to take another tack.

I felt for my cellphone and finally found it. I pressed the home button. When the pane lit, I tapped in my passcode. No service, of course. But it was one o'clock. More than an hour since I'd left Mom to go search for Dad. She had to be really worried. Maybe enough to call for help. They could be on their way right now.

Or not. With the air in the crawlspace warming with my presence, and the day, I needed to continue my effort to escape. The trail of whoever had done this was growing colder by the moment, unless, of course, they were still here. That thought was not comforting. But if they were here, they couldn't stay forever.

I reached out and felt for the little casket. Although I couldn't see, I worked at the hasp, finding it still hopelessly locked. Whatever was inside was not meant to be found. This was a secret someone needed kept. I wondered if whomever had entombed me knew of its existence. But I was pretty sure they did.

Lifting the casket in one hand, I judged it to weigh two or three pounds. Its bottom was about the size of a sheet of writing paper, and the chest itself stood about ten inches tall. It indeed was made of old, cracked leather over wood, with metal corners.

I tucked it under one arm and dragged my body over the dirt and pebbles to the cabin foundation. I settled under the largest hole I could see, roughly the size of quarter. Putting on eyeball to the opening, I peered out. Thick vines and grass blocked most of my vision. Using one hand to pry and push at the edges of stones all the way around the hole, I met unyielding resistance. But I learned the rocks were held together by a kind of rough, sandy mortar, which shed sharp grit when rubbed. My heart quickened. If I felt as far as possible around the inside of the foundation, maybe I would find a place where the mortar was old enough and compromised enough to allow a rock to be dislodged.

Before I started what could still be a dead-end search, I put my mouth to the small hole in the mortar and yelled.

"Hey! Anybody there? Help!" I paused, waiting for any response. Maybe from the river people. Somewhere a squirrel scolded, in short, low, staccato growls. Farther out, a scrub jay scolded the squirrel. The building heat made everyone cranky, including me.

"Help! Can anybody her me? I'm under the cabin. HELLLLP!"

The trees absorbed the sound, shaking their leaves in dismissal. They just wanted to get along, to be left to their lovely green lives, the fresh air, the morning dew and evening breeze.

It was time to start searching for a workable chink in the mortar.

Sweat wet my face, arms and torso as I crawled and dragged myself a foot at a time, over stiff and torn tarpaper, sand and gravel, around the shallow prison. My elbows and forearms stung with scratches. My fingernails shredded as I picked at line after gritty line of mortar. Lots of grit popped out, along with dry moss, dead grass, spiders and other invertebrates. A lizard skittered up and over my back at one point. I didn't mind. They represented life, and a certain freedom—which I soon hoped to reclaim for myself.

I had to work around random rocks, and masonry blocks and aligned joists. But for the most part, aside from the spiders and a bony mound of what may have been a dead rat, I had the place to myself.

To myself, that is, until I angered the skunk.

My hand brushed a pile of weeds and twigs surrounding a narrow depression. I briefly touched plush fur. As I jerked my hand away, a noxious cloud of damp spray enveloped me, burning my eyes and throat, making it hard to breathe.

"Shit," I barked, scrambling backward, tears streaming, fire searing my throat. The stench of burning tires cloaked me like a second skin.

I kept lurching backward on my knees until I hit the opposite rock wall with my heels, and paused to assess the damage. I could barely breathe. Every inhalation was a sword stuck down my throat. But I was alive. Kind of. The penetrating odor now was part of me, and I, of it.

Rubbing my face and arms with sandy dirt, hoping it would absorb at least some of the stink, I turned awkwardly around on my skinned knees to face the low rock wall before me. I saw a hole the size of a quarter. I put my face up to it and stared out.

A pair of large black boots stood in the weeds not six feet away.

21

My eyes flooded. I felt both soaring hope and paralyzing fear. Was this a rescuer? Or had the entomber come back to finish the job? There was no way I could escape, that I could see. And if no one found me, I'd die anyway. Oh, it would take a while without water and in chokingly stale air. But a smart killer would make sure I couldn't talk if someone did find me. Just as he'd silenced the other woman.

Hoping he didn't know I was on this side of the crawlspace, I breathed so shallowly that I felt lightheaded. As seconds ticked by, my pulse ticked up.

Blinking away my tears, I lowered my chin to the dirt and squinted through the tiny hole, trying to get an idea of whose feet might be in those cowboy boots, the tops of which were sheathed in dark jeans. Trying to get an idea of my fate.

A rustle to my right made me wince. The skunk, leaving? Or another furred threat? Silence followed. It had given me pause, but it was nothing compared to the threat that might await outside the hole. I focused on that again.

The boots rocked back and forth directly in front of the hole as if their owner were deciding what to do next. As if he knew I was peering through the hole. As if he were going to kneel for a better look.

I shrank back as silently as I could into the dark. A shiver shook me. I whispered a prayer through a mouth dry as ash.

"Lord, *Tunkashila,* save me." I still had no idea who this was, or their plan.

Sure enough, a pair of large, tan hands descended into view in the crushed weeds about a yard from the hole. The hands braced on their palms, long forearms stretching above them. Not a reassuring sight. Eyes would appear next.

With icy fingers, I felt behind my waist for my revolver. The idea was to silently unholster it, aim at the hole and fire fast enough to blind or kill.

But how do you pull a Velcro strap silently off a holster? It's a question soldiers and police have asked for years. A question that, if answered properly, could save threatened lives.

It had to be done all in one move. Rip away the Velcro strap, pull out the gun, aim through the hole and squeeze the trigger. There was no safety on my .38 Crimson Trace S&W, so that, at least, would be no problem. I'd count to three, then rip, draw, point, fire. I had to squeeze forcefully or the red laser-thread would shine through the hole, announcing my intent.

Rolling onto my left shoulder, wrapping my left hand around my belly to grip the holster strap with my fingertips. I lay my right hand on the holster, poised to pull out the revolver once it was free of the strap.

One … the head outside my hiding place was a dark blob, backlit by the light, slowly lowering itself into viewing position.

Two … labored breathing and a deep, "Uh-uh" grunt as a heavy male chest dropped to the ground. His head was haloed in a thin rim of outside light.

Three …now!

I ripped and drew. But as I pulled back a few inches to jam pistol tip into the hole, my right hand froze. I stared in shock at the outline of the head, one eye surely trained in my direction. A sickening realization filled me.

I knew that silhouette. My hand trembled. I lowered the gun.

Sonny Chief. Come to find me. And I had nearly killed him.

"Sonny?" my voice quavered, dredged up from some bottomless swamp of fear.

"What are you doing in there, Pepper?" His voice drifted in on a question that drew my eye back to the hole. I stared in relief and disbelief as his head drew back. I saw Sonny's deep-chocolate eyes crinkled at the corners while staring at my one eye against the hole. His lips parted in the most blinding-white grin I'd seen, even on him.

"I was looking for Dad," I rasped, still breathing through my mouth because of the putrid odor. "He's been missing more than three hours. We're really scared."

"No doubt."

"I also was looking for a box I saw down here before. Somebody came in and trapped me. Might still be around."

He half rose, and seemed to glance around before again looking at the hole.

"Phew! Got skunked, eh?" He waved a hand past his face.

Before I could answer, Sonny pushed up to his feet. I'd been far too scared to recognize those size-13 Tony Lama boots. The next moment he was gone I heard him moving around outside the cabin, crackling through brush, taking his time. Surely he was checking to see if we were alone. Then he hopped onto the porch, strode into the cabin and walked to the back, making the floor above me creak.

I shimmied on hands and knees as fast as I could, damn the stinging cuts on my hands, knees and elbows. I rushed toward where it sounded like him lifting the arm-chair off the broken floorboard. The heavy chair hit a wall and dropped to the floor with a thud that shook the cabin. Next came the eerie screeches of the split plank being pried upward, followed by a half-dozen sharp bangs as it was flung across the bedroom. A blinding slab of daylight hit my face as a whoosh of fresh air swirled around me.

Taking a deep breath, I gazed up admiringly at endless legs in tight, black jeans, and at muscled arms and shoulders. Sonny wore one of his favored black tees, stamped with the winged "W" associated with Waylon Jennings, of all people. He stood silhouetted like Superman against a silver square of window.

The next moment Sonny knelt as I turned my body and pushed the torso up through the long narrow hole as easily as a bread slice in a toaster slot. I felt only a small scrape against my breasts when his arms wrapped me under the armpits and pulled me up. I melted into his embrace, a sob bubbling up from deep inside me.

After a moment I jerked away and held up my hands.

"Sorry," I said. "Now you'll smell like burning tires. Let's get out of here and run me a baking soda-and-bleach bath." Catsup was good for deskunking dogs. But I preferred my catsup on a hamburger.

Sonny threw his head back and laughed. I loved the deep, booming sound of it. He gave me his serious look. The way his head lowered, how his eyebrows tilted into an inverted V, it was a little-boy-hurt look. A six-foot-six, 44-year-old little boy.

"What?" he raised his hands, pale palms up and long fingers spread. "That's the thanks I get? That's no way to say *pilamaya,*_thank you. I wasn't quite done there."

"That may be," I said. "But my stink can't be fun for you, Sonny. Will you take a rain check on my thanking you properly?"

"It is a little strong," he chuckled, pinching his nose. "But now you are gifted with skunk power. Don't have to fear, or fight. The energy you give off will be enough." His lips quirked.

"Don't I wish. Man, you almost gave me a heart attack. I thought whoever shut me in there was back. I almost shot you. You shoulda said something."

"Didn't know for sure it was you were down there."

Before we left, Sonny did more recon around the cabin and down by the river as I suggested. I dropped back into the hole, found the box and hauled myself back up, hugging it under one arm. As I stepped on the porch Sonny returned, pushing aside saplings like they were broomsticks.

"See anybody?" I said. "No sign of Dad, I take it."

"Nope. But the gravel looked trampled, moss on the rocks disturbed, signs of a picnic." He held up a chicken drumstick with the meat mostly gnawed off. It startled me to see what remained of the flesh looked un-cooked.

"Who eats raw chicken?" I said.

"Coyotes," he said. "Other animals."

"See anything else down there?"

"Just reefer butts. I noticed there's a little grow behind the cabin."

"Supports my theory about squatters. Or a cult. Remember that beheaded chicken I called you about Monday? The note? What is it that connects these people?"

He tossed the chicken bone and put an arm around my shoulders.

"Whatcha got?" he said, looking at the weathered chest under my arm.

"That's what we're going to find out," I said. "Once we open the lock."

"Might be something police would be interested in."

"In good time," I said. "But I want to see for myself, first. And we've got to find what happened with my father. Let's go and call, then go back to the house. Maybe he's turned up."

He gave me a look from under raised eyebrows.

"Let's hope so. What about the box?"

I looked at him from under lowered eyebrows.

"It's coming with us." When he put a hand on my shoulder, I pulled away.

He cocked his head and folded his arms.

"Assume you have a plan." That look of his was back.

"Don't worry. I'll figure out what to do so neither of us gets in trouble."

Sonny said nothing more. He'd made his opinion known. He knew better than to argue with me when my mind was made up. When I got that look of my own—a look that he claimed could melt iron.

"What I don't get," I said as we walked into the hall, "is why whoever shut me in the crawlspace, leaving me to die, didn't take this box. It isn't dusty, so it appears to have been recently handled."

"They left it there for safekeeping?" he said.

"Or didn't know about it."

As we walked to where I could call 911 to report my entrapment, I allowed myself to offload my pent-up despair over my lost father, his occasional bouts of forgetfulness. Another visit to the neurologist was in order once we found him. Now that my crisis was over, worry about him again constricted my chest.

Sonny said Mom already told him those things when he stopped by their house on the way to mine in

Gold Hill. He liked to surprise me when he came to visit—an annoyance I oddly enjoyed. Just as oddly, his timing often was impeccable. He credited the "spirits," as a traditional Indian might do.

But he also knew I'd been threatened for looking into the murder and related issues. He had offered to come down Friday when I'd first told him about it.

We walked briskly across the field. I told him more about the river people. He took it in without comment. I elaborated on why I'd gone into that crawlspace in the first place. Prayed that he'd buy it. But I didn't care a whole lot if he didn't.

"The split floorboard was pushed open," I said. "I thought that odd. I looked into the crawlspace, wanted to see if Dad slipped in. Thought he might be unconscious."

Sonny took this in, not questioning a thing. At least not out loud.

Near my parents' fence I made the 911 call and told almost all. The dispatcher said they'd send someone soon to talk with me about my father, the river people and my entrapment. I didn't mention the little box.

We went through the barbed-wire fence. A breeze came up, taking the swelter out of the day. We fell silent as we walked hand in hand, lost in thought.

What were the river people really up to, I wondered? Where was my father? Did I have to enter that disgusting crawlspace to search for him? A lump of worry rose in my chest and lodged there. I was scared of being charged with interfering with a murder investigation. But scared more that someone had entrapped me with intent to kill.

I looked toward my folks' house and gripped Sonny's hand tighter. I'd better get my story in order for police. Or I'd be trapped again, and this time with no one to save me.

22

An hour later, back at my parents' and freshly bathed and scrubbed, I ran a hand over my still-damp hair. A call from the sheriff almost as soon as we'd hit the kitchen brought the welcome news that they'd found Dad and were bringing him home after a brief physical and mental examination.

I looked over at an also-bathed Sonny, now relaxing with a cup of coffee and outstretched legs at the other end of the leather couch in the living room. He looked preoccupied and plainly tired. His long drive, my rescue, concern about my missing father as well as about his own issues, whatever they were—had taken a toll. He even looked a few pounds thinner than the last time I'd seen him.

The TV was on low. Wild-eyed plaintiffs pleaded their case before some black-robed judge whose thickly mascara'ed gaze often shot skyward, followed by a stern warning. I couldn't help sometimes being mesmerized by such shows. Guilty pleasures.

The scent of lemon-verbena soap still clung to my wrist. Along with subtle notes of skunk that hopefully only I could smell.

Mom, lounging in a red Western chair, one of a pair framing the front window, tapped her fingers on the chair arms and looked outside for the tenth time. Old Heller lay at her feet as if to lend support. His snoring could have wakened the dead.

"Don't know what's taking them so damn long," Mom said, also for the tenth time. "They called to say they were bringing him at least an hour ago."

I felt another stab of worry. Maybe it wasn't him they found. Or maybe he was injured and they took him to the hospital.

But I said nothing. I didn't want to add to her stress. We all knew what happened the last time worry got the best of her. A major stroke. One's parents growing older is not for sissies—to put a new spin on a time-worn adage.

As if on cue the sheriff's unit rolled up, followed by another vehicle. A familiar uniformed figure emerged, went around, helped my father out and escorted him up the porch steps. I rushed toward the door. Mom rose with difficulty and shouted, "Thank the Lord. Come in, come in."

Heller rose, and barked perfunctorily. The handle clicked and the door opened. Sheriff Welles leaned back to let Dad hobble past him. A Search and Rescue unit was parked behind the sheriff's vehicle, but no one got out.

"Dad," I cried, hugging him hard. I felt his heart beating a little too fast. But at least it was beating. I would have died if we had lost him. My Dad. My rock.

Sonny rose from the couch, and Mom reached out to join in my hug of a haggard-looking Dad with dirt stains on his pant legs.

"Gus," she breathed. "You all right? You had us worried to death. Where on earth have you been?" She looked him up and down, and brushed his legs as well as the back of his shirt. He either had fallen, or lay down for a rest.

"Don't know what the fuss is all about," he snorted, swatting away her hands and pulling back "I knew where I was. Looking over the Robertson place. Might've taken a wrong turn, having a looksee up by the highway. Got turned around. But no matter, thanks to this guy."

Dad clapped the sheriff on the shoulder. He got a curt smile for his effort. Then he gamely faced Mom, who peppered him with reprisals.

Sheriff Welles clasped his hands in front and squared his shoulders. He took us all in with his deep-set eyes. He let his gaze linger on mine.

"You OK, Miss Kane?" he said. "After what happened at the cabin? Require any medical attention?"

"No, no, just a few scratches," I said, waving a hand and making sure my robe was secured around me. "Plus, I had a little argument with a skunk."

He drew back his chin and raised his eyebrows.

"Nothing a good bath couldn't cure," I said, then immediately blushed.

Welles reached over to extend a hand to Sonny, who strode forward to give the sheriff a firm, single handshake, Indian style.

"Good to see you again, Chief," Welles said. "To what do we owe the honor?"

"Hey," Sonny said, glancing at me by way of an answer.

They nodded at each other without smiling. Equals. At least, to Sonny.

A shadow flickered across Welles' face. I had no idea of his opinion of tribal police, but I but guessed it was less than positive. Cases with disputed jurisdictions abounded, sometimes with disastrous results. In the Dakota pipeline protests, for example, encounters between feds and state police with tribal law-enforcement quickly shifted from measured talk into verbal and occasionally physical sparring matches, egged on by Native supporters and the goons hired by pipeline officials.

Sonny arranged his frame to emphasize his superior height, if only by an inch or two. He smiled lazily at me before looking back at Welles. Although Sonny's deliberate movement secretly pleased me, I tried not to show it.

"To answer your question as to why I'm here," Sonny said, "Pepper's been having some trouble, as you know. I was due for a road trip anyway."

He watched Welles carefully, almost as if challenging him. Had Sonny sensed the electricity, however minuscule, between the sheriff and me?

"She seems pretty capable to me," Welles countered without blinking. He raised his chin and gave a tight smile that animated deep dimples beside his lips.

I mentally rolled my eyes. Was Welles' attitude as defensive as it sounded? It struck me I might be enjoying this interchange a bit too much. But what woman didn't like to be sparred over, in a figurative sense? No harm, no foul. My heart belonged to Mister Chief.

"Yeah," said Sonny. "She's all that and then some."

The look in Welles' eyes changed abruptly from one of controlled amusement to professional concern. He turned his back to the room, keyed his shoulder mic and spoke a few sentences that included "father" and "family." When he turned back he glanced out the window. A familiar looking blue pickup rolled into view and parked behind the Sheriff and the Search and Rescue unit.

"Detective Frank James, OSP," Welles said to me. "You know him. Lead investigator for the murder. We're just glad you're safe and that we were able to find your father." He touched his hat and walked to the porch while Detective James climbed the steps. They chatted briefly before James' knuckles rapped the door frame.

Mom motioned him inside. Dad shook his hand in greeting.

I lingered sheepishly in my robe, wishing I'd changed into real clothes before this party began. But frankly, I wasn't quite of sound mind or body after Dad's walkabout, my ordeal in the cabin, not to mention the de-skunking. No matter. Wouldn't be the first time police interviewed people in robes, or less. Wouldn't be the last.

"Miss Kane, Sheriff Welles tells me you're okay?" A question from the murder's lead investigator, not a statement.

"Affirmative, Detective James. Got one helluva scare. Thank God my boyfriend decided he needed a road trip and got me out. Sonny Chief, Lakota Tribal Police."

Sonny took a step forward and they shook hands.

The detective looked around the room and then back at me.

"Can we go somewhere to sit and talk about what happened today?" James said, nodding toward the kitchen visible through the archway.

I walked to the kitchen with him and Sonny in my wake.

"Would you like coffee?" said Mom, holding Dad's arm as she stepped forward.

"That would be nice, Mrs. Kane," said James. "Thanks."

After James, Sonny and I were seated around the table, with Mom at the counter and Old Heller warming my feet, I told all that happened leading up to, during and after my imprisonment in the crawlspace.

"That must have been horrible for you," said James, finally setting aside his pen and notepad. He watched Mom drift up with the carafe and pour him steaming mug of coffee. When she offered cream he held up his hand. After a few contemplative sips of java, he let a smile soften his heretofore tight lips. He jotted some-thing on his pad.

"Would you care for a piece of pie?" Mom said. "Fresh baked."

Dad motioned he was going down the hallway. Mom waved him away. James set down his pen and notepad and looked up at her.

"Pie would be nice," James nodded. "Missed lunch."

He sighed, rolled his shoulders and looked back at me. "So why, again, did you return to that cabin? Go into the crawlspace? Help me understand your thinking."

"It was just as I told you," I said, the image of the hidden chest filling my mind. "I was looking for Dad. He could have crawled in there, or fallen in. The broken plank was pushed down. I shined my phone light down there, didn't see him but—"

"I don't need to tell you that place isn't safe on so many levels," James said. His black eyes held a look of concern. "You said you shined your cellphone light in there and didn't see him. Why go in at all?"

My pulse pounded in my temples. My cheeks heated up.

"He might have been unconscious, out of sight," I said, almost truthfully, not mentioning my curiosity about the box. "I was just going down to have a quick look. I did have my gun."

The detective took a deep breath, blew it out slowly and savored another mouthful of coffee. He looked at the pie slice Mom had set before him, as if considering a bite. Instead, he took a glance at me from under lowered brows. I dreaded what was coming. The glance held. I tried not to cave.

"You really should have let—should let—police handle it. Sheriff Welles was notified about your father. And the Patrol is still actively investigating the murder."

"But…"

James raised his hand, palm forward.

"I understand your impatience to find answers to the murder, happening so near to your folks, and the arsons, warning note. Also, your need to find your father. I have a daughter like you. Impatient. Gutsy."

"Do you?" I said, not happy about where this was headed.

"But please, Miss Kane. Don't put yourself and your family at risk. I shouldn't have to tell you obstructing an investigation is a serious crime."

"Yes, you're right."

<u>Good. Appear humble. Toss James a bone.</u>

"So you cannot go over there again. Keep out. Understand? We're handling it. We don't need another dead body."

I bowed my head and closed my eyes. Sonny shifted in his chair next to me. He lay his hand atop my two, clasped tightly on the table.

"Yes," I said again. I pulled one hand out, patted Sonny's, and looked up.

The detective's next question caught me by surprise.

"Were you looking for something there besides your father?"

My breath caught. The room turned shockingly still. Even Mom, who'd been rattling dishes at the sink, was still. Time inched by as I considered my answer.

"Maybe," I said, feeling a weight lift slightly. Should I, would I, tell about the chest? If I did so now, I would have to hand it over, and with it, any clue it held for me? Of course I would turn it over. I planned to. But first I still had to see what was inside.

"Go on, Miss Kane. I appreciate your cooperation. May I call you Pepper?"

"Yes," I said. "I just wanted to find Dad, as I said. And while doing so, I thought I might see something there that I hadn't your crime-scene investigators—"

"Really? Something they might have missed?" James sat back in his chair and shook his head. He tapped his pencil on the table. "What did you think you might find?"

I'd already said I was looking for random, previously unnoticed details. As if unnoticed details were possible, as thorough as the OSP forensics unit would have been.

"Nothing," I said, shutting the door, looking down at my hands, which suddenly seemed extremely large, as if they belonged to someone else. "Just the wall."

"Help me out here, Miss Kane. What exactly do you mean, 'the wall?'"

"The wall ... of my own stupidity, I guess." I gave what I hoped looked like a chastened shrug. "If you don't go too far, how do you know how far you can go?"

He stretched his neck from side to side and looked up at the ceiling. I stole a glance at it, too, and saw a moth flutter in a spider web attached to the light mount. I looked back at James.

"Why me?" he muttered. He gave me what looked like a resigned grin. "I'm sure I don't need to stress the importance of telling the truth. So save us all some grief. Tell us everything. You never know what will move us all closer to solving this." He picked up a fork.

Between taking notes and, during pauses, taking quick bites of pie, the detective asked a few questions of Sonny, and warned me again about staying away from the cabin. He said it was still an extremely active, high-priority case. In other words, butt out. Or face serious legal action.

I'd heard words to that effect before, from Sheriff Jack Henning in my own Jackson County, when I'd investigated who killed a show horse at Brassbottom Barn. And another time after I'd witnessed a fall off Table Rock near Medford.

●

Well, no matter. I took such warnings as par for the course. Which meant I'd probably continue doing my own investigating, but be far more circumspect about it.

23

I got to my afternoon shift at The Horsehouse late again. Sonny had peeled off at the turn to my place in Gold Hill, where he'd tend to chores I'd long postponed. Such as burning branches that had accumulated in my half-wild side yard over winter. And brush-hogging the fence lines. He liked hard physical work, and did it well.

Tulip had been briefed by cellphone while the little chest and I were en route to the store. But once we stood face to face in our home-away-from-home, and I'd told her about my near entombment, she heaved a sigh and took me by the shoulders. Luckily I'd hidden the chest under a newspaper in the back of my crew cab, to be opened in private. If she'd seen it, she'd have skinned me alive for tampering with potential evidence.

"All right," she said in her best ex-schoolmarm tone. She glared down at me. "That does it. You all are officially done going to that property until the dead woman is identified and her murderer is found. Do you understand? D-o-n-e."

"But, Tule, I had to find Dad, and …"

"No ifs, ands or buts. This is nothing to mess with. Not sure we should even try to purchase the place, explore financing, right now."

She glanced away. I may have given her a wounded puppy dog look.

"I guess it was dumb to go into the cabin. Or, at least, the crawlspace. But look, Tule. Let's go ahead with the bank meeting tomorrow. At least we'll have our financial ducks in a row when and if we decide to go ahead."

She glanced round the shop before speaking. Her eyes looked resigned, softer.

"Yeah, okay. What can it hurt? But no more snooping, Missy. Promise?"

I nodded, chastened but not deterred.

After Tulip left I made myself concentrate on selling. It wasn't that hard. Customers trickled in throughout the afternoon, some there to buy a shirt or cowgirl baseball cap, others there for fly spray. It was getting to be that time of year. Flies in the Valley worried horses and their peeps with the persistence of World War II kamikaze pilots. I tucked away several cans of insecticide for my own equines.

Between swipes of the credit-card reader and clangs of the cash-register drawer, I reflected on the horrible events earlier that day. Who had tried to seal me off from investigating the cabin, from living the rest of my life? Likely it was someone who knew nothing of the box, or they would have taken it. Maybe.

Or someone protecting the box.

Every time I was alone for a few minutes and tempted to retrieve the chest and pick its lock, someone came into the store to shop or chat. I couldn't bear not opening that chest immediately. But I'd have to wait for that night at my ranchita, with Sonny by my side.

Shortly before five I took a call from Cleve Robertson. My heart did a flip. I'd forgotten I'd agreed to meet him after work at his parents' old house. He'd be there in an hour.

Filled with fear and questions, because I was pretty sure Cleve might be the one who'd tried to cut short my life that day, I phoned Sonny. I told him I needed to meet the guy, that Tulip hadn't texted me back, and would Sonny go with me. My hands trembled all the while.

"I really don't want to go over there," I said. "This Cleve guy, or his weird grandson, might be involved in our case."

"No need for you to go," Sonny said.

"But I have to talk to him. Tulip and I meet with our banker in the morning, and we have to nail down his price for the place."

"Can do that over the phone."

"I want to see him face to face, feel him out about things, watch for reactions. Stuff you can't get over the phone. And I want you to go with."

Sonny gave a heavy sigh.

"It might be best to let some things go, Pepper. Things that can bring more trouble." His voice lowered, and hardened. "Focus on learning the price. Over the phone."

I pictured Sonny setting his jaw, working his cheek muscles. I was making him mad. In effect, challenging his opinions and expertise. Not a good place to be.

"I can't just have a phone chat. We're talking about the ranch. Our dream. The warnings, the murder, the box, are tied together. I need to see if I can eliminate Cleve."

Silence. Then the sound of something, a fingertip, tapping wood.

"Sonny?"

"*Ho.*"

"I've talked to him by phone already. I need to see the dude in person. He won't do anything if you're with me, and I pretend I know nothing."

"Police would have contacted him about the incident today. If he's the one who locked you under there…"

"Maybe they haven't talked to him, are still gathering evidence, making sure how to approach him. I have to talk to him now."

A low groan on the other end of the line.

"Just if you—if we—go," said Sonny, "best not to think about or picture what happened today. That will show. Still no proof it was him."

"Who else?" I said. "His father? Mother? Son?" I heard my voice grow louder and gain an octave.

Another sigh.

"You also said that realtor friend of yours is too interested in a sale," Sonny offered. "And that contractor you know."

Sonny was trying to calm or distract me. So I had the edge.

"OK," I said. "I'm good now. We'll talk about it later. Pick you up in five."

I drove too fast the short distance home. Hugged Sonny mechanically, then softened it with a kiss. We hopped into Black Beauty, his steel road pony. I fiddled with the radio and AC dials, trying to gather my wits as he drove us to Grants Pass. I usually went there once a week. Now it had morphed into a daily commute.

The sun, low on the hilly horizon, burned my jaw and forearms as I sat rigid on the passenger seat. Seven miles from town, when we passed the city of Rogue River with its single-arch bridge over gleaming water, I reached back to touch the rifles mounted in the truck's rear window. Hopefully we wouldn't need them or the .38 inside my concealed-carry purse.

We'd just keep the conversation casual, a quick, informal meeting so Robertson and I could agree on a price. Real cool. With an army of ants gnawing my gut.

I could barely breathe when we hit Grants Pass Parkway in late rush hour. We soon drove south on Highway 199 which, before I-5 was completed in 1962, a scenic "Gateway" to the Redwoods, Golden Gate Bridge and San Francisco. I'd mostly composed myself by the time we headed further south onto Jerome Prairie Road.

We turned up a short incline and emerged from a small stand of oak and fir at the white cottage. Robertson, a taciturn-looking guy in a plaid shirt and suspenders like his dad wore, stood by a grey pickup with a canopy. His eyebrows did seem conjoined.

Managing a smile and a relaxed posture as I got out of Black Beauty, and making sure Sonny was a step behind, I walked up to extend my hand.

"Pleased to meet you at last," I said as Robertson took my hand in one largish, work-roughened paw. "My friend, Sonny Chief."

Robertson tilted his head to look up at Sonny's unsmiling face. The men shook hands. Pulling away, Robertson shifted his weight and nodded at Sonny's gleaming, chromed-out truck.

"Nice rig," he said curtly. I considered it an attempt to break the cool, rigid atmosphere that had settled over us. He motioned us toward the cottage. As we made our way there, he passed, turned a key in the lock, opened the door and let us in.

I heard him lock the door behind us. I tensed, hearing hammer blows in my ears. Was he locking it on purpose? Or from habit? He seemed the type who routinely expected trouble. I couldn't shake the feeling that I was inches from a killer.

The near-empty living room smelled of dust and disuse. Our footsteps were muffled by dingy, wall-to-wall blue carpet. That would have to go, if Tulip and I ever bought this place and called it home. Hopefully there was hardwood under the rug.

But I liked the airiness of the living room, and the character of the chinked, white-painted fireplace flanked by built-in bookcases with small windows above.

The reality of why we were here bumped those happier thoughts aside.

With the rolling, confident gait of a man used to getting tough jobs done fast—felling trees, overhauling cars and trucks—Robertson strode to the living- and dining-room windows to open and the drapes. The rooms were flooded with fiery late-day light.

Two white-plastic chairs sat in a dining-room corner. Through that window you could just glimpse the barn beyond the back lawn, and, to one side, the lightly wooded slope abutting the river. I caught sparkles of sun-touched water between branches.

Sitting in the nearest chair, I saw Robertson hesitate beside the one opposite.

"Mr. Chief?" he said, nodding at the chair.

"I'll stand," said Sonny, positioning himself partly between Robertson and me.

Robertson thumped down into the chair and patted its arms.

"My folks said to say hello," he wheezed, covering his mouth with a fist while giving a short cough. "They enjoyed meeting you."

Nice opening. Whether genuine, or calculated to appear so.

"They seem like really nice people," I countered. "Too bad the place became too much for them."

"Among other things," he said, frowning, and looking out the window.

I champed at the bit to know what he knew about, or may even been party to, today's incident at the cabin. No way to tell unless I asked. But I I wasn't about to do that. Sonny had warned me to not even picture it. For once I'd have to be patient. I looked up at Sonny. A movement of his jaw showed him to be grinding his teeth.

I focused back on Robertson.

"No more trouble here since that fire?" I ventured.

"Not that I know of," Robertson said matter-of-factly. Not even an eye blink. "All OK at your folks'?"

"Little problem today. My Dad has memory issues at times. He went for a walk, got lost, and we all went out looking for him."

Robertson shifted in his chair, and glanced at a black ashtray on the windowsill.

"Everything turn out OK with him?"

"Sheriff found him out near the highway," I said. "Seemed OK. Think he'd gone to your back acreage and got turned around. As he says, old age ain't for sissies."

"True." He didn't sound concerned with my attempt to feel him out about the day's crises. But his hands rubbed his knees as if they hurt. Then he rolled his neck. Perhaps physical exertions that day had gotten to him. At work? Or at the cabin?

Out of the corner of my eye I saw Sonny move to peer through the window at the barn some hundred feet away.

"Nice barn, there," Sonny said. "Looks old."

"That author guy mighta built it when he put up his cabin," Robertson said.

I saw another opening.

"So, Mr. Robertson," I began. "Someone also said, maybe a neighbor, or former owner, that they thought you might be distantly related to Preston O'Hara? Is that so?"

Robertson huffed, and shook his head.

"Don't we wish," he said.

Was he telling the truth?

"His books still sell well, I understand," I encouraged. "I just bought some online. Couldn't afford signed first editions, though. Those are crazy expensive."

Robertson raised his hand and gave a dismissive wave.

"Pah. So they say."

I briefly reflected on his words, gestures, facial expressions. They seemed stock and genuine on the surface, but carried slightly exaggerated energy. Robertson was either a crafty fox, or an unrefined rustic innocent. Time to get down to business.

"So did you all come up with a price?" I asked.

Now he leaned forward with a grunt. Using his left hand, he pulled a folded paper from his pants pocket. He carefully unfolded the sheet, smoothed it with his left hand and offered it to me. His hands looked strong, with age spots making inroads. Creases on the underside of his fingers looked raw, as if they'd recently scraped something sharp. Protruding nail heads? Splintered wooden planks?

I swallowed and blinked to keep the day's dark memories in check. Forcing a smile, looking into Robertson's blank eyes, I took the paper, trying to keep my hands from shaking. On the paper were photos and a description of the property including a short sentence about the "famous Hollywood writer" who'd lived there.

"Historic Significance," blared a headline over the sentence telling of Preston O'Hara's better life and times.

Black bullet-marks pointed out property features: Three hundred feet of prime riverfront. Full water rights. Perfect growing soil. Secluded, yet close to town. Fenced, barn, good well. Live in/rent out "while building your dream home." No superlative had been ignored. Had Gloria Allende helped him craft this? It did look professionally made.

Large, boldfaced figures at sheet's bottom read, "A steal at $1.4 Million."

My heart sank into my boots. So that was his asking price. He probably would take a bit more than a mill, but even that would stretch Tulip's and my budget if we decided to buy. And if we were approved for a loan covering the amount above our half-million down payment,. it would leave nothing for improvements.

I looked back at Robertson. His eyes were dark ciphers, the black eyebrows dotted with a few silver hairs, immobile.

"That's a little high, Mr. Robertson," I began. "A real-estate friend of mine placed it quite a bit below a million. Working from comps."

"Yes, I met with Mrs. Allende this morning," he said. "I don't know where she gets the figures she gave you. I've done research, too. This is the price. Low, ask me."

I took a deep breath and let it out slowly, not taking my eyes off him. He'd already talked with Allende. Or she had talked to him. That didn't set my heels clicking together with joy. Was she really my friend? Was he being straight? Time to get tough.

"I agree you have a wonderful place," I said. "My friend and I have admired it for a long time. That dogleg of land on the river is a great feature. But maybe you are a little too attached, don't really want to let it go? There was trouble selling it in the past, due to the alleged curse and all. Now the murder..." I let my voice trail off, for emphasis.

I noticed that breathing had become harder for me. My little soliloquy seemed to have sucked the air from the room.

Sonny shifted his bulk by the window, his back now turned to it. He clasped his fists in front of his hips like a proper officer of the law. A not-so-subtle but effective posture calculated to announce authority.

"Does raise questions," Sonny said almost inaudibly.

Robertson scowled up at him.

"Hey, you with law enforcement or something?" he said. "Get the feeling I'm being cross-examined here.

It's a fair price." The energy in the room definitely had changed, and not in a good way.

"Tribal police," Sonny said. "Not my jurisdiction. I'm here as a friend."

A weak smile cracked Robertson's lips. He looked back at me.

"I get it. Backup. Well, don't worry. Not trying to beat you up because you're a woman." He gave Sonny a wink. Sonny's face was a granite carving.

Where did that statement come from? I hadn't even considered that angle.

Up to now the encounter with Robertson had been fairly neutral. Cordial, businesslike. Even ho-hum. Early on I'd glommed onto words or behaviors that might indicate depravity or guilt. Now, even with the "weaker woman" thing, I really had no clear idea of his being a killer or entomber. But did have a clear picture of his being greedy.

That's when another idea seeped into my mind.

"Mr. Robertson," I said, "I understand you love this place. Don't really want to sell it because you want to buy it yourself but can't afford it. Is that why it's priced so high? So it won't sell or that your feelings will be soothed if for some reason it must?"

His faced shaded into red. He coughed into a fist, folded his arms and leaned back in his chair. With jerky gestures, he smoothed the thighs of his pants.

"Mind if I smoke?" Before we could answer, he reached into his shirt pocket to draw out a pack of unfiltered cigarettes. He shook one out, took it between his teeth, and picked a match from a book in the pack's liner. Striking the match with a thumbnail, he touched the flare to the cigarette. After three short puffs to ensure it was lit, he inhaled a lungful of smoke and blew it toward my face.

I held his gaze, refusing to blink or cough. But my cheeks burned.

"You know, Mr. Robertson," I said, reaching for a possible safety cord. "That'll stunt your growth."

He glared. Obviously in no joking mood.

"Hey, I'm not here to argue," Robertson finally said. "That's my price. Do you want to make an offer, or not?"

I blinked against the smoke now, but plowed ahead.

"We're meeting with our banker tomorrow," I said. "We or our representative will bring you a formal offer afterward. But let's say it will be around six-fifty. With a contingency. To wit, the murder's being solved."

He rolled the cigarette to the other side of his lips and lowered his brows.

"Huh. You must think me an idiot. Know what? I think you're trying to take advantage of an elderly couple who needs the money."

I kept my eyelids open as I stared him down.

"That will be our offer, or close to it. This place won't be an easy sell with what's gone on here, now and for years. The curse, the frequent turnover."

Robertson threw back his head and guffawed. He laughed so hard the skinny legs of the chair wobbled dangerously. He tipped sideways, then squared up the chair while letting his laughter drop to a head-shaking chuckle.

"You were a former reporter, right?" he said, eyes twinkling.

"Of course. But I don't see what—"

"You have an excellent imagination."

I saw where this was going. Downhill. As in, fast.

"I am just trying to reach a reasonable price for both of us," I said. "That's all."

Sonny stepped forward, hands still clasped. I'd almost forgotten he was there.

"It seems someone has poked a hornet's nest," he said, raising an eyebrow and looking at each of us in turn. "The man named his price, Pepper."

Oooh, that stung. Or was Sonny trying to appear neutral, even on Robertson's side, to defuse the situation, perhaps keep me from incurring further unpleasantness? Knowing Sonny, I decided it was the latter.

And I took the hint.

"All right, Mr. Robertson," I said. "Let me discuss this with my business partner. As I say, we're talking to a lender. But our best offer will be well below a million."

Robertson fixed me with a gaze tinged with amusement. He drew on his cigarette, blew the smoke to one side and continued staring.

I fought off the urge to squirm. Didn't know what to make of that look. But it felt as if he were trying to breach my soul.

24

Sonny and I phone-ordered a pizza to pick up in Gold Hill before we got on the freeway and headed for my house. As he drove, we briefly went over our meeting with Robertson, agreeing that his price was ridiculous, but coming up with no clear ideas about his guilt or innocence regarding my cabin entombment.

When we subsided into friendly silence, I turned the radio on to our favorite country station and thought of the locked chest waiting for us at home. I could hardly stand not knowing what was in it. Soon we would find out.

Sure, it was wrong to have it. But we had it. I'd wanted to open it at once, at my folks' or at our store. But I didn't want my parents or anyone else involved and we would need to use extra care and special tools. It looked as if rough handling might destroy it. Plus we wanted to leave it looking virtually untouched, to police.

Having spied the chest, Mom merely shook her head and muttered, "I hope you know what the hell you're doing." I had not replied. I had no good answer, anyway.

Now, as Sonny and I wound among the hills, we encountered little traffic other than semi tractor-trailers and late commuters. I considered asking what was happening with Sonny and his ex-wife in Seattle. And about the "health issue" he'd mentioned. In the end I decided another time would be better. We had enough on our plate.

"So," I said, choosing a neutral topic. "How did you manage to snag time off from working the new pipeline protests?" He was only a part-time tribal policeman, on call as needed, which suited this commitment-phobic man just fine. However keeping peace at the pipeline had kept him busy much of the year.

"My uncle, Arvol Chief, knows I need to spend time with *oyate,* my relatives. He still has big pull." Sonny slid his gaze sideways to give me a teasing look.

I angled him a look of my own, as if to say, "So, I'm family?"

His gaze returned to the road. He gunned Black Beauty and pulled out, passing a Queen Mary-sized RV towing a compact Lexus. Road warriors of a different kind.

Back in the so-called slow lane, in which most drivers were doing at least ten miles over the 65 mph limit, Sonny relaxed against the seat back.

"There're always those working against my uncle," said Sonny, ignoring my "family" question. "These guys would rather have the pull. They say the elders don't keep up with changing times."

"Probably meaning he's not militant enough," I said. "What do you think?"

Sonny kept his fingers wrapped over the wheel, but tapped his thumbs against it. He shook his thick braid back over his right shoulder. I loved that hair. In fact, l was the one who'd persuaded him to grow it long, traditional style. Before we met he'd kept it short, identifying then more with dominant-society law enforcement.

"My uncle is truly traditional," he said. "That's how he says we keep our identity as a people. Our chiefs and spiritual leaders from the Old Days many times advocated peaceful solutions. Called wisdom."

"Which, in a way, led to their downfall," I said. "Calming the war chiefs and younger followers hot to defend their land and people, to kill or drive off invaders."

"Appeasement sometimes added to our losses," Sonny conceded. He paused. "That, and invention of the Gatling gun."

"Bows and arrows are no match for what amounted to machine guns," I said.

For a moment the only sound in the cab was of Willie Nelson crooning "Blue Eyes Crying in the Rain." Sonny and I had danced to that, a time or two.

"Anyhow," Sonny sighed. "He and another uncle on the council fix it so I can do peacekeeping as needed, where needed. Even for our people off the rez."

"And spend time with your loved ones," I said.

He reached over and took my left hand into his. As he held it, the warmth and strength of his palm and fingers momentarily dispelled any doubt I held about us.

A few miles before we rolled off the freeway and into Gold Hill, I gave Mom a call to make sure Dad was okay after his walkabout.

"Say anything more about his day?" I put her on speaker.

"Told me everywhere he'd gone," she said. "The river, the cabin, the highway. Saw a weird party at the river. He didn't let them see him."

"Weird in what way Mom?"

"He didn't elaborate. Something about seeing bloody animal flesh and a sword."

"Yikes. I talked to those weirdos, and got the hell away. I should research cults in the area. Can I talk to Dad?"

"He hit the hay. Claims he knew where he was all the time. Couldn't understand the fuss. But I told him in no uncertain terms he can't poke his nose into that property any more. Same goes for you, baby girl."

"I know." I looked over at Sonny. He turned his head toward me and arched an eyebrow. "I promise, Mom. I won't go there again." At least until we figure out what's happening, I told myself.

After we disconnected, I called Tulip, told her about my talk with Robertson, and reminded her of our upcoming meeting with our banker.

"I've got my financial info ready to go," she said. "Give my love to Sonny."

He leaned over and spoke to my cell phone.

"Hey, Tulip."

"Hey, Crazy Horse. "Glad you've come down to keep an eye on our girl. Hope you brought a straitjacket."

I winced at her racial epithet. Sonny ignored it. As a distant relative of the great Lakota warrior, he thought the appellation amusing. I was not so taken with it.

"What kind of thing is that to say," I snapped. "See ya tomorrow."

Sonny and I detoured into Gold Hill for the pizza, and then drove the last mile in pizza-perfume heaven.

At home Sonny and I poured ourselves root beer, grabbed a roll of paper towels, and tore open the card-board takeout box to attack our galaxy-sized Italian pie. Aptly named "Kitchen Sink" because it had everything you'd ever want in a pizza and then some. It featured a double crust filled with mozzarella and a top smothered with three meats, green and red sweet-peppers, black ol-ives, onions, mushrooms and sun-dried tomatoes. Plus a dusting of Parmesan. I added hot-pepper flakes for good measure.

The Boston terriers circled and whined like wolves.

"Sorry, guys," I said through a mouthful. "People food. Don't want you stinking up the house all night."

Sonny set crumbs of pizza to one edge on his plate. I followed suit, again admiring such traditional

Lakota practices, similar to those of other spiritual traditions. Observing them filled me with a bittersweet joy as I pictured aunts, uncles, grandparents—even a sweet, funny female cousin about my age, who'd died far too young.

As we ate, the ancient, leather-covered wood chest sat between us on the dining table. I could hardly take my eyes off it. All in good time, I thought. All in good time. Sonny and I talked of the murder investigation, mine and the police's, about the arson fires, the river revelers, the pot grow back of the cabin, and our persons of interest – including the entire Robertson family – and even budding realtor, Gloria Allende. I did mention my having called the bookshop in Seattle, having asked Chili to look up O'Hara's family connections, and talking with Sam Jenkins about the mystery woman seen at the Farm Co-op last week.

"All good stuff," he nodded.

Chewing my last pizza bite, I rose to fill white-china bowls with lime sherbet that had been in my freezer since dinosaurs roamed the earth. Sitting back down, I took dainty spoonfuls, savoring every bite as I looked forward to but also dreaded opening the little chest. Who knew what Pandora's folly we'd find inside?

"Bottom line," I said, "we've got to establish the identity of the victim. She will lead us to her killer." I stroked the rough, domed lid of the chest. "Time to open this, see what treasure it contains."

Sonny nodded, and stared at the object as if it held a malevolent spirit.

"I trust you have a plan to get the box to police," he said. Somewhat sternly, I thought. His broad, often unreadable face looked troubled, his brows drawn together.

"Working on it," I said, feeling surprising warmth in the old, hard leather under my palm. Then I withdrew my hand as if the chest were a hot stove. "I'll think of a way."

Sonny let his eyes drift to one side as if he saw or heard something I did not. What I did hear was the chiming of the gilded clock striking nine. The time could or could not be nine, considering the unreliability of that cantankerous object.

"We need to purify and bless this box," he said. "You have sage and tobacco?"

If the dead woman's spirit still were attached to the box, assuming it had been hers, or if a murderer's spirit were, either way we'd want to respect and appease it. No use inviting further anger or reprisal. I still didn't know if I believed in the curse thing. But I wasn't about to take chances. Bless the doggone box, we would.

An abalone half-shell containing shredded sage from the rez and covered with a brown-tipped white eagle feather sat on a shelf above the chiming clock. Some time ago Sonny had given me the feather—though non-Indians legally were not supposed to own eagle feathers—and taught me how to "smudge" or cleanse myself and objects of evil.

I fetched the shell, found a box of long wooden matches and sat back down.

"Washte." He nodded. "Good. You do it."

Cradling the shell and feather in my left hand, I struck a match on the side of the matchbox and coaxed a small flame in the sage. I dropped the match into the leaves, took the feather by its stem in my right hand and rapidly fanned the hot spot to produce a cloud of fragrant grey smoke. I fanned it around myself, Sonny and the little box.

"Tunkashila, Grandfather, cleanse and bless this box, its contents and whoever it belonged to ... or belongs to," I said. "Protect us, guide us. We only mean to help."

"_Aho,_" said Sonny, scooping smoke toward his chest and guiding it over his head and shoulders. He finished with, "_Pilamaya, Tunkashila._ Thank you."

"_Mitakuye oyasin,_" I finished, fanning smoke around myself and the box, and then setting down the shell and feather "All my relatives."

The sage continued smoldering, but now we focused on the box.

"Got plastic gloves that might fit my hand?" he said. "So far only your fingerprints are on this. And those of whoever last touched it."

"No," I said. "How about plastic wrap?"

"Might leave residue. But at least it won't leave my fingerprints."

I rose, tore a sheet of plastic wrap off a roll by the refrigerator, and lay it on the table for him to wrap around his box-steadying hand.

Sonny fished in his jeans-pocket for a folding knife. As he opened it, I admired its elk-antler casing and its profusion of tiny tools, from a screwdriver and corkscrew to several sizes of knife. The casing bore his initials in abalone of a warrior on a horse. It represented sensitivity, strength and courage. We would need plenty of the last, as he worked carefully to open the lock without scratching it.

"Could use some WD-40," he said, now prodding the small brass screws holding the lock to the top front of the box.

"I have some in the utility room," I said.

He held out one hand, palm forward.

"Joking," he said, looking at me with concern. "You need to relax, honey. It's best not to contaminate this more than we already have. If we're going to turn it in."

I felt my shoulders lower. I stroked his bicep. When he glanced up, I gave him my warmest smile.

He went back to the task. With the care of a surgeon, he worked one tiny screw loose, then a second, and finally a third. The fourth screw was missing, and I noticed a tiny crack in the leather there. Did it mean anything other than this box was ancient, and had probably been opened and closed, possibly impatiently?

"Let me finish doing it," I said.

Sonny sat back as I reached forward. Scarcely breathing, I grasped the box and pulled it toward the table edge. I worked one of my fingernails under the lock mount, picked at it, but had no luck. Sonny handed me his knife with the tiny screwdriver extended. I took it and gently edged the tip under the metal, and then jimmied upward, feeling a give. When the lock was off, I placed trembling hands on either side of the domed lid and raised it until it was fully open.

My heart sank. The box, lined with faded, stained fabric in a cowboy-and-Indian print popular in the 1950s, was empty.

I felt as empty.

"I don't believe it," I said. "It has to have contained something important or it would not have been stashed there. Money, papers, something."

Sonny nodded while staring at the box.

"Huh," was all he said. "Maybe whoever trapped you in the crawl space was there before you, and took something out."

"But why didn't they take the whole box, if it contained something valuable, or incriminating?" I looked at him and then again studied the box.

The domed lid. The lining bulged below it.

"Look at that," I said, lightly stroking the fabric.

The lining was silky, frayed, water-spotted. Held with glue around its edges to the wooden box interior. The glue made the edges of the lining feel brittle and crackly to my touch. There were lines and daubs of what looked like new glue poking out here and there beneath the hemmed edges. I pushed my knuckles against the bulge. It rustled, crackled and resisted depressing. Clearly some folded papers lay beneath.

As I rotated the box onto its back side so the lid's inside faced me, a chill filled the dining room. I shivered.

"Do you feel that, Sonny?" I whispered, looking over his shoulder to see if we'd left the sliding door open a crack when we let out the dogs. We had not.

He merely nodded. I had no idea what that meant, but he didn't seem bothered.

I then slowly chipped away at the lining's upper edge until I could peel it open. There was a ripping whisper when I pulled the dry fabric toward me. I tugged some more, so the cavity was fully exposed. A handful of brittle, folded papers, some of which were old news clippings, tumbled out. They lay half in, half out of, the box.

25

I reached my right hand toward the papers. Sonny's left hand grasped it before I touched them.

"Do you have thin cotton gloves?" he said.

I understood his implication. My fingerprints were on the box. Even if we wiped it, traces might remain. Plus the box covering was fragile enough. It might not survive a serious wiping. But my fingerprints weren't on the papers. If we put them back beneath the lid lining, reglued them and replaced the lock, no one need ever know I'd seen them.

My man was a step ahead, looking out for both our interests. One more thing to love about the guy.

"I think I do have some gloves like that," I said. I hurried to the sock-and-glove drawer in my bedroom chest, rustled around and found a pair of silky black numbers I'd bought for some formal occasion. Maybe a divorce party. They were crumpled in the drawer's rear left corner.

"Sexy," Sonny said when I brought them back to him. He fingered the embroidered fleur-de-lys on the top of the gloves. "How come you never wore these for me? With your other lacies?"

A smile teased the corners of his lips. He was trying to lighten up the situation, put me at ease. Maybe I didn't want to be lightened up right then. Instead, I put on the gloves, sat back down in front and fanned through the papers. First was a folded, dogeared print of O'Hara's official author photo seen on many dust jackets, a small leather notebook and yellowed clippings. Then what looked like a folded letter, his cream-colored birth certificate with ornate edges, and O'Hara's obituary—how had that gotten in there?

"Wow," I breathed. Wow didn't begin to cover it.

Looked like we'd hit the jackpot. My dangerous digging and probing might be about to pay off. Clippings, the diary, a letter, some them placed there recently. Hopefully it'd help us solve the death on the Applegate. And the attempted murder of me. I was sure my crawlspace entrapment was not meant merely as a warning. I'd already been warned by the "chicken" note.

I picked my reading glasses off a stack of magazines. Quickly scanning pages, eager to learn what the box and their presence implied, I caught a headline here, a sentence there. The clippings were notices of O'Hara's Hollywood blacklisting and abandonment by lawyers. A mention of his alleged homosexuality. Plus, a copy of his New York Times profile obituary from 1953.

I held the items up one by one for Sonny to see.

"Huh," he muttered, noncommittally.

"That's bizarre," I said. "Everything else is old. But O'Hara's obit was put here by someone after his death, and this other obit is brand new." The latter was from the West River Eagle, a newspaper in Eagle Butte, South Dakota, for Marguerite Louise Shopbell, aged 87, dead after a "lengthy illness." The small head-shot showed the woman still handsome in her 60s, a broad smile not extending to her sad eyes.

Sonny peered at it and nodded.

"My home-town paper."

"Really?"

"We had Shopbells on the rez when I was a kid. Many moved away. Some were adopted by whites thinking to give them a 'better' life.' Don't get me started."

"Thank the Indian Child Welfare Act for putting the brakes on those adoptions," I said. "Supposed to keep Indian kids with relatives, in touch with their culture."

"But then some kids returned to the rez were abused by relatives that were supposed to help them," Sonny said. "And some adopted out didn't feel welcome in white *or* Indian society. Lost their way, or got into drugs, prostitution. Told you not to get me started."

"When, again, Sonny, was the ICWA passed?"

"1978. Still controversial."

I turned back to the grandma's obituary, puzzled as to why it was in the chest.

"A daughter, Lela, predeceased Mrs. Shopbell," I said. "The grandma's survivors include her grandchildren, Sidney and Melissa. No last names."

Sonny looked into the near distance. "Somebody's *unci,* grandma. Wonder how her obit came to be in this box."

"Maybe a somebody who knew of or was close to O'Hara?" I said. "But put here by a somebody who knew about the legacy. Maybe even about the murder."

We fell silent for a moment. The dogs snored softly under the table.

"Wait," I said, struck by another thought. "Sidney was O'Hara's real first name. He used his middle name of Preston as his first name after he went to Hollywood."

"Mmmm." Sonny sipped coffee and leaned over to read the obit.

I slid it closer to him.

"I can't believe it," I said, my gaze frozen to the page. "It says the grandchildren are 'of Oregon and Washington.' Doesn't name cities. But this means whoever kept or found the chest, possibly a grandchild, might live not far away."

"And had a reason to keep it all hidden," Sonny said.

The import of all this left me temporarily speechless. My head buzzed, my tongue felt glued to the roof of my mouth. I gulped down coffee without tasting it.

"We're looking at the cache of a killer, or someone who knows a killer," I said. "A very incriminating cache." I searched through the other papers. "That woman. She was too old to be one of the Mrs. Shopbell's grandchildren. But may have known the grandchildren, known about the letter, gone to find the stash and been killed for it."

"Very good." Sonny tapped his fingers on the tabletop.

Next I tackled the notebook the size of a thin cigarette pack. It was an old diary with the initials "S.P.O." printed in silver on a dry, curled, black-leather cover.

"No way," I breathed. "O'Hara's diary."

Sonny reached out to run his thumb over the embossed initials.

"This calls for *pejuta sapa,*" he said, rising. "Black medicine." He rustled about making coffee while, heart racing, I let out the dogs, polished my glasses with a napkin, and sat back down at the table.

The diary pages were all filled with the tiniest printing I had ever seen, in fine-tipped pencil. In fact when I opened the book a miniature pencil slid out, hit the tabletop and clicked to the floor. I picked it up in my gloved hands and turned it over. A bridge pencil. My parents used one like it to keep score playing bridge eons ago.

I squinted to read the diary's writing. The entries were brief, dated, cryptic. Tiny sketches of rifles, hunting knives and animals accompanied them. Two-dimensional sketches that resembled Indian ledger drawings.

One page read, "May 1: Shot bull elk. Field dressed. Hardest thing ever." No year was given. The entry was so cryptic, different than O'Hara's formal writing. Almost as if penned by someone else.

I skimmed the other pages—there were a hundred. I'd read them in detail later. But several stood out:

"July 14: Bastille Day. Oh la la."

"November 20: Cold as hell. River partly froze. Ice fishing!"

I zeroed in on one page in particular.

"January 2: Son born. Sickly. Hard time aborning. Mom not well."

I caught my breath. The diary lined up with what I knew of O'Hara. Hunter, fisher, father of a son doomed to early death and a wife who died not long after.

Setting down the diary, I unfolded a letter written on lined notebook paper. At the top was a ledger-style sketch of a war-bonneted warrior astride a running horse and brandishing an eagle staff, done in colored pencil. The horse had a lightning bolt on a shoulder.

"Whoa," I said, eyes racing through the words. "A letter from that grandma to her grandkids. A grandma who knew she was dying. Marguerite Shopbell. My God!"

Sonny sat next to me with our steaming coffees. Mine smelled like he'd added mint creamer to my coveted Kona. But I had no appetite for it just then.

When I began to read the letter aloud, my pulse pounded in my temples. Written in red pencil and shaky block printing, the letter said:

"Dear *Takojas*, my grandchildren, Melissa and Sidney. (You each get the same letter.) You don't know me. But I feel strongly our connection. The *wasichu,* whites, took my baby Lela—your *ina,* mother—in 1954 gave her and you a better life than I could. But you are still my blood *takojas,* and I will always love you."

Sonny took my hand. It felt cold and numb even in the pretty glove. I blinked back a stinging tear before again reading aloud.

"The Wheelers did not want us ever to contact them. They had an attorney in Seattle notify me in 1994, when Lela died giving birth to you. They would raise you, wanting no further contact. But now, as I am dying, I had a lawyer send this letter to them to forward to you. My last wish is for you, my beloved *takojas,* to claim your grampa's legacy if you still can.'"

Sonny sat still as a statue. His jaw moved slightly. Then he nodded.

"Aho."

I studied his face, discerning resignation but also a suggestion of anger.

"So there was a kind of family," I whispered. "And there *is* a legacy."

He took a slow sip of coffee.

"Or there was."

I read on, my voice quaking but my mind empowered by this message virtually from the grave.

"'Very long time ago I had a letter from your *tunkashila,* or grandfather—Preston O'Hara, who wrote books—before he died. We had a fire and lost it when Lela, our love child, was born. But in it he told of a precious ring, his diary and an unpublished book hidden at his cabin in Oregon.'"

I became aware of the ticking of the old gilt-trimmed clock in the living-room hutch. It sounded like soldiers marching. Had it always been this noisy?

Swallowing hard, I continued reading aloud.

"'A relative went to look for the treasures years ago but found nothing. I wrote the Wheelers but my letters came back unopened. I had a lawyer send this so hopefully it will find you. Your grampa's last wish was for his seed to know their heritage, never know want. I fear his treasures are long gone. But if by some miracle they are still around, my last wish is for you to find them.'"

I gulped as I read aloud her final words:

"'Your loving *unci,* grandmother, Marguerite Louise Shopbell.'"

Setting down the letter, I stroked Sonny's forearm. We looked at each other one long moment before speaking.

"So," I said, "This grandma had an illegitimate daughter, Lela, by O'Hara in1954. The girl was adopted by whites, and bore two children. Those kids would be in their mid-twenties now."

Sonny drank more coffee, cradling the mug with both hands as if it were a baby bird. It was a big mug but his hands made it look small. He'd chosen the red-and-black one from Seattle Mystery Bookshop. The one like the mug I'd photographed near the dead woman. The woman who "looked Indian."

I shoved my chair back and looked out the glass slider. Night had taken hold. The moon was just past full. An owl glided across the pale orb.

"Sonny," I whispered. "The dead woman I found must have known of the *takojas,* and this letter. Maybe she put it there."

"Could be." He pressed his lips together.

I sat dazed. What finds, this journal, that letter. And the promise of a ring and an unpublished O'Hara manuscript, possibly still hidden in the cabin. Or under it.

"I wonder if the ring and manuscript originally were put in this chest by O'Hara," I said. "There was room for them in the body of the box."

"Maybe," he said. "And whoever found the box and put in the new papers, hid the other things somewhere else. To be on the safe side."

"If that grandma was right," I said, "and the O'Hara legacy still exists, it could be worth a hundred thousand dollars or more, to the right publisher or collector. Worth killing for. And if it's all gone, at least this chest and O'Hara's diary will be worth a pretty penny.."

"No doubt," Sonny agreed. "Question is, why someone kept the chest and papers hidden in the cabin."

"I have my own theories, Sonny. But I'd like to hear yours first."

He flattened one hand and rubbed it on the table.

"It was dangerous if the chest and papers were to come to light now," he said.

I took a few more swigs of coffee and tapped the papers with my gloved finger.

"You're saying if the dead woman or her killer found this stuff, they felt it had to stay hidden or be moved around because it would be incriminating?"

Sonny raised his head to look at me. His expression was still undecipherable. I wondered what he was feeling, if he were still ruminating on the adoption issue and its multi-generation fallout.

"Ho."

"They could've pawned the ring," I said. "But maybe it had O'Hara's initials."

"He or she might have had another reason to keep them hidden," Sonny said.

"Like they were afraid someone else close to them would see them, and planned to come back after all this fuss died down."

Sonny gave me a languid smile. "I like how you think, lady. We make a good team." A shadow crossed his eyes, but then vanished as he raised my hand to his lips and kissed it.

"We do," I said, happy for the distraction. "Make a good team." I let that sink in. "Now we have some answers, but new questions."

The mood had shifted. I felt my blood pressure returning to semi-normal. I riffled through the remaining papers and picked up the O'Hara diary again. It thrilled me to hold something he had held. I felt I knew him so well now. The image of his face filled my mind. I couldn't get over those sad yet haunting hopeful eyes of his. He'd wanted his things to benefit not his own white relatives, which suggested none remained or at least none he cared about, but his Indian offspring.

Collectors of O'Hara memorabilia—would crawl over broken glass to get their hands on these items from the chest. Especially the diary. Probably pay thousands for such souvenirs.

What other treasures lay among the last papers here?

The copy of the birth certificate, of course. I picked it up. The document was dated 1912 and generated in Orange County, California, identifying both parents and their child as male, Caucasian. Sidney Preston O'Hara.

"So, I said, "he grew up, read and wrote wild-West and modern adventure novels, married an Indian. Produced a half-breed with her."

"He would've been criticized back then for marrying an Indian," Sonny said.

An idea came to me, making me sit up straighter.

The heroine of "Rogue Princess" was named Marguerite. A nod to his last love.

"I remember telling you I had an aunt who was sterilized," Sonny was saying. "They did that so we wouldn't breed."

"A woman friend in Seattle," I said, "told me at the white school they washed her mouth with soap and beat her if she spoke her native tongue."

Sonny stared into the living room. A worry line deepened between his brows.

"Bad times," he said.

I put my arm around him and stroked his back. He gave me a wan smile.

"No wonder some Indian kids suffer from low self-esteem and bullying," I said. "Good you broke the cycle winning athletic scholarships, getting a higher education."

I leaned over and kissed his neck, savoring its silken warmth and faint smell of musk tinged with cinnamon. His pulse beat strong and steady against my lips.

"I was one of the lucky ones," he said. "Wish it were over, or mostly."

"Mostly?"

"We got back our ways like sundance, sweat lodge, *yuwipi* healing ceremony. But there are still streets and mascots with demeaning Indian names."

"Luckily that's changing."

Sonny gave me a coffee-scented kiss. "Then there's people like you."

I blushed, and cleared my throat.

We spent another half hour going over the papers. We skimmed the clips about the Hollywood blacklisting era, which O'Hara had dubbed "The Hollywood Horrors." Finally we agreed to call it a night.

As I got ready for bed and Sonny washed up in the guest bathroom, I thought of how another big day lay ahead. An early ride at Brassbottom Barn—still had to prepare for the Seattle show. Meet with our banker. But mainly see if the Mystery Bookshop or Chili had turned up anything useful to an investigation that now seemed close to being solved.

I also had to return the little chest and its contents. But when? Where? And not indemnify myself or my partner in the process.

Sonny and I turned in around eleven, steamrollered by the day. But before dropping off to sleep, I grabbed a remote and switched on the wall TV. I had to see if we or our case were in the news.

He had just rolled onto his side and slid one arm under my neck. When I settled against it, he placed his other hand softly on my cheek and combed my hair with his fingers. The Bostons snored peacefully at the foot of the mattress.

"Mmmm," I murmured, my eyes on the TV screen where the female anchor was introducing the day's big local stories. "Hold on, honey. I want to hear this."

Sonny fluffed his pillow next to mine but kept his fingers in my hair while we focused on the screen.

The lead story showed senators fomenting about federal plans to shrink the size of Siskiyou National Monument to our east, to allow more logging and agricultural activity that would bolster local economies. A few other stories followed.

Finally, there it was: A whole two minutes given to my cabin entombment. The anchor tossed the segment to Shane Chapelle of the slicked hair and station-logo jacket, collar turned chicly up.

"That's right, Andrea. I'm here with Cleve Robertson, whose family owns the Grants Pass farm where a woman's body was found Friday."

The shot, recorded that afternoon, showed the men standing by the Robertson cottage where Sonny and I had met Cleve earlier. Robertson had done the interview before he and I had talked, yet he had said nothing about it.

"We hear there was a fire set in your trash cans, like someone did at your neighbors'," said the newsman. "And today police say the woman who found the body had an accident at the cabin, got trapped inside. Can you tell us what you know?"

Robertson folded his arms and screwed up his features, as if he were in pain.

"Alls I know is, my folks and I are rattled," he said. "We heard the lady was looking for her father. She fell through rotten floorboards and got somehow trapped."

"Police say she's all right, though," Chapelle said, "and that a friend found her. What does this mean for your plans to sell the property? Is the cabin curse still active?"

Robertson unfolded his arms and stared into the camera.

"Not sure," he said. "Maybe for people who believe in curses."

Chapelle tossed the segment back to the studio anchor.

Sonny and I looked at each other.

"Did you get any texts or voicemails?" he asked.

I reached to my right for the cell phone on the nightstand. Then I remembered I'd deleted a dozen media texts when I'd called in our order for pizza. I still had to time for rude reporters.

"Deleted them." I looked at Sonny, now up on one elbow, and shrugged. "I don't have time or inclination to answer them."

He nodded, his face ghostly in the TV's glare.

"Maybe best to talk to the major media types," he said. "Help them get the story straight. No need to give the newshounds more to chew on. Speculation's a bad deal."

"I know," I sighed. "It's ugly now, and bound to get even uglier. We just have to figure out who the dead woman was, and who wanted her dead. And quick."

"And photo the papers, get the box to law enforcement," Sonny said. He drew his forefinger down my arm. "Knew it was wrong. Shouldn't have gone along with it."

"Yet you did, Sonny. Why?" I stared at his profile.

A pause. He slowly turned his face toward mine. I felt warmth emanating from his eyes. I sure felt warm where his hand lay on my bicep.

"Maybe because I like you," he said. "And trust you know what you're doing."

I pushed up on one elbow and met his gaze.

"Like me, Sonny? LIKE me?"

"Love you," he corrected, pulling me atop him. He curled his fingers in the curls around my face and positioned my head so my lips were inches from his. His breath drifted like a blessing breeze over my face.

The question of his ex-wife and any legal issues in Seattle hovered between us for a moment. Then it vanished. I held out the remote and clicked off the TV.

We kissed tentatively, suddenly shy. Like schoolkids. Then something changed. Our kisses became more urgent, reaching deeply, prodding tenderly, then dancing over each other's face and neck.

I took his head in my hands. With trembling fingers I unwound the ribbon from his braid and heard his long, sweet-smelling hair cascade across the pillow. I buried my face in the black lushness. He stroked my hips and rained kisses on my shoulder. I took his earlobe between my teeth and gently sucked it.

He moaned softly.

I rose on one elbow and lifted his face toward my chest. I gasped as he tongued first one nipple, then the other. Warm tingling sensations suffused my core.

Ten minutes ago I thought we were too tired for this. Now it was the only thing I wanted. Our panting and rocking by turns excited and soothed me.

But it was too much for the dogs. They snorted, and leaped off the bed for calmer sleeping quarters.

Meanwhile our journey to release turned steep. It slowed as it approached the top. I hung there a moment, not breathing. Then lightning flashed behind my eyelids.

I gasped, seeing the world, my whole life, as if from a very high place. The view from there was breathtaking.

26

"Sonny?" I said, sitting up to a bright room and an empty space beside me.

No answer. I looked at my phone. Six-thirty. He must be down at the barn feeding Bob and Lucy. The dogs must be with him.

Man, had I zonked out. But now I felt great. I hoped Sonny did, too. We'd grab a java and a fast breakfast, then go our separate ways for the day. I had to slam in a ride on Choc at Brassbottom, meet Tulip at the bank and work my afternoon shift.

My heart sped up when I thought about last night's stunning discoveries in the little chest. The obituaries, the diary, letter from the grandma to the *takojas*. At least one of them seemed to have found it. Now it sat innocently enough on the dining table.

Somewhere in this day I had to figure out a way to get the chest and its contents to the police without having my butt thrown in jail for messing with a criminal investigation. As I saw it, I was helping. Too bad the law didn't see it that way.

I had to ensure that neither Sonny nor my folks were implicated regarding the chest. That might be tricky. I'd come up with something. Maybe.

As a professional courtesy, I sent TV reporter Shane Chapelle a text.

"Accidentally deleted your texts. Can answer questions, but keep them short."

That should do it.

I turned on the radio and did a little line dance while making coffee and frying bacon and eggs. I needed a hearty breakfast. Yesterday had zapped every ounce of my energy—though that last late workout had been pure joy.

Sonny and the Bostons blew through the back door. They brought the scent of alfalfa and pine bedding-pellets with them. I put out food bowls for the dogs and bacon and eggs with nuked freezer-biscuits for Sonny and me.

"You're up," he said, smiling large. "Smells good in here."

I gave him a hug and a kiss, lingering against him a moment. Aahhh. Fresh air, clean man, with just a hint of warm horse. Nothing finer.

"Mmmm, another Sonny day," I said. "My favorite kind."

He stroked my hair and searched my eyes.

"How you feeling today, pretty lady? What're your plans?"

I sat down across from him, avoiding looking at the chest. I'd photographed the contents, tucked them back inside and re-glued the lining before going to bed.

"Find a way to get that thing back where it belongs and somehow tip off police without incriminating myself," I said. "Although I doubt that's possible. This will blow the case wide open."

"Remember, I know nothing about it."

"Right." I sighed, starting to eat. In a moment my ladylike portion was gone. I went for a second helping. I noticed Sonny had put a spirit offering at the edge of his plate, and was eating more slowly than usual. Probably worried about the chest.

He looked up.

"You're going with Tulip to the bank today?" he said.

"Yes, but first I have to ride Choc. Then make calls about our mystery, and work at The Horsehouse. How about you?"

"Gonna see if cousin Deputy Boo's heard anything over the Jackson County Sheriff's grapevine about our little problem in Josephine County."

"Yeah," I said. "Like, how come that reporter Shane Chapelle is so tight with Welles. And like, if any OSP types drop that guy crumbs about crime stories."

Sonny nodded and picked up his coffee mug. He stared into the black liquid as if admiring his reflection, which I wouldn't have blamed him for doing. He wasn't using the SMB mug, but a red, black, white and yellow Circle-of-Life mug from Pendleton. He emptied it, and tucked the last bit of bacon into his mouth.

"Really good bacon."

"You only ate one piece," I said.

"Trying to eat more healthy." He patted his stomach, flat as ever, if not flatter.

"Always good," I said. "So what was your take on our meeting with Cleve yesterday? I still can't believe his asking price on the place."

"Seemed a little tense, reactive," Sonny said.

"Robertson seemed like he was trying to hide something."

"Or control his temper. Which looks to be on a short fuse."

"Your personal, or your law enforcement opinion, Sonny?"

"There's a difference?" He stood and took his dishes to the sink.

"Well, I'm definitely packing," I said.

"As you should."

Hearing some romantic ballad playing on the radio, I drifted in for a hug. Sonny pulled me close and danced us into a little Texas Two-Step. When he stopped, he wound his fingers through my curls and gave them a playful yank.

"Ouch," I said, tugging on his re-tied braid.

"We should go dancing some night," he said.

"Doubletree Lounge has a bluegrass-pop band this weekend."

"Sounds good." As we stood apart, he slid his gaze out the sliding door.

"What dog is that?" he said.

Through the glass I saw Alice, the Days' border collie, running nose to ground in my pasture. That set the horses running and bucking. Why wouldn't Alice stay home?

"Neighbor dog," I said. "Rescue. They're not real happy with her."

"Needs more training. Understanding. Love."

"Especially love," I said, tracing his lips with my forefinger. He nibbled it.

The living-room clock rudely chimed. I hadn't wanted our moment to end. We had really begun to connect these past twenty-four hours, as if we'd never been apart. Had it only been twenty-four hours?

"I'd better get a move on," Sonny said. "I'll call my kids and cousins in Seattle. See if anyone knows a Melissa Shopbell. I mean, Wheeler. Or whatever O'Hara's granddaughter uses for a last name now."

"Great idea," I said. "You have a lot of connections in that community."

"Finding her or her brother is key to our case," he said. "Good instinct, getting that box. Take care getting it back."

When we kissed goodbye, I flashed on my failure to ask about his ex-wife and their situation in Seattle. But them, I reflected. Sonny was with me, wasn't he? He'd come right down when he knew I was in trouble.

Maybe I didn't need to know the details now. All I needed to know, he'd told me by his being here, by acting as he always did. We could talk later. I truly did need to explore our future. Talk about whether our relationship would always be this way, and if that would be enough.

For now he was mine. I would figure out a way to make that "now" stretch into the future. Working together as we were today, relying on each other for practical as well as emotional support, only strengthened the foundation.

As I watched him drive off in Black Beauty and re-secure my gates, I wanted to smack myself. I'd forgotten to show him the amazing O'Hara poster I'd tucked into a closet. Although upon seeing its Indian-ghost image, he mightn't have been amused.

OK. Maybe it was wrong of me to buy it. The piece was expensive, something we couldn't afford at the moment. But it still struck me as some kind of windfall, message, or lucky charm. To me, at least, it seemed to send off positive vibes.

Jill Benetton called it "creepy." Was I so in love with it, that I failed to see that?

I'd have to give interpretation more thought. Just not right now.

* * *

Brassbottom Barn was a hive of activity. Though it was only 8:30, this was the weekend before the Tuesday we'd haul up to the Northwest Open Western Show, or NOWS. This was the critical time to nail practices and take final coaching from the Grandeens. Winning a thousand-dollar jackpot or two would help pay Tulip's and my show expenses and add bucks to our guest-ranch war chest.

I marched down the aisle, dodging buddies taking horses to the arena. Enduring curious stares and brisk greetings, I bumped into Freddie Uffenpinscher leading his charcoal-grey horse.

"Hey, Freddie," I said. "What brings you out from your salon on a busy Friday? By the way I need my nails touched up tomorrow or Monday."

He grimaced, and froze in mid-stride. Poppin jumped, clipping my right toe.

"What's wrong, Freddie?" I hopped on one foot until the pain subsided.

"Working through back pain. Crunch week before a big show always messes with me." He stretched his torso this way and that.

"I'm sorry."

"I need my Carlos. He's a horse chiropractor, in addition to being assistant trainer for Royce and Rogers in Texas. Nice little sideline. Ouch!"

Little Stewie stopped as he and Jeanne Allende led their clopping horses toward us, bound for the outdoor arena. We were to have a mock Western Pleasure-horse class, but with Freddie riding English-hunter style.

"My mom fixes backs in her physical therapy job," said the boy, beaming. He reached up to straighten his horse's forelock that, to me, looked perfectly straight. "You want me to see if she's still in the parking lot, Freddie?"

"That's OK, Stewie. Donna's going to show me how to fake a good ride with a bad back."

"Donna's the expert," I said. "Remember her crushed disc from a horse fall? She had to wear a support belt, but also found a way to ride that masked the pain."

"Drugs are always an option," Freddie laughed. He patted his horse, which was tacked up English. "So how's your murder investigation going?"

I glanced down at Stewie, whose bright eyes narrowed.

"Decided to leave it up to police," I lied for all our benefit. "How's your report on Preston O'Hara going, Stewie?"

"OK," he said, worry lines connecting his forehead freckles. "Teacher says I need more color."

"What do you mean?"

"Like how he felt losing his wife and kid," he said. "Take poetic ... license? Something like that. And write some sentences how he would write them."

Oh, my, I thought. Impressive. So the boy was learning about poetic license.

"Those are excellent ideas," I said.

"Yeah. So did you find out who that dead lady was?"

I looked at Freddie. He widened his eyes. Jeanne leaned in. This conversation had taken an unwelcome turn.

"Not yet, Stewie. I don't think anyone knows." Suddenly I felt saucy, wanting to end this chat and get on with our riding practice. "Do you?"

"Jeanne and I have some good ideas." He raised his chin as if daring me to ask.

"Well," I said, "don't keep me in suspenders. Let's hear them." I winked at Jeanne, who smiled and shrugged.

"We think she knew about the legacy that old newspaper story talked about. Money or something. And came to find it. Then got whacked by somebody else who knew about it." He looked at Jeanne, who nodded and looked away.

I felt gut punched. Had Stewie, aided by savvy Jeanne, read my thinking of late? Either that, or he was wise beyond his years. Maybe ten going on thirty?

"How would she or they know about it, Stewie? If that's what happened, which no one knows." I waited expectantly. This had to be good. I had a box and a letter.

Little Stewie had only his young imagination augmented by Jeanne's opinions.

"I was hoping you'd tell me. TV last night said you went to the cabin and got trapped in the crawlspace. On purpose? By the killer? Jeanne says so. My paper's due Monday, by the way."

With that, Stewie motioned to Jeanne. They led their horses away.

Jeanne whispered as she passed, "Sorry. We were just kicking around ideas."

Freddie whooshed out a breath and watched them go outside.

"Holy crap," he said, mustache quivering. "Those kids are scary. Remind me not to try to keep any secrets from them."

Freddie's dramatic ways bespoke an early fling on the off-Broadway stage. Now he made do with an occasional foray into community theater. But then, horse shows also were a kind of theater. With lights, costumes, action, and a stage made of sand.

"Tell me about it," I said. "I just wish the media would not get so involved in the case. They're making it a big deal, making me into a celebrity. And not the kind I want to be."

"Know what you mean. I have friends in the media. Pretty tight with a few folks at KMFD. Andrea Carmichael, Shane Chapelle, Adam—"

"You know Chapelle?" I said. "He's the worst. Got some 'in' with Sheriff Welles in Josephine County. What an idiot. Shane's been on my case like the plague."

"Well, word is, Shane's hot to get on a national network news show," Freddie said. "Needs to score big stories. Wife's dead against it. She wears the pants. Which probably is why they're getting a divorce. Although Shane's been known to go both ways."

"TMI, Freddie," I said, looking down the empty aisle. I had to go saddle Choc.

"I just wish Chapelle would make it snappy, and get the hell out of town," I said. "What an a-hole."

"Nah, Shane's cool," Freddie said. "He just knows big stories make big names. Not to mention serious money. Can't blame the guy. I'd probably do the same, myself."

27

I opened my stall door, haltered Choc and led him into the aisle. There I stopped and stroked his head. His tall, elegant body was just so beautiful, it took me away from my troubles. I stared lovingly at his rich light mahogany coat with purple glints, sleek as a seal's. How had I gotten so lucky, as to have an equine partner such as he?

Providence, I thought. I'd been through tough times, and would be again. But Creator had blessed me with this beautiful boy, to enjoy and win with. And win I did.

After a quick grooming, I joined the other riders in the outdoor arena, where a clouded sun beamed down.

"Pepper," called Donna from the center of the ring, where she, togged in a hot pink top and cap with charcoal jeans and boots, coached riders.

"Yo," I said, opening and closing the gate, Choc following me at reins' length.

"Just in time for a Western pleasure run-through," she said. Her head swiveled to take in the dozen horse-and-rider pairs including Tulip, jogging around on the rail. "Finish your warmups. Five minutes, everyone."

Shoot. That wasn't enough time to get our minds and muscles ready to go. It took ten or fifteen minutes, at the very least. I shouldn't have taken time to chat with Freddie and Stewie. I'd better suck it up, focus on steps directly ahead, rather than obsess about the murder and related problems.

I toed the stirrup of my roughout Western saddle and swung up. I legged Choc into the center, pulled his head to one side and jogged small circles. Then we went the other way, varying the size of our circles. I often changed the arc of his neck and body by pressing my calves to different spots on his ribs to push his hip or shoulder in or out.

About halfway through my warmup, I saw Tulip pivoting her horse at the far end of the space. She was a vision in head-to-toe chambray, with sparkles. We waved, and then went back to work. I burned to tell her about the chest and its contents. And about Sonny. And Cleve. She must not have heard about my cabin fright yesterday.

Maybe Tommy Lee was back in town early. She and I would talk later.

I halted Choc and backed lightly, squeezing harder with my legs and releasing to cue him to stop. We also did 360s—circles in place with hind legs anchored in one spot. Finally, I sat back, pressed my calf into his side and sent him into a slow, rolling lope. A big rocking chair come to life.

"OK, everyone," Donna shouted. "Ride to an open spot along the rail and halt, left shoulder to the inside. Remember. Every moment you're in the arena or near it, you are showing. You never know when a judge is watching."

I urged Choc to an open spot on the white-vinyl rail and squeezed him to a halt. He bowed his head. The weight of the reins alone, and a light fingering of them, directed his head left or right, up or down. The trick in showing was not to let a judge see you working the reins or the spur. Or at least not working them too hard. You had to make everything look easy. Like a perfect ballet pas de deux.

My chest tightened, my heart-rate increased. This was Donna's intent: Make it feel as if it were a real show class that you'd spent hundreds of hours and thousands of dollars preparing for.

"Now, wa-alk," said Donna, sounding like a proper horse-show announcer. "Walk your horses, please."

I took a steadying breath, lifted my chin and squared my shoulders. I thought "walk." This activated my body enough for Choc to feel a cue coming. Then I lifted the reins and gently "flagged" his sides with my lower legs, signaling him to walk forward.

We circled the arena, with Donna calling out instructions and corrections, while mourning doves called to mates in trees outside the arena.

"Victoria, loosen your reins," she shouted. "But not too much." She addressed our barn vixen, the one who considered horses more reliable than men. I smiled.

"Freddie, you're not practicing hunter-under-saddle. Look as if you're riding to hounds. Walk Poppin out with a long stride, and encourage him to 'hunt' the bit. Make his nose reach to where slack leaves the reins. Tuck your butt, ride on your pelvic bones and lift your ribs to lessen pressure on your lower back."

Soon we were all jogging smoothly. Damp spots wetted my underarms and back. Why was making it look easy such doggone hard work?

"Stewie, don't let his head drop too low," Donna shouted. "And get out in the open where the judge can get a good look at you."

Stewie had been riding next to the rail, half-hidden by Jeanne and her horse jogging closer to the center.

"Tulip, don't pick at the reins. Hold your hand steady over his neck."

When it came time to lope, we were as loose as noodles and mentally ready. I pressed my right heel behind Choc's cinch and rocked my hips. Choc responded by rounding up and flowing forward into the perfect Western three-beat lope.

The "draped" split reins swung rhythmically, in perfect cadence, a pretty exclamation point to this toughest of Western Pleasure gaits. They call it the "money gait" because few horses and riders execute it to perfection. It's what wins you the jackpots.

After an hour the lesson was over. We'd done well, and I had momentarily forgotten about the murder, Sonny, the little chest. Now it all came stampeding back to me. Tension ratcheted up my spine. But at least the lesson was over, and had been a success.

"Well done, everyone," Donna exclaimed. "I think you're ready for Seattle."

Everyone rode out of the arena and back toward the barn. I took a little detour to the trails around the farm's pens and pastures. A twenty-minute relaxation ride would help put everything in perspective, and let reminders from our practice sink in.

I swept my gaze around the valley, letting it linger on twin Table Rock mesas looming long and black from farmlands to the south. I imagined how Tulip and I would create trails on our guest ranch. I might even take Choc or Bob there for a planning ride after we returned from Seattle. I could just see guests taking an evening trot across the fields, wading in the river, stopping at the cabin for s'mores and ghost stories.

The way to this dream faced many challenges and roadblocks—many to be handled today. I'd been threatened. My family and I were still at risk. But somehow I needed to make it all go away. This dream of ours absolutely must come true.

Tulip rode up beside me and Choc as we circled back to the barn.

"Better light a fire under it, girl," she said. "Our bank meeting is in a half hour."

* * *

Traffic was a brick going into Medford that late on a Friday morning. I found myself cursing as I drove Tulip and myself into the downtown area, where rigs like my dually fought for space among smaller pickups and snappy compacts. But the drive offered me a chance to hear about her boyfriend's coming back to see her a day early.

And to tell Tulip about my amazing past twenty-four hours, including Sonny's rescuing me from under the cabin, and our meeting with Cleve. She couldn't believe the asking price for the place. But she was sure he'd drop it.

I didn't tell her about the chest hidden under a newspaper in the extended cab's footwell. The fewer who knew, the better. I could tell her after I delivered the goods.

Hearing of my other adventures, she sat, mouth open, eyes staring.

"You could have been killed," she exclaimed.

"Thought I would be."

"Damn good thing Sonny showed. Maybe O'Hara's ghost had a hand." She angled me a look.

"Like the ghost in the poster. Although that was an Indian ghost."

"But O'Hara lived and thought Indian."

"True." I thought not only of his lifestyle and books, his wife and their child, but also of his affair with Marguerite Shopbell, their illegitimate daughter, and the *takojas*. I wished I could tell Tulip more, but was not sure I was ready. The chest had to be returned safely, first.

It took an eternity to find a parking space downtown. Even those at the bank were full. At last a spot appeared on the next one-way street, two blocks away.

We were late to our appointment. We explained to our banker we'd had to clean up from horsing around, and change into town clothes in the barn lounge. And then, there was that traffic.

Kendra Willis, an attractive brunette in a navy pantsuit and white blouse, smiled warmly as she ushered us into her small but well organized office. She brought us coffee, pulled out our chairs and went through the preliminaries easily enough. She scanned our financial records, consulted her computer monitor, jotted notes, asked the usual questions about debt-to-income ratio, though she must have known it by heart from our previous dealings with her regarding the tack store.

"I'll check with our underwriters," she finally said, steepling her hands and sitting back in her plush leather chair. "And there will be an appraisal of the property and a title search. But, barring unforeseen circumstances, I think you'll be qualified for a five hundred thousand purchase-and-improvement loan to add to the five hundred-thousand down payment you already have."

I nodded, feeling my heartbeat quicken.

"So," I said, "that means we would have another hundred-fifty thousand above the five what we already have, for a purchase price of up to six hundred fifty thousand, leaving us three-fifty for improvements."

"That's right."

Tulip looked at me. She shifted in her chair, and not only because of her too-tight white slacks, but probably also because of the reality of the financial limb we were going out on. I felt squeezed, myself. The purchase price likely would be higher, the needed improvements more costly. But it was what it was.

We thanked Kendra, left her with our paperwork and hurried out into the hall.

"I hope it's going to be enough," I whispered as we walked toward glass doors leading outside. "We have to talk Cleve down, and also try to qualify for more money."

"It'll be OK, Pep. Maybe we can bring in some silent partners. Tommy Lee. Bet he'd kick in something. The Allendes. Isn't Gloria's husband a high-dollar lawyer? Owns some posh inn and spa in Ashland?"

I spun around to face Tulip.

"Little late to think of that now," I said. "But, actually, those are damn good ideas."

"Not gonna lie," she said, pushing open the glass doors and letting in a wall of noon city heat. "I'm scared as hell, too, now we're doing this. Feels like we're rushing toward a cliff. Like Thelma and Louise in their convertible."

"I'm scared, too, Tule. It's a huge step, a life-changer. But ready or not, we're off and running. Let's just picture that convertible as a flying car."

28

I turned Red Ryder 's AC to flash freeze when we climbed back into Red Ryder to return from Medford to Brassbottom Barn where Tulip had left Peggy Sue, her vintage pink pickup.

On the way we rehashed our bank appointment, pretty certain we would qualify for a mortgage loan big enough to buy and develop the ranch as we envisioned. Then I heard more about her friend Tommy Lee Jaymes' visit the previous night. Probably more than I wanted to know. I never shared quite as much about Sonny and me. But I zipped my lip and listened to Tulip's torrid tale.

"And you know what?" she said. "I might just take TLJ up on his offer to go on the road with him for tribute acting gigs. Lose weight, dye my hair to match Sarandon's."

"Or wear a wig," I said. "Your mop's been dyed enough for one lifetime."

Before we got back to the barn I told her about Stewie and Jeanne's theories about the dead woman, why she was in the cabin and why she'd died.

Tulip's mouth fell open. She flapped her salon-enhanced lashes.

"I declare," she gasped. "What do y'all think of his theory?"

"I'd say it's pretty near the target."

"Think so? Any particular reason?"

"Just a hunch."

We'd reached the barn. I unlocked the passenger door. As she slid out of Red Ryder and headed for Peggy Sue, I called after her.

"Hey, maybe you and Tommy Lee can go dancing with Sonny and me this weekend at the Doubletree."

She hopped into her pickup and gave me a thumb up.

When I came through The Horsehouse back door, I saw Karen Mikulski flipping through Western catalogs at the counter. She'd filled in for Tulip that morning. I smelled coffee brewing, heard country tunes playing and saw a Jack Russell puppy romping between racks. The dog barked and ran up, his stubby tail waggling stiffly.

I fondled his ears. He snuffled my pant legs. I couldn't wait to don comfortable jeans for my afternoon work shift.

"New kid on the block?" I asked Karen.

She stood, smiled and scooped him into her arms.

"Meet the Reverend," she said. "Rev, for short."

"Pretty cute. Bringing him when you house sit for me next week?"

"If you don't mind." She kissed the dog's head and set him down.

"Not if he's crate-trained and housebroken," I said. I'm sure my dogs would love a puppy to play with."

After Karen left, I found a lemonade, a dried-out "everything" bagel and a bit of cream cheese in the store fridge, and sat down to enjoy them sat at the counter. Lucky there were no customers. I was desperate to call Sonny and my folks with the good news from the bank, and follow up on my calls to Chili and the Seattle Mystery Bookshop.

Easy things first. I called Sonny. He had wrapped up lunch in Medford with his cousin. He was glad to hear about our encouraging meeting at the bank. But he'd learned nothing new from Boo about the murder investigation in Josephine County.

Mom was at Freddie's Manes 'n Tales salon in Grants Pass, being primped and entertained by Freddie himself. Dad was at a doctor appointment. Something about the new meds for his memory lapses. They hadn't yet given them an official diagnosis. She'd pick him up in an hour.

Next I called SMB. As usual, J.T. answered. He sounded distracted.

"Seattle Mystery Bookshop, J.T., hold on … J.T."

"Hi, J.T. This is Pepper Kane. Calling back to see if you'd remembered, or one of your staff knew anything, about the woman I called about Tuesday?"

Silence, followed by the sound of papers shuffling.

"Lauren," he said, sounding as if he were holding the phone away from him. "Can you take this?" Then back to me. "Hang on. Someone's coming."

"Hello, Lauren speaking," said a low, silken voice.

"Hi, Lauren, this is Pepper Kane, a former customer. I used to write—"

"I know who you are. How can I help you?"

"I'm in Grants Pass, trying to learn if one of your people recently worked with a middle-aged, Indian-looking female customer who might have been interested in books by Preston O'Hara? Bought one of your mugs? It's important."

"That's so weird," she said. "Because someone else from down there called with the same question. Police. What's the story?"

My cheeks heated up. I told her as quickly as possible about the woman I found in the cabin, how I'd gone there as a potential buyer for the property, and that I'd noticed details about the scene including her age, apparel, overweight appearance and the mug.

"Wow, that's more than they'd tell me," she said. "What a shock for you. But why are you looking into it? Isn't that their job?"

I locked up, seeking a decent response but finding none. Drumming my fingertips on the counter, I decided on the truth.

"I am a person of interest," I said "The place is next to my folks', so we are all at risk, and want answers. Plus, it's my nature. Did you know such a woman? I understand she had a Celtic tattoo on one arm and was missing a front tooth."

I dropped my shoulders, took a sip of lemonade, and waited.

"Oh, dear," Lauren said. "Well, I actually did interact with a woman like that."

I pressed the phone harder to my ear and scooted forward in the chair, as if doing so would let me hear her answer sooner.

"I don't remember a tattoo or a missing tooth. But she did want to know about O'Hara. Mostly his books and their value."

"What day?"

"I think a little before Memorial Day weekend. Maybe the Tuesday."

Closing my eyes, I blew out the breath I'd been holding.

"OK. Did she buy anything?"

I heard a clatter and a curse in the background. Books, falling? There was a pause before Lauren spoke again.

"Didn't buy anything," Lauren said. "But after she left, we saw a mug was missing. That happens sometimes. Or a book will disappear. As you know, in Pioneer

Square we get some street people, mostly wanting to come in out of the rain."

Now we were getting somewhere. Maybe.

"So you think she was homeless," I said.

"Possibly," she said. "She looked like she'd worn those clothes awhile."

"Did she give a name?"

"Not that any of us recalls. I told the police all this already."

"But she was just as I described?"

"Yes. Wait. Did you say she was in her late forties or early fifties?"

"Correct."

"That's odd," said Lauren. "At the time I thought she was older because of how hard she looked. But now I remember thinking how her voice and her sad, dark eyes reminded me of a girl's. She might've been in her twenties, though all else squares up."

"Kind of odd someone that young, and sounding undereducated, would know about Preston O'Hara."

"That does seem odd, Lauren. A lot of younger people don't read books these days, or at least not literary Westerns or old adventuring tales. But I can't get over that you now think she was in her twenties: The dead woman was twice that. "

This changed everything. We were talking about two different people, but with similar clothes, hair, height, weight. I thought of the *takojas* mentioned by the dying grandma, Marguerite Shopbell. The grandma who had two blood-*takojas* raised by a white couple. *Takojas* who'd be in their twenties.

The woman in the cabin could have been a friend of the granddaughter. An imposter. Maybe one who had seen or discussed a certain important letter.

My cheeks burned with excitement. After jotting notes on my talk with Lauren, I called my daughter, hoping she'd found useful intel via her Internet ancestry and name search. Or hack. Whatever.

Pride swelled in my chest as Chili answered in a tone that hinted of success.

"How weird, Mom," she said. "I was just going to call you. You won't believe what came back from our little, um, project."

"Try me, Chills."

"OK. That Marguerite Shopbell person? She was the sister of Preston O'Hara's first wife, Rose, who died in 1948 after losing her son a year earlier."

"Have that."

"Marguerite had a girl fathered by O'Hara in 1954. On Standing Rock rez. A Lela Shopbell. Adopted out to whites named Wheeler. Didn't O'Hara die in 1953? "

"Believe it or not, Chills, I have that, too."

"Really?"

I ran my fingertips up and down the frayed side seam of my jeans, and swiveled around in the captain's chair at the Horsehouse counter. I looked out the front window and saw someone sitting in a fancy, low-slung silver car by the curb. It looked to be a man, talking on a cell phone, but unidentifiable because of lightly tinted windows.

"Quick," I said. "I may have a customer about to come in. A well-heeled one, judging from the car."

"So this Lela Shopbell died at age 40 in an alcohol treatment facility after having twins. Custody went to Lela's adoptive parents. A Clancy and Jane Wheeler, Caucasians, Seattle. Actually, Bellevue. West side of I-405."

"Hmm, the money side," I muttered. "What I need is their contact info."

"I delayed calling you until I had all that, Mom. They moved a few times. He worked for Boeing. A high-level executive."

The man in the car outside had stopped talking on his phone. His head, seen in shadowed profile, rotated from side to side as if he were scoping out the neighborhood, an enclave of modest shanties and once-proud Victorian homes. There was an orange flare near the steering wheel. He'd lit a cigarette.

I got a bad feeling in my gut. This was no customer.

"Chili," I said. "I need their info. Now!"

She recited the couple's latest address and phone number. I marveled that they still had a land line with a vintage prefix. But, then, they were older, if they'd adopted children in the 1950s. Long-held habits didn't die gladly.

"What are their adopted grandchildren's full names? What is their other info?"

"Jees, Mom, slow down. OK. Melissa Marguerite Wheeler and Sidney O'Hara Wheeler. I saw both kids when they turned 21 changed their surnames to Shopbell. Like their mom's original surname. Little weird."

"It happens sometimes."

I was expecting something like that. Marguerite Shopbell's letter had hinted that Lela and the *takojas* were estranged from their adoptive parents and grandparents.

"You did good, Chills. No. You did great. I'm all over this. See you in Seattle."

I called Sonny to tell him the news. He was in Grants Pass, at my parents', after chatting with Sheriff Welles. I could hardly hear him for hammering in the background.

"What's going on?" I shouted.

"Oh, that's just your boyfriend, Jesse Banks," he said. "We're in the arena. He opened a wall to fix a sparking outlet."

"What? Even if Jesse Banks were the last man on Earth—"

"You at the store, Pepper? Taken the chest back yet?"

"Listen, Sonny I just talked with Seattle Mystery Bookshop, and Chili. I think we have the info we need to begin to solve the murder." I ran through my findings.

"Haven't had time to call Uncle about Shopbells on the rez. Will do. Then I might run back up to Seattle. See if I can find this Melissa. Tend to other business."

"I'm contacting the adoptive parents, or grand-parents, Sonny. But I need to hear if you found out any-thing from local law enforcement peeps."

Sonny waited until Jesse's hammering changed to prying-wood sounds.

"Welles told me you have something in your pos-session that could implicate you in the murder. I played dumb."

I smacked the counter with my palm. A Horsehouse-logo pen jumped, rolled over the edge and hit the floor.

"No. How would they know that, Sonny?" I shook my hand in a fruitless attempt to drive out the pain, and stooped to retrieve the pen.

"No idea," he said, sounding calm but a tad irked. "Where is the box now?"

"Out in my truck."

"But maybe partly in view." His words were clipped, challenging.

I bristled at the implication that I'd been careless. And stupid to have taken the chest in the first place, even though he'd gone along with it. Reluctantly, I had to ad-mit.

"It's covered it with newspaper. I was going to drop it somewhere at the Robertsons' after my shift. Hadn't quite worked that out yet. Been a little busy."

"Welles says they're looking into cult activity on the Applegate. Thinks there's something to that theory on a curse at the cabin. Cleve's grandson hooked up with a group that sacrifices animals."

I sat up straighter in the captain's chair.

"Whoa. I knew those river people were evil. Have you talked to Cleve?"

"Will if I find time."

"Good. Well, take care, Sonny. Love you."

"You, too. Later."

When we disconnected, I punched the number Chili had given me for Jane and Clancy Wheeler of Bellevue. Waiting for someone or voice mail to pick up, I let my gaze slide to the front window. The silver Italian job was gone.

But when I closed up the shop at five, I found a silver Post-It note on Red Ryder's windshield: "You have something of mine. Leave it on the Robertson porch, say nothing and there will be no more trouble."

29

I drove in silence at a gutsy 80 mph, keeping pace with I-5 rush-hour traffic toward Grants Pass. My palms and underarms were soaked, despite the AC blowing out a snowless blizzard. As I went over and over the case, how I'd handled or mishandled it, my fingers tapped out a Morse-code SOS on the steering wheel.

Who the hell besides Sonny and me knew about the box I'd found in the cabin? The old crackled box, re-locked, that now sat—still covered by newspaper—in the passenger footwell of my dually? I'd moved it from the back for fast access.

If I knew the answer to who else knew about the box, I probably had my killer. So to speak. I was still in danger, and plenty of it.

And what if the killer had been tailing me, or otherwise keeping track of me? Maybe even sitting outside my house or shop? I flashed on the silver car outside The Horsehouse this afternoon. The shadowy figure inside. It prodded a notion inside my agitated mind. But I was unable to pinpoint the memory or what it meant.

I turned on the radio and tried to get into the '70s country tunes. But today Mr. Jennings et al were unable to calm or distract me. I turned the radio off.

The Wheelers had neither answered my call nor responded to my voice mail. I looked down at my phone. Should I call again? Was it even the right number? Maybe I could persuade Chili to drive over to the east side of Lake Washington, which ran the whole 30-mile eastern side of Seattle, to pay them a visit.

I was almost through Grants Pass, headed south-west on Highway 199 to Jerome Prairie. But I still had no plan. I would get rid of the chest. I knew that much. After all, I had photos of all the papers and the diary pages in my phone and laptop files. I had even printed out the letter and stashed it in my manila folder on the case. And I'd left Tulip a message telling her what I was doing, if only sketchily. She didn't need to know everything just yet.

Another call to Sonny went to voicemail. I was getting a lot of that lately. Was he still at my parents'?

I was scared to death to have to go onto the Robertson property alone. Again. That windshield note meant someone knew what I had to do, where I had to go.

If I didn't take the box back soon, I would be dogged and threatened until I did. The owner or discoverer of the chest wasn't taking "no" for an answer. He might even go back on his promise of "no more trouble." In fact, the more I thought about it, the more I was sure he would take it to extremes, and punish me.

I decided to stall while figuring out my best course. Maybe I wouldn't even take back the chest to the Robertson place. Just call or go straight to police. 'Fess up, plead temporary insanity, face the consequences. I'd been in similar jams before and always emerged relatively unscathed.

But down deep, I knew I wouldn't take that route. I was in this deep. I might as well go all the way. Besides. Confessing to mistakes or frailties was not in my DNA.

The Farm Co-op came into view ahead on the left. I waited through the light, then circled the store and drove into the lot. My mouth was as dry as a dust mouse and my brain needed a blood-sugar boost. I'd buy water and a vanilla ice-cream Drumstick.

The Co-op was fairly empty of customers. Sam Jenkins tried to catch my eye as I got my brightly wrapped, waffle-cone treat from the freezer by the cash registers. He waited with a grin behind the checkout counter.

"Heard they're getting close to solving the case," he said amiably. "Should be a relief for you and your folks."

"How'd the heck did you hear that?" I said, showing him my Co-op card and sliding my debit card into the chip-reading gizmo. The one that could round up your $1.99 purchase to $2.00, with the extra penny going to 4-H and FFA programs.

"Walt Walters, your folks' neighbor?" Jenkins said. "Came in for wild birdseed. Said he'd seen something on the noon news. Sheriff Welles saying OSP tentatively ID'd the woman who has a record in Seattle. Maybe that ol' gal I saw in here last week."

"Really. He or the news say how they found out?"

"Nope. Just gave a name. Selena. Serena. Something like that."

Selena. Lauren at the bookshop had mentioned a younger woman dressed like the woman in the cabin. I'd guessed that younger one was Melissa, one of the *takojas*. The dead woman was twice her age, yet resembled her in features and dress. That suggested she was an imposter or another interloper. One who knew about the O'Hara legacy, and got axed for her it. But by whom? Someone known, or a stranger?

* * *

The sun baked my arms and threatened to make short work of the frozen Drumstick as I sat in my truck outside the Co-op and frantically tackled the sweet. I was one lick ahead of the sweet, creamy droplets and chopped peanuts sliding down the sugary cone toward my fingers. The wrapper didn't catch them all, and soon my lap and hand were overtaken by a tiny avalanche of ice cream, nuts and hard chocolate.

Of course that's exactly when my cell phone erupted with Waylon's rockin' vocals and guitar riffs. I propped the remainder of the Drumstick in the console cupholder, napkinned my hands, and answered. The caller ID showed a Bellevue prefix.

"Joyce Wheeler returning your call?" said a pebbly voice.

My heart skipped a beat.

"So glad to hear from you, Mrs. Wheeler. Do you remember me from my picture and byline in the Seattle newspaper?"

As a reporter, I used that gambit to win trust in a hurry with a phone-interview subject. It worked 99 percent of the time. People felt they knew you, said things they'd tell a friend. Or at least a trusted acquaintance.

"Oh, yes. Pepper Kane. You were on the front page a lot. Haven't seen your byline lately."

"I moved back to my hometown of Grants Pass, Oregon."

"Lovely down there. So what can I help you with? Are you freelancing ? Hopefully a story on Bellevue Arts Museum's fabulous new acquisition?"

"Something a bit more personal, I'm afraid."

She didn't need to know I was not working on a story.

"Oh, dear. Is it what police contacted me about today? About our granddaughter, Melissa? They wanted to know if I had information on a ... friend ... of hers that was killed down your way."

A friend or "known associate" of Melissa's. An older female who may have dressed like Melissa. Bingo. I pressed on, eager to learn more.

"I am, er, am helping with the investigation, Mrs. Wheeler. What did police say about Melissa or this friend?"

"Was I in contact with either one. Did I know if Missy had been in trouble, since she was a known associate of this friend. Selena. Sorry I didn't return your call sooner, by the way. I spend a lot of time visiting my husband at the nursing home."

"I'm sorry."

"Thank you. I said we've been unable to reach Melissa for five or six years. Or her twin brother, Sidney. I think Sidney's using a different name. Shopbell. It was their surname before we adopted them."

Something stirred in my deeper mind when she said "Shopbell." While trying to get ahold of that something, I glanced at the newspaper-covered mound in the footwell. The paper had slid off a corner of the chest. Had that happened during my helter-skelter drive here, or before? I looked around the parking lot, filling with shoppers stocking up on home-and-garden supplies for weekend projects.

But back to the matter at hand.

"So you have no idea as to your grandchildren's whereabouts, Mrs. Wheeler?"

"We had an awful falling-out when they were in their teens. They didn't feel like they fit in at school, despite our giving them the best of everything. I think it was Sidney who researched their birth-family background, but they both became obsessed with Indian culture. Though they didn't want to actually live on the rez, or anything."

"Too different from the life they'd known, probably." I meant that to strike her as understanding, empathetic. Although I wasn't feeling it.

"Sidney had a minority scholarship to University of Oregon, we heard, when he came to us for money. He might still live in Oregon, but never wanted us to contact him."

"What about Missy?"

"I think she's still in Seattle, in the projects, with that friend. She used to come by for money, too, but refused to give her contact information." She sniffled, coughed, and then resumed the conversation. "We don't know what we did to alienate them so."

"I'm sorry," I said, feeling the hurt all around. "I'm sure it wasn't your fault."

This wasn't going as helpfully as I hoped. I genuinely felt Joyce Wheeler's pain. Losing a child, and then the grandchildren you'd raised, would leave a huge hole in your heart. And endless self-blame. True of Indian couples, as much as non-Indians.

"Pepper?"

"Still here."

"We were shocked when a letter came to the house for Missy about two weeks ago. From Eagle Butte. No return address. I forwarded it to Seattle Indian Health Center hoping she might come in for some reason and they'd give it to her."

That hit me like a mule-kick to the head.

I watched the Drumstick dissolve into a brown-and-white puddle in Red Ryder's cupholder. My hope for answers about the murder was doing much the same in my sorry brain. I wadded up napkins from the truck door-pocket and stuffed them in the holder.

"Try to remember, Mrs. Wheeler, anything police said about that friend."

"She was Indian, like Missy, but older. They first thought she was Missy's mother. Then they implied Missy was, well, working for her."

I picked a chip of chocolate from the mess in the cupholder and popped it in my mouth. The bittersweet shock gave me a pleasant jolt.

"On the street, you mean? As a prostitute?"

"That was my understanding." Then a raspy sigh. "I just don't know how Missy could do that. We were crushed. It led to my husband's downfall."

"I'm sorry. But don't be hard on yourself. People have their reasons. And it might not be what you think. But so, to your knowledge, Missy is still around?"

"Haven't heard otherwise. Think you can you help us find her?"

I hesitated a tick before speaking.

"Not if she doesn't want to be found." Harsh to say, but true.

I was processing all this as fast as I could. Right now that seemed be a losing battle. As with the sunshine and the Drumstick. But I had to try to salvage something.

"Mrs. Wheeler?"

"Yes?"

"Thank you for being so open. If I find out anything more about your grandchildren, I certainly will let you know. "

"I would appreciate that, Pepper."

I hurried back inside the Co-op, used the bathroom and called Sonny again. I had to leave another voice mail—this one with what I'd learned from Joyce Wheeler. I also texted him.

"Leaving Co-op now to return our find," I said. "I may need backup."

30

I got back into Red Ryder, glanced at the chest and drove toward the exit of the Co-op parking lot. An aged black pickup pulled in front of me. It reached the exit first, but paused before tuning on the street behind the store.

A slow burn heated my face as I waited. I so wanted to be on my way and have this all over and done with.

Fortified now by fat, sugar and protein, I planned to just cowgirl up, roll into the Robertsons' place, drop the chest and get the hell out. I had no idea where I'd leave that chest. On the house porch? Or at the turn onto the driveway? Whoever knew about the chest and left me the note could be watching for me, planning to punish me, and maybe fixing to silence me for good.

Who was it, really? My first thought was of Cleve Robertson. But, considering all possibilities, it might be almost anyone who'd come under my scrutiny: the whole Robertson family including the old folks, Cleve, or his son, the alleged cult member. Likely the one shooting video—and God knew what else—on the banks of the Applegate after our Memorial Day barbecue.

These were a stretch, but it could even be my cash-strapped contractor pal, Jesse Banks, or my budding realtor-friend, Gloria Allende, hoping to score a major sale for her broker, and secure a small fortune in kick-backs for herself. I knew she'd already scoped out the property—including the ill-fated cabin—with one or all of the Robertsons.

The pickup in front of me finally lurched forward, leaving a cloud of smoke in its wake, and turned onto the street. Grimacing at the odor of rank exhaust, I glanced in my rear-view mirror as I let him get well ahead before I exited and followed.

In the rear-few mirror I saw a low-slung silver car with tinted windows pull in close behind my truck. A silver car like the one parked outside my store that afternoon.

Silver car, silver car. A creepy feeing prickled my skin. Hadn't old Walt Walters, recalled seeing such a car at the Robertson place recently? Gloria Allende had a silver Mercedes, but this was lower, sleeker, clearly built for speed.

I floored it. Red Ryder hesitated a split-second, then roared forward as I steered it onto the side street, and then onto Highway 199 back toward town. Glancing often at my mirrors, I wove in and out of traffic and broke every driving law in the books.

Hanging an eye-blink right through a red light, barely missing a homeless man with a towering backpack, I drove onto a road fronting a strip mall anchored by a chain supermarket. Horns honked and tires squealed behind me. I cut a another right into the parking lot.

Customers pushing store carts or talking on cell phones dove out of the way as I cruised at a steady 15-mph down the parking lanes. The silver car hung back and dodged many of the same obstacles, but continued to follow.

When I bumped my dually back onto the road and hung a left onto the fast lane of Highway 199, I pushed Red Ryder past 60 mph, cutting in front of a retirement-home van. But I slowed when I came upon a log truck laboring up the highway. I stomped the brakes, unable to pass on the right because of the retirement-home van.

The second a decent gap opened between the vehicles, I punched it, crowded into an eight-foot-wide space between them, and roared forward. The retirement van swerved to the right, and the truck driver favored me with a long blast from his horn while I accelerated around him and back into the fast lane.

A glance in the mirror showed the silver car nicely stuck behind the truck, now signaling for a return to the slow lane.

I drove like a bat out of hell for another mile, and then slowed to leave 199 for the snaky left exit onto Demaray Drive. Hitting the straightaway again, I gunned it. The left onto Jerome Prairie Road came up in a flash, and I whipped the dually onto it.

Immediately I heard a bleat of sirens behind me. The sound grew louder. A rainbow of flashing strobes lit up my rear-view mirror. The vehicles were about an eighth of a mile back but gaining fast. I pulled over to the narrow shoulder and settled the slipped newspaper back over the little chest.

Shit. They were coming for me, ostensibly for reckless driving. But they were sure to notice the chest and learn from my plates and ID who I was, what I'd been up to regarding the hottest case in Josephine County—if not the state of Oregon.

A moment later a medical response van and sheriff's police roared by, hell bent for somewhere else in Jerome Prairie.

I whooped out a sigh and dropped my chin to my chest. When I opened my eyes again I looked in the rearview mirror. The silver car mysteriously had vanished, as if I'd only imagined it. Where had it gone? Was it lurking just out of sight, lying low until the emergency vehicles and any that followed were well out of the picture?

My gaze dropped to the passenger footwell. The chest, a lump hunkering under newspaper in there, suddenly seemed radioactive. My gut told me to get rid of it now, fast, however I could, and get the hell away. Not even go to the Robertson cottage. Maybe just drop the box in the ditch with a note telling the Robertson address.

Last night this chest was my ally, the key to solving the murder and to making things right for the ones deprived of a loved one, and those entitled to any remaining O'Hara legacy. Now the chest oozed malevolence. It was going to be my undoing.

O'Hara had filled it with treasure before he died. But had he included it in his cabin curse, as well?

31

While the dually idled, I looked at houses and farmland around the roadside. Homes on small acreages, some with cattle or horses, looked modest but well-tended, blinds open, windows shined. Mailboxes stood in soldierly ranks by driveways on the right, while ancient oaks extended shading arms overhead.

Homes on the left were much the same—front or side pastures still green and lush from spring rains and warm weather. A few llamas and more horses dotted the fields, and RVs or trailers stood beside garages and other outbuildings.

About a quarter-mile up the road, what looked like a bicycling group pedaled toward where I waited, trying to decide how to dispose of the chest without anyone seeing me.

It stuck me that they, or a neighbor, might remember a loitering vehicle that looked out of place, as Walt Walters had seen near the Robertsons'.

This was not a good spot. Nowhere would be. I might as well cowgirl up, take the damned chest back where it belonged and scurry next door to my parents' as if nothing unusual had happened. Maybe Sonny was still there.

We'd call the sheriff. I'd confess my deeds, and face the consequences. I'd been in worse situations and come through relatively unscathed. No big.

Or not. Maybe it would be better to just stick with Plan A, pick up a burner phone on my way back through town and leave OSP or the sheriff an anonymous text about the chest and its whereabouts. I'd work it out after doing what I had to do now.

Driving forward again toward the Robertson place, doing an unremarkable 40 mph, I grew increasingly tense and uncertain. I began to sweat, and heavily, despite the cool air whispering over my face from the dash vents. The steering wheel was slick beneath my fingers. I made myself focus on my mission.

Hang on. You got this. Everything will be fine.

Within three hundred feet of the Robertsons', I slowed the truck. Good. No other people or vehicles in sight. Keeping my eyes front I hung a quick left up the short gravel drive between the oaks and pines.

The white cottage came into view, its roof and siding dappled with shade. No signs of visitors or other activity. I flashed on how cool the inside of that house would feel even in late-day, like now.

Driving a tight, right 180, I parked and left the truck idling, faced back toward the road in case I needed to leave in a hurry. I grabbed the chest, slid out and kept the door open as I hurried to the porch. I would just leave the box and run.

The chest would be safe on the porch for as long as it took its keeper to retrieve it, or for responders to come. But I tucked it behind one pillar so it couldn't be seen from the drive. Almost done. Then I was so outta there.

Almost.

A hand gripped my left arm and spun me around. Shane Chapelle's smiling face and blocky 9 mm Glock met my astonished gaze. The scent of herbal aftershave wafted past me. From this vantage point I glimpsed the back of a low silver car down among a neighbor's trees to the right of the drive. I'd been so focused on the garage, house and yard that I'd blown right past it.

"I believe that's mine," Chapelle said, jerking his head toward the chest on the porch. "Pick it up and hand it over. Be quick, now."

My heart threatened to burst through my ribs. Time seemed to stall, even slide backward. I looked around, running through my options. My gun was jammed into the back of my waistband, under my summer top. If I distracted him, and then acted fast...

"So, how did you know I had the chest?" I said, faking casual air designed to disguise my feelings, catch him off guard. "What do you mean, it's yours?"

He snorted, and shook his head. But his gun stayed steady, pointed at my chest.

"The chest, Pepper? I don't have all day."

"So it was you, all along. Never would have guessed. Appearing to be chasing the big story, but actually the cause of it. No wonder you seemed to have an inside track on the investigation. So much for journalistic integrity."

His handsome face clouded.

"Wrong again." He gestured with the gun, indicating I should pick up the chest.

"That was you outside my store and the Co-op," I said. "I suppose you figured I'd taken it after I was trapped in the crawlspace. Was it you who trapped me?"

"No comment."

"Or you saw the chest in my truck because I didn't cover it well enough. Tipped off Sheriff Welles. I'm dying to know your story. I mean, as a fellow journalist."

Chapelle stiffened. A scowl marred his features.

"Throw the gun on the lawn, and give me the chest," he said. "Now." His dark eyes looked cold as basalt in winter. A scrub jay screeched, mad about something. Just like me.

I took a deep breath and exhaled slowly to buy time. I had to figure something out, but couldn't let Chapelle see my indecision. That would show weakness.

"You killed that woman, didn't you, Shane? The one from Seattle who came looking for the legacy. And now you want the chest. Did you know about it before the murder, or after?"

I let that settle in while my mind teemed with theories and questions.

He sneered. Not a good look for an upwardly bound TV newsman. "I don't know what the you're talking about."

"Just answer me."

He clicked the safety off the pistol and steadied the weapon with his other hand.

"You're wasting my time. Let's go." His angry eyes for a moment took on a hint of sadness, a whisper of doubt. Just as quickly that vulnerable look vanished.

The buzz of rising blood pressure filled my ears. A hush came over the scene. Even the scrub jay was silent. It dawned on me who Chapelle might be and how he'd known about the chest.

I knew those eyes. They stared out of many old author photos. And that name. Chapelle. A surname that may have been used by a French trapper when such men took Indian wives, and later Americanized by the homonym "Shopbell."

"My God," I said. "Are you O'Hara's grandson? Who renounced his adopted grandparents and got that letter from his blood grandma? Sidney Shopbell? Chapelle sounds like Shopbell, but more upmarket. And O'Hara also disliked his first name. I talked with Joyce Wheeler today and she told me everything."

Chapelle's face was a stone carving. It reminded me of Sonny's when he wanted to keep something locked inside.

"Your gun? The chest?" Chapelle snapped, motioning sharply with his pistol.

I raised my hands in a "why me?" gesture. Then I felt anger and power surge through my body. My skin tingled as if from an electric shock. I refused to let my voice quake as I tried to appeal to his vanity and higher self.

"Shane." I growled. "Or Sidney. Whoever you are. You don't want to go through with this. You're a fabulous reporter. Have worked all your life to get where you are, and higher. Freddie Uffenpinscher told me all about you, your national network dreams. Call State Police. Confess. They will go easier on you. Don't throw everything away."

He kept the gun pointed at my chest. But the tip wavered. A chink in the armor. He was good with a microphone, intimidating subjects into talking. But with a gun? He must be desperate. He wanted what was in the box and to be free to pursue his dreams, more than he wanted to kill me and be prosecuted for homicide. Or did he? He'd killed that woman, hadn't he?

"Shut up," he snapped. "Just give me your gun. And that chest."

Stepping back, I squared my shoulders and shot him a hard look.

"Why? I texted law enforcement about it, where to find it. But if you're going to kill me, at least share what's going on, as a courtesy, with a fellow reporter."

His smooth tan forehead had turned shiny in the literal and figurative heat. A hank of blue-black hair, no match for the rising temperature, dropped onto one temple. He brushed it back with his free hand.

"Don't be ridiculous," he sneered. "Welles is about to officially name you a person of interest in the murder."

"So you do have an 'in' with him," I said, raising my chin. "How does he owe you? He doesn't seem the bribable type."

His face darkened. He lunged forward, threw his free arm around my neck, and yanked the revolver from my waistband. Throwing a hip into my side, he shoved me off the porch into a waist-high yew shrub.

I hit the branches face down, sinking halfway in, a hundred needles pricking my face and arms. The smell of crushed evergreen filled my nose. A drop of warm blood ran into my mouth. I spat and clambered out of the bush. When Chapelle stopped to retrieve the chest, I launched myself at him. We tumbled to the concrete, a grappling mass of arms, legs, blood and spit.

A shout from the lawn froze us in place.

"That's enough. Get your asses up. I'm through playing games."

Cleve Robertson!

Chapelle and I disentangled ourselves and turned to face Robertson. Standing thirty feet away. He held a sawed-off shotgun on us. His face was mottled red. A lit cigarette stuck out from between clenched teeth. He gave off the smell of cigarette smoke and stale sweat, as f he'd been waiting a long time in a hot place.

"Hands on your head, "Robertson barked. "Both of you."

Chapelle reached out his hands to show him the chest.

"But we had deal," he said. "What the fuck?"

The words hit me like a chunk of concrete. What deal? What was Robertson talking about? I stared at Chapelle. Looking stunned, his hair roughed up around his face, he took a hesitant step forward.

Robertson's face shaded dangerously to crimson. He cocked he shotgun.

"This is still my property. March to the barn. No tricks now."

As we stepped off the porch and began a slow walk toward the old structure, Robertson picked up our dropped guns and shoved them into his back pockets. Then, one hand holding the shotgun on us, he hopped on-to the porch and opened the door to put the chest and guns inside.

"What deal?" I rasped to Chapelle on my left. My mind jumped with possible explanations for Robertson's appearance. I hated every one.

Chapelle halted and let his head fall backward. Then he straightened and resumed walking.

"OK," he said. "Since we're probably going to die, anyway. I was shocked to get that letter two weeks ago. Some tribal lawyer found my address."

Glancing over my shoulder, I saw Robertson put the chest and guns inside the house. He turned with the shotgun, stepped off the porch and motioned us on.

"Either of you tries anything," he yelled, "I'll shoot to kill."

Chapelle and I plodded more slowly, arms touching.

"I came to the property as if I were a buyer," Chapelle said. "He showed me to the barn and let me go on to the cabin. I did a thorough job searching for the so-called legacy, pulling out chimney rocks, looking in the crawlspace. I found the chest buried under tarpaper. O'Hara'd hidden it good."

"With the ring and manuscript inside? What'd you do with those?"

"Re-buried them in a corner, to pick up later."

I looked back toward Robertson, thirty feet back. We walked faster, as if that would keep us safe.

"But why keep it there? " I said. "And what about the woman? A friend of your sister, by the way."

"Gathered that, from police."

Out of the corner of my eye, I saw Robertson and the shotgun draw closer.

"My wife and I are divorcing," said Chapelle. "Didn't want her to know about the legacy. Plus as it's the Robertsons' land, they could claim anything found there. I've been talking to lawyers."

"Still don't know where Robertson comes in."

Chapelle stumbled and fell to his knees. I knew it was staged. I stooped to help him. I took my time, watching Robertson. He was about fifteen steps away, and lighting another cigarette, one-handed. As if he had all the time in the world.

"Cleve found me with the chest," said Chapelle, brushing his pants and walking again. "I said I could prove I was entitled to the legacy, worth a fortune. I'd cut him in if he'd help me keep it hidden until after my divorce. I'd also share with my sister."

A shotgun tip slammed into my back. I lurched forward, flailing to keep upright. I was glad for Chapelle's steadying hand. A dull ache throbbed in my back.

"What the hell are you chickens clucking about?" Robertson barked. "Walk."

The barn lay a few steps ahead. We let ourselves be herded inside, with Robertson still brandishing his shotgun.

Cool darkness slashed by arrows of sunlight enveloped us. A sparrow fluttered out a gold rectangle that was the upper half of the rear Dutch door. Peaceful, as it had been when I'd first visited it. But peaceful now as the crypt.

I considered making a dash for that door. But its latch looked locked. And I wasn't sure I could vault over the open half before being shot.

"In there," Robertson snapped from behind and to our left.

"The tack room. Be quick." Again the thrust of a shotgun barrel against my ribs, again a whiff of cigarette smoke and stale sweat.

Nausea swept me. It felt like a boa constrictor squeezing my gut.

Chapelle and I hung our heads and filed into the windowless room where stiff bridles, saddles, a folded horse-blanket and the dusty grooming bucket stood solemn witness to our fate.

The door slammed behind us. Then came the sound of a rusted lock being keyed shut, stubbornly. The sound of heavy footsteps moving away. Finally, silence.

I heard Chapelle stir somewhere in front of me.

"You said you texted people where you were going, and why," he whispered. "Sheriff Welles? Your boyfriend?"

I wondered if he meant Welles was my boyfriend, or if he meant Sonny.

"I lied."

"You have your phone?" he whispered.

"In the truck."

"Any idea how we can get out of here?"

"None.," I stage-whispered. "We're dead. So tell me. Did you kill that woman?"

"Hell no," he said with a flare of anger. "Didn't even know about it until I heard it over the newsroom scanner."

"So you didn't learn it from Welles? Thought you had an in with him."

"Sometime he tells me stuff. Nothing vital."

I heard a noise outside the barn. Like objects being moved around.

"Did you confront Cleve about it?"

"Played dumb."

"Know why he didn't remove the body or murder weapon?"

"My take is, he wanted to incriminate me. I got questioned, too, you know."

I hadn't considered this until now. It lent more credence to Chapelle's claim he had no "in" with law enforcement.

"They found things that implicated me," he continued. "Probably from when I first visited the cabin. I wasn't careful about fingerprints. Didn't think I needed to be."

The footsteps returned. Slow, heavy. Then a man's cough. Robertson was back. But was there someone with him? A woman?

Through the old, dried-pine door, I heard a falsetto voice say, "You tried to cheat me out of what's mine."

The voice was breathy, like Robertson's, but sounded female. Or like someone mocking him in a female voice. Someone who well knew how he sounded. Could it be Gloria? Jesse? Maybe Cleve's son?

Two coughs from Chapelle ended my speculating.

"We gotta get out of here," he said. "Dust is messing with my voice."

I harrumphed.

"A lot more's going to mess with it if Cleve gets away with whatever he plans for us...Sidney. Why'd you change your first name to Shane?"

"Which sounds more glam for national TV?"

A shout blasted through the locked door. Unmistakably Robertson, this time.

"Hey. Shut the fuck up in there. This ain't no hen party."

More footsteps, closer now. Along with the sound of papers being crumpled. Liquid being poured.

Glug, tinny echo, glug. Liquid being poured from a large, echoing container.

My breath caught. This meant only one thing. The former firefighter had come to the forefront of the action, again. Setting fires in trash cans was not enough. Now he had a bigger target. Old structures containing volatile oils, straw and dry timber spontaneously combusted all the time. Too bad if a pair of snoopy trespassers just happened to be inside.

My eyes had adjusted to the dark. Enough so, that I saw a faint line of light showing beneath the door. But the light was orange, and fluttery. Like flames.

"Shit," I said. "He's set the barn on fire." As the import of my words computed, a weight dropped over me. One I couldn't work myself out from under. We were going to die. Burned alive. All because of a letter, a little chest, and maybe a long-ago curse.

The smell of gasoline, woodsmoke and burning straw seeped under the door. These were accompanied by crackling sounds. Everything unfolded in slow motion.

I heard the doorknob rattle from our side. Chapelle, testing the lock.

"The screws feel loose," he said. "Maybe I can wrench them out."

"Not as easy as opening the chest," I said. "Quick. Find that horse blanket. We need to cover the crack and keep the smoke out as long as possible."

While Chapelle was busy with that, I bent down and scrabbled around the floor for that old cobwebby grooming bucket. After a few seconds my hand bumped its rim. I rummaged inside, tossing out brushes and currycombs along with a dead spiders and horseshoe nails.

Despite the crack under the door being blocked by the horse blanket, the smoke grew thicker. The flickering orange light originally spied under the door, grew brighter around the door's frame. Feeling a burn and tickle in my throat, I coughed.

But I now held a screwdriver, probably once used as a hoof pick. I straightened, felt for the door, and found three rough screw heads holding the lock in place. I wrenched the screwdriver handle, and felt them given a little. But the screwdriver tip repeatedly shot away from the screw heads.

Desperate, I began to pick jab and pry at the lock plate and old, wood around the it. A few splinters gave way. But not enough to get us out before that blaze really took off.

Heart pounding, I stabbed and pried harder, again and again. My fingers and wrist ached from jolts and twists. I coughed again, finding it even harder to breathe.

A soft, heavy weight hit my back. Then horse-smelly cloth slid over my head as Chapelle tried to partly cover me with a second smelly blanket. I heard and felt him panting under it at my back.

"Let me do it," he said, grasping my right wrist. "I'm taller and stronger."

I bristled momentarily, but then let that go. I jerked my hand away.

"I've almost got it," I gasped, redoubling my efforts.

By now my nose and the back of my throat burned from inhaling smoke fumes. They were strongest by the door, seeping toward me as I poked, jimmied and pried. My back ran with sweat. My forearms ached and throbbed.

I paused, touching my palm to the door. Almost immediately I whipped it away. The wood was blazing hot.

Even if I did pry off the lock, we'd face an inferno. One from which there was little likelihood of escape. Yet I had to try.

One final, thrusting jab and wrench did the trick. The lock came loose and rotated downward. I gave it a final blow and plunged my fingers into the searing hole where it had been.

"*Hoka hey!*" I yelled, voicing the traditional Lakota war cry. "Let's go!"

I threw my blanket-wrapped body into a boiling, black-and-orange hell. I felt Chapelle at my back, stumbling as desperately forward as I.

Giant tongues of flame licked out of the smoke. Whooshes and rumbles roared somewhere inside the inferno. I shut my eyes and crashed to the cement floor, dragging my body toward where I thought the back door was. I hoped Chapelle was close behind, although I no longer felt him.

A sharp pain and a smell of singed skin and hair pierced my panic. I scrambled on, shoving back the pain, feeling for the bottom of the Dutch door. When my fingers bumped it, I heard a heavy board, then another, hit the concrete behind me.

The hayloft, collapsing. I might be killed by falling lumber before I was consumed by fire and smoke.

I grasped a handful of horse blanket for protection and raised myself enough in the roaring, acrid cloud to pull at the door handle. It wouldn't budge. I screamed, and pulled again, putting my whole bodyweight into it.

The door swung outward. So did the smoke and flames, thundering overhead.

I threw myself forward on the ground, clawed dirt and rocks, and bucked like a saddle bronc on meth. I set myself on a straight course through the choking storm, and pulled life-saving distance toward me. I heard Chapelle grunting somewhere behind.

My journey from the inferno seemed to take hours. I thought it would never end. It was probably only moments.

All I knew was that I'd skittered and stumbled like a tossed firecracker over a field, through a jungle and into the blessed, cooling water of the Applegate River.

I lay immobile. Rocks now supported me, pressing hard against my knees, hipbones and chest. As I lay prone, head barely above water, I spotted Chapelle similarly positioned off to my left.

Scrapes, burns and bruises shot painful shards through my exposed skin. Icy liquid slapped my face and sluiced over my back. My limbs were numb with cold.

But we were alive.

We were alive.

EPILOGUE

June 1, 2017

I leaned on the spectator rail with the border collie, Alice, at my side. The south Seattle horse-show arena felt as airy, and looked as bright, spacious and welcoming as I recalled. I envisioned Choc and me gliding through a Western pleasure class, then being called to the center to accept a thousand-dollar win check.

Now country music played softly over loudspeakers. Colorful pennants and an American flag hung from rafters high overhead. A scatter of spectators lounged in steep grandstand seats behind me, and riders schooled equines in the enormous arena below.

A true Palace of the Horse. It rivaled any I'd seen, even in California and Texas. How blessed I felt to be here. In fact, after Friday, to be anywhere.

Choc was enjoying his evening feeding in the Grandeen bloc of the rows of stables flanking both sides of the arena. We had all rolled in with our horses, show clothes, silver-trimmed saddles and long horse trailers at three, giving us just enough time to unload our horses and gear, bed stalls, fill water buckets and lightly work and bathe our horses before hitting the prep and practice grind tomorrow. Classes started Thursday.

I glanced at my watch. Six-fifteen. Time to go freshen up in the living-quarters horse trailer Tulip and I used as a traveling Best Little Horsehouse. At seven we'd meet the Grandeens, our buddies and Sonny at a swank steakhouse overlooking Puget Sound and the Olympic Mountains.

Thinking of the trailer and how this likely was our last year of hauling it to regional shows to sell clothes, tack and grooming supplies, I felt a ripple of sadness.

But I also felt elation. Though it might be our last year with the Horsehouse trailer or freestanding store, it also would make way for a new year of developing our guest ranch on the Applegate, where the new Horsehouse would also rise.

Bruises, scrapes and scorches from the barn fire still marked my head, back and arms. But they would heal. And the hair would grow back on the back of my head, although doctors had given no guarantee.

For now I kept the spot medicated, and covered by a cap. I'd already tried on my 100X Western show hat. Its sharp-shaped crown just cleared the burn zone.

It was a miracle I was even alive. A miracle that Shane Chapelle, nee Shopbell, was alive, too, after the inferno. Luckily Walt Walters down the road had seen the smoke and called 911, bringing firefighters, EMTs and law enforcement to the scene mere minutes after our escape.

We were all over the Friday late-evening TV news, as viewed from a hospital bed, with my parents, Tulip, with her handsome Tommy Lee at my side. Mom and Dad left at nine. Shortly before ten, Sonny finally called. From Seattle, where he'd gone to search for the missing granddaughter. I told him everything in a tired rush of words, imagining myself safe in his embrace.

"Glad you're OK, honey," he said. "I knew that box would get you in trouble."

"Love you, too," I said. "Let me know if you find that *takoja*. See you soon."

When we disconnected, I focused on the TV news.

"Sheriff Welles stopped Robertson and took him in for questioning as he drove from the fire scene," said the TV news anchor. "Reportedly he had firearms and a suspicious chest in the back of his vehicle. He is being held on suspicion of several counts of arson, as well as murder and attempted homicide."

They rolled video of firefighters knocking down the blaze, with much of the barn still miraculously standing.

I called Robertson's parents the next day to offer a lame condolence about their son, and tell them Tulip and I were still interested in their property. I then called Gloria Allende and asked her to deliver our offer of six hundred-thousand dollars.

Shane Chapelle had occupied the hospital room next to mine. He and I were questioned separately by police Saturday after the fire. I had not needed skin grafts; Chapelle had. Luckily the flames had not touched his camera-loving face.

Unluckily his immediate future was not so certain. He likely would be charged as an accessory to murder, though plea-bargaining would reduce his sentence.

I called him Sunday from my home, where I was prepping and packing show clothes and tack. I was grateful that Karen Mikulski could tend my livestock and dogs during my short stay in the hospital. She house-sat for me now, while I was in Seattle.

Her phone call Friday after she arrived at my ranchita had unsettled me.

First she told me Stewie won the $50.00 for his Preston O'Hara paper.

"Excellent," I said. "I thought he would."

Before signing off, she dropped a small bomb.

"What should I do with this skinny border collie whining at the door?" she said.

"Call the Days, my neighbors," I said. "Their number is on the whiteboard."

Later that night she texted me.

"They say if you can't find room for that—and I quote—'dumb, neurotic hound,' take her back to Southern Oregon Humane Society."

I texted back, "Bring her in and feed her skinny butt."

As for Melissa, the missing *takoja* in Seattle, Sonny had visited the Seattle Indian Health Center, the low-income projects, and street people known to be occasionally cooperative. Talked to a cousin who had a cousin who had a cousin.

Missy went into rehab Monday and, according to Sonny, was ecstatic at the promise of a new life made possible by her grandfather's legacy. She and Chapelle planned to reconnect with the Wheelers, and share their windfall with Indian youth. Scholarships would be in the works.

Sonny promised to take me to meet Missy after the show. He'd also treat me and his kids to a Mariners game. Chili and Serrano would round out our party.

While I was lost in such thoughts, someone rudely bumped my hip. Alice growled. I turned to give the person a dirty look.

"Hey, pretty lady," said a familiar voice. Sonny's pleasing male scent—mixed with essence of horse, tanbark and Northwest fresh air—floated around me.

I raised my eyes to take in his teasing smile.

"Man," I said. "Don't do that. I was about to chew somebody a new behind." I gave him a hip bump. "Wondered if I'd see you again, even at dinner. All these phone calls ain't doin' it."

"Well, if you really want to chew my behind ..."

"So did you get answers to your other questions?"

I felt an anxious flutter in my heart. After making sure Missy was on a healing path, Sonny had met with his ex and his doctors. A minor heart attack weeks ago had sent him to the hospital and later, an attorney, with Sonny making out his will. So far the blood-pressure meds he'd been prescribed, were doing their job.

"I couldn't tell you until we worked it out," he said. "Didn't want you to worry. And had to make sure that if I died, my kids would get what they're entitled to—my share of the family's cattle ranch."

I searched his eyes, feeling a rush of relief. I lay my head on his chest and encircled his waist with my arms.

"Anyway, I'm glad we all had a happy outcome," I said. "We might have to talk about our own future, one day soon."

The look in his eyes melted me.

"I might be open to that," he said.

He pulled my hands away, kissed them, and leaned down to nuzzle my neck. His lips worked around to mine, tickling my chin in the process. The feel of his mouth opening, his tongue-tip darting against mine, sent shivers down my core.

This time it was my turn to pull away. Blushing, I looked around, not used to public displays of lust. Seeing three show-girls I knew in the stands behind us, I gave them a sheepish smile.

But Sonny enjoyed such displays, as if daring any observers to be so lucky. He grabbed my arms and pulled them around his waist. We snugged together for only a moment before pain hopscotched across my skin.

"Ow," I squealed, pulling away. "Burn spots."

"Sorry," he said. "You OK?"

"Gotta cowgirl up. There's no crying at horse shows."

He picked up my left hand and held it to his chest.

"Think there's time," he said, "for us to slip back to the trailer before dinner to tend to those burns ... and other business?"

I looked at him through what I hoped were seductively lowered lashes. Then, puckering my lips, I blew out a breath toward his face. I followed that with a wink.

"Like, you have to ask?"

* * * * * * * * *

Meet our author

Carole T. Beers

Born in Portland, Ore., to descendants of Oregon Trail pioneers, Carole T. Beers fell in love with writing as soon as she could read, and with horses as soon as she could ride. After earning a B.A. in Journalism at University of Washington, she taught at private schools, wrote for romance magazines and worked for 32 years as a reporter/critic for the Pulitzer Prize-winning Seattle Times newspaper. Several of her pieces won awards. Along the way she competed on a women's shooting team and earned a pilot's license. She also worked in marketing and retail—great sources of story and character ideas!

Carole now lives in Southern Oregon where she writes "New West Mysteries with Heart." These include the fast, fun Pepper Kane novels featuring a spirited ex-reporter who shows Western horses, sells tack, and solves crimes with the aid of her Lakota-police partner, Sonny Chief. Set in the Pacific Northwest but sometimes venturing into the Southwest, her books showcase Carole's love of nature, time spent with animal or human friends, mind-teasing puzzles and hopeful endings.

Soon Carole will publish a novella, "The Stone Horse," inspired by Zuni carvings of spirit animals. Years ago she mentored Indian youth, sang on a drum and danced in pow-wows with the support of Lakota, Cree and Northwest Coast friends. She still holds these friendships dear to her heart.

Her free-time pursuits include dancing, hiking, playing games and watching the Seattle Seahawks with her husband, Richard. She also likes to attend Bethany Presbyterian Church, hang with her Boston Terriers and ride her American Paint horse, Shiny Good Bar ("Brad"). Though retired from showing, she still rides as if she may show next week.

Reach Carole on her website. http://www.caroletbeers.com or her Facebook:http://www.facebook.com/caroletbeersauthor

89789650R00176

Made in the USA
Lexington, KY
03 June 2018